The Black Beacon Book of Horror

OTHER TITLES FROM BLACK BEACON BOOKS

Anthologies:

The Second Black Beacon Book of Mystery
Tales from the Ruins
A Hint of Hitchcock
Murder and Machinery
The Black Beacon Book of Mystery
Shelter from the Storm
Lighthouses
Subtropical Suspense

Books by Cameron Trost:

Oscar Tremont, Investigator of the Strange and Inexplicable
The Animal Inside
Letterbox
Hoffman's Creeper and Other Disturbing Tales
The Tunnel Runner

www.blackbeaconbooks.com

the
BLACK BEACON BOOK
of
HORROR

The Black Beacon Book of Horror
Published by Black Beacon Books
Edited by Cameron Trost
Cover art by Greg Chapman
Copyright © Black Beacon Books, 2023

The Guisers © David Turnbull
The House on the Bluff © Edward Lodi
The Choir © Kev Harrison
Ruby's Syzygy © Matthew R. Davis
Humus © Sam Dawson
(First published in *Urges*, Huntiegouke Press, 1997)
Questions a Man Ought Not to Ask © Elizabeth Broadbent
(First published in *Dark Horses #7,* August 2022)
Marjorie © Meg Belviso
Children of Blood © Greg Chapman
(First published in *The Pulp Book of Phobias*, LVP Publications, 2019)
Quiver © Angelique Fawns
Cameo © Deborah Sheldon
The Great Invocation © David Schembri
Dominion © Jeff Wood
Divine Liquor © C.C. Adams
Landslide © Harris Coverley
Holiday Home © Cameron Trost
Her Mother's Lullaby © Micah Castle

Black Beacon Books
blackbeaconbooks.com

ISBN: 978-0-6452471-3-8

The Black Beacon Book of Horror features dark and disturbing tales from some of the most original and imaginative authors writing in the genre today. These tales of psychological, supernatural, folk, gothic, and cosmic horror will usher you into the darkest of realms and leave you there to fend for yourself. You'll lose your way in abandoned houses and hospitals, and be trapped on stormy beaches and along foggy country roads. There are haunted dolls, creepy-crawlies, malevolent spirits, creatures of legend, Lovecraftian terrors, and the demons within our own minds. But as varied as the settings and themes are, each tale has that one essential trait; the power to make you glance over your shoulder just to be sure the terror hasn't found a way to leave the page.

- Cameron Trost, editor

Black Beacon Books would like to thank our patrons, whose passion for great fiction and independent publishing helped make this anthology happen.

If you'd like to join the team and reap the benefits, subscribe on our Patreon page at: *patreon.com/blackbeaconbooks*

The five patronage tiers are
Shipwreck Survivor, Moonlight Smuggler, Sea Witch, Assistant Keeper, and *Lighthouse Keeper.*

The Guisers by David Turnbull...9

The House on the Bluff by Edward Lodi...27

The Choir by Kev Harrison...36

Ruby's Syzygy by Matthew R. Davis...51

Humus by Sam Dawson...71

Questions a Man Ought Not to Ask by Elizabeth Broadbent...79

Marjorie by Meg Belviso...92

Children of Blood by Greg Chapman...100

Quiver by Angelique Fawns...113

Cameo by Deborah Sheldon...125

The Great Invocation by David Schembri...138

Dominion by Jeff Wood...156

Divine Liquor by C.C. Adams...171

Landslide by Harris Coverley...180

Holiday Home by Cameron Trost...192

Her Mother's Lullaby by Micah Castle...211

Author Biographies

THE GUISERS
David Turnbull

'If the guisers come chapping on the door, just ignore them,' said his host. 'If you indulge them, they'll keep coming back.' Sarah Monroe was a small redheaded woman with a lilting highland accent. She was dressed casually in an anorak and jeans, sturdy mountain boots on her feet.

'*Guisers?*' asked Jack, holding the little Airbnb folder she'd given him with instructions on how to operate the cottage's central heating and kitchen utilities.

'From the word *disguise*,' said Sarah.

Jack shrugged, not understanding what she was talking about.

'There's always guisers round these parts,' said Sarah. 'Dressed up to look like something else. Especially after the clocks change.'

'You mean like *trick-or-treaters*?' asked Jack, finally cottoning on. 'Halloween was ages ago.'

'The tradition existed here for centuries before the Americans commercialised it and started putting it in movies,' said Sarah, fetching her car key from the pocket of her denims. 'It was Scottish immigrants who brought it with them across the Atlantic.'

'I see,' said Jack. 'And what's *chapping*?'

Sarah raised her hand and made a small pink fist around the car key. 'It's what we call knocking. As in knocking at the door.'

'So, if the *guisers chap* on the door, I'm just to ignore them?'

'That would be the best strategy,' said Sarah.

'But it's the middle of December,' said Jack. 'Why would anyone still be celebrating Halloween?'

'It's the dark they're marking,' she said. 'They start coming out around Halloween. But they carry on until the winter solstice.'

'That's tomorrow, isn't it?'

Sarah nodded. 'Just ignore them till then.'

She turned and made her way towards the front door. 'I'd best be off before the road back down to the village gets too frosty.'

#

Jack unpacked and made himself a coffee. He thought he should really make a start on the first draft of his report. The whole idea of renting this remote cottage was to give him time, without distractions, to complete it. If he could get it done in the next couple of days, he could drive back home and relax over Christmas before he had to deliver the presentation in January. But the car journey from London had been gruelling, even with an overnight stopover in Newcastle. First thing in the morning, he told himself, easing down into an armchair and resting his feet on a little leather stool.

Intermittently sipping the coffee, he went over the structure of the report in his head. Jack had an instinctive ability to visualise the layout of anything he needed to write down on paper or commit to a laptop screen. Even if the fine details were not quite there, he could clearly see how the sections of his PowerPoint, the headings, the bullets, the charts, and graphics would pan out.

He'd been over it in his head at least a dozen times as he navigated his route to the highlands. One last run through before he fired up his laptop in the morning wouldn't do any harm. But his weariness was rapidly getting the better of him. Yawning, he set down the coffee cup and closed his eyes. Sleep rushed in on him like an incoming wave. The room seemed to sway as he surrendered himself to the fatigue.

He had almost drifted off completely when the knock on the door roused him. The *tack-tack-tack* was sharp, as if someone had used a stone to knock rather than a bare first.

His immediate assumption was that Sarah had forgotten to tell him something and had made a U-turn somewhere on the narrow, winding road down to the village. In his sleepiness, he'd missed the sound of her four-wheel pulling into the gravel drive. Somewhat drowsily, he rose to his feet, almost knocking the coffee cup over in the process.

The knock came again.

Tack-tack-tack.

Maybe Sarah was using her car keys to make sure he heard her. On the other hand, that sure sounded like something you might describe as a *chap*. Recalling what she had said about ignoring the *guisers* if they came *chapping* at the door, he pressed his eye to the glass spyhole.

The slightly distorted image revealed what appeared to be two children in fusty looking costumes. The first was tall and lanky, dressed in a rather bedraggled looking rabbit costume, face covered by a cheap Bugs Bunny mask. The second, much shorter, wore a tattered bowler hat, face obscured, and a blazer several sizes too big, with oversized padded shoulders and tainted brass buttons, mildew on the dirty white collar of his shirt.

Jack took a step back, remembering what had been said about never getting rid of them if he didn't ignore them. They must have heard the crack of the floorboard, because they immediately broke into a discordant little chant. 'We are the guisers. The guisers. The guisers. We are the guisers, come to sing a song.'

Jack didn't think he'd particularly savour any song they might choose to sing. They were out of key and barely in time with each other. There was an unsettlingly high-pitched tone to their voices that grated and put him on edge. It seemed to vibrate uncomfortably inside his inner ears. He wondered if this was how a dog might feel on hearing a dog whistle.

He backed himself to the stairs and quietly edged his way up. When he peeked from behind the net curtains of the bedroom, he saw the two figures walking along the driveway toward the main road. A thick mist was rolling down from the mountainside, swirling like wraiths between the tall trunks of the conifers. In the gloom by the cottage gate, he could make out the indistinct silhouette of what he assumed to be an adult. What kind of parent would drive their kids all the way up here just for the sake of some scarcely remembered tradition?

When he looked again, all three of them were gone. He listened for the sound of a car pulling out into the road. But the silence of the mountainside around the cottage was all-engulfing. They surely couldn't have walked all the way up from the village, could they? It was freezing outside. His weariness returned. None of this was important. Not in the grand shape of things. A bed was waiting for him, and more than anything, he just wanted to lie down and sleep.

#

In the morning, after a breakfast of scrambled eggs and orange juice, he sat at the kitchen table, cracked his knuckles, and prepared to get stuck into his report and the PowerPoint presentation that was to go with it. The restaurant chain he worked for had big plans to diversify. Tea was going to be the new coffee. Modern tea houses, with a variety of blends, were going to challenge the global coffee shop brands for dominance in high streets and city centres. There would be the usual selection of cakes. But the speciality would be four different types of scones, sold with jam, in a range of flavours, accompanied by little jars of clotted cream. That would be the unique selling point of the brand. The fact that the jars were designed to be recycled was an added bonus that had gone down extremely well in the focus groups the company had set up.

Jack had been placed in charge of the pilot project at half a dozen trial locations. His report and presentation would focus on their success and profitability, extensive customer feedback and consumer surveys, and the franchise business model that would provide the backbone of the proposed expansion. There was no doubt in his mind that the board would endorse the plan, and when they did, he'd be in the running for the position as head of operations in the new tea house division.

But for some reason, he just couldn't focus. His fingers felt fat and awkward on the keyboard. The words on the screen seemed to constantly blur and swirl. That dreadful guiser song had burrowed into his head like an earworm, repeating over and over in the discordant tone of those kids who'd chapped on the door.

'We are the guisers. The guisers. The guisers...'

After fifteen minutes of this, he gave up and closed the lid of the laptop. A walk was what he needed. Get the blood circulating after being cramped in the car for most of yesterday. Breathe in some fresh mountain air. Clear his head. Refocus his thoughts.

The leaf mulch at the verge of the road made it slippery in places. He walked at a cautious pace. It was around ten in the morning and shafts of wintery sunlight were glinting down between the tall branches of the conifers. There was still a residual frostiness in the air, accompanied by a strong stench of rotting vegetation. Jack imagined the stiff corpse of a summer long gone lay mouldering in a ditch and waiting to be buried beneath the snows of the dominant winter.

As he walked, he began to feel an overwhelming sense that he was being watched. That nagging, itchy feeling you get when you feel certain you ought to look over your shoulder. He succumbed—he looked—and sure enough, there was child halfway up the hillside, among the pines. He or she was wearing a black balaclava with little pointy woollen bat ears sewn onto the side, and a long cloak that looked as if it had been cut out of the scuffed leather upholstery of an old sofa.

'Good morning,' said Jack, waving as he passed.

The child spread its arms wide, unfurling the cloak like ragged wings.

'Nice one,' said Jack. He chuckled to himself as he walked on. When he glanced back over his shoulder, the child was gone. With a shrug, he pushed on, consciously keeping to the side of the steep road so he would see a vehicle heading downhill if it came around one of the many sharp corners.

He reached a clearing strewn with what at first appeared to be rocks but on closer inspection turned out to be the moss-covered remains of a long-abandoned cottage. Another child stood among the ruins, by a hollow stack of bricks that looked as if it had once been a fireplace.

This one wore a pink tutu speckled with greenish algae and white tights full of rips and holes. Jack assumed it was a girl. But he couldn't tell for sure because she had a striped bobble hat with holes cut for eyes and mouth pulled over her face. In one hand, she held a small plastic container, and in the other, a little wand with a hoop on the end. She dipped the wand into the container, swished it around, raised it to her lips, and blew. A cluster of bubbles danced and bobbed around her, reflecting the December sunlight.

She began to sing under her breath.

That same horrible chant.

'We are the guisers. The guisers. The guisers.'

Jack felt a twinge in his inner ear. The muscles in his abdomen tightened.

'Good morning to you,' he called, fighting down the nausea that rose at the back of his throat. The child turned and looked at him, then squealed horribly, like a startled piglet, and fled into the trees.

'Suit yourself,' he called after her, wondering if these two kids, and the other two who had come chapping at the cottage door, might be the offspring of some local farmer. It seemed strange that they'd be wandering around up here by themselves, so far from the village. Maybe they were travellers? Maybe somewhere nearby, in a cove or gully, there was an impromptu caravan site, Landrovers and trailers set out in a circle, like covered wagons in old western movie, scrawny dogs yapping and chasing their tails.

Who cared? It was none of his business really.

It was time to get back to the cottage and get stuck into the report. He retraced his footsteps along the road, distracting himself by kicking fallen pinecones and indulging himself in a little childish fantasy, imagining he was a striker scoring the winning goal in the cup final at Wembley.

He had only gone a few yards when a stone clattered onto the road in front of him. He looked to the hillside, expecting to see the child in the makeshift bat costume, but there was nothing but the pines, dark green needles on the layered branches eerily swaying and whispering in the cold breeze that was steadily whipping up.

A sound behind him suggested another stone had been lobbed down onto the road.

'Very funny!' called Jack.

The next stone hit his shoulder, startling him. Jack's head snapped toward the hillside.

'Just quit that right now,' he warned, adopting the sternest voice he could muster. He thought he saw a shadowy figure dash from one tree to another. Another stone hit the road and ricocheted away onto the verge.

'I'm warning you,' Jack yelled, well and truly riled now. 'Just quit while you're ahead.'

Then the singing started. It seemed to come from all sides, as if he were surrounded.

'We are the guisers. The guisers. The guisers. We are the guisers. Come to sing a song.'

A volley of stones hit the road in front of him. Some of them bounced back like shrapnel and peppered his ankles. If he hadn't been wearing denims, they might have broken the skin.

'Okay,' said Jack, picking up his pace. 'You've had your fun. But it's gone too far.'

Another hail came at him. This time one of the stones hit him square on the forehead. Stars flashed before his eyes. He stumbled, hand rising to the bump that was already swelling. There was wet blood on his fingers. 'Fucking little shits,' he roared, losing it now and swinging round on his heels.

There came another nerve-shattering porcine squeal—several voices at once. He saw a series of rapid blurs dashing back into the sloping woods.

Christ, how many of them were there?

'You better run!' he called after them, feeling the warmth of his blood trickle over the bridge of his nose. 'If you know what's good for you, you better hope I don't catch you.'

#

He dabbed the blood away from the lesion that split the angry purple bump on his forehead and winced as he applied a sticking plaster to the wound. He was furious. This was assault. He ought to report it to the police. But what could they do? He had no idea who those little delinquents were. Instead, he phoned Sarah on the mobile number she'd given him.

'Everything okay up there?' she asked.

'There's been a bit of trouble,' said Jack.

A slight pause on the other end of the line.

'What kind of trouble?'

'Kids,' explained Jack. 'Dressed in some sort of fancy dress. Throwing stones out on the road. I got hit on the head.'

'Are you okay?' She asked. 'Do you need a doctor, or anything?'

'I'm fine,' said Jack, playing it down. 'A bit of a bump. Grazed flesh. But I'm far from happy.'

'You went outside?' It sounded like an accusation rather than a question.

'For a walk,' replied Jack. 'It's allowed.'

'It's just…well, I thought you said you had a lot of work to do.'

'I do, but I needed a bit of fresh air to clear my head.'

'It would really be better if you didn't go out on foot. Not at this time of the year.'

Jack narrowed his eyes. 'What's that supposed to mean?'

Another pause. 'The mist rolls down quickly. It can get pretty dense. If a car was coming along, they'd never see you.'

'I was careful.'

A longer pause this time. 'You said there were kids in fancy dress? Did they chap on the door? You didn't answer it, did you?'

There was something in her tone. He couldn't quite put his finger on it. But it almost sounded as if she harboured some underlying desire that he had answered the door. He dismissed the notion. He wasn't thinking straight. Probably something to do with the blow to the head.

'I'm more worried about the ones who were pelting me with stones,' he said. 'Is there a family that lives up here? I can't see how else they'd have come up all this way themselves. I'm pretty sure there was an adult with the ones who knocked—*chapped*—on the door last night. But the ones this morning weren't under any sort of supervision.'

'Just ignore them,' said Sarah. 'If they think they're getting to you, you'll never get rid of them.'

'You know them, then?'

Her answer gave nothing away. 'Just locals. Up to mischief. Ignore them.'

'I was hoping there might be a village police station you could report them to. I'm sure the sight of a patrol car making its way up here would scare them into behaving themselves.'

'My cousin Kenny is in mountain rescue. I could get him to take a drive up there later.'

'I don't need rescuing,' said Jack.

'Just to check on you,' she said. 'If the little buggers are still

16

pestering you, Kenny can call the police from the cottage phone.'

#

Late morning dragged into early afternoon and still he couldn't get into the swing of things. He wrote paragraphs, endlessly spell-checked them, then deleted entire pages and started from scratch. The angry bump on his head throbbed incessantly and gave him a pulsing headache that even a heavy dose of paracetamol didn't address.

He wondered if he'd made a mistake coming up here.

Maybe he should have just stayed in his apartment and worked from there. Although he lived by himself, he had a big circle of friends who always had something going on at the weekends. No matter how much he protested about having a work assignment to complete, they'd have somehow enticed him away from his PC.

Coming here was a sound plan, he reassured himself.

He needed the space.

He needed the peace and solitude.

If only he could focus.

If only that annoying rhyme would stop echoing in his head.

He closed the laptop again, made himself some toast and a mug of coffee, and sat down in front of the TV. There wasn't much to choose from. The news, an episode of a soap opera, a convoluted games show hosted by some minor celebrity whose name he couldn't quite recall. He settled on a tacky old, politically incorrect, monochrome western, replete with gunslingers, white extras made up to look like marauding red Indians, and the US cavalry galloping in to save the day to the sound of the requisite bugle call.

The closing credits were just rolling when the sound made him jump—

Tack-tack-tack, on the door.

Tack-tack-tack, again.

Those kids were back.

He was about to storm along the corridor, yank the door open, and confront them, but he checked himself. He was still furious about what had happened out on the road. Still in pain from the injury that the stone had caused. What if he grabbed one of them in a fit of

17

anger? What if he hit one of them? That wouldn't go down well. No matter what they'd done, they were kids. He was an adult. He couldn't go swinging his fists at kids. Even if they were delinquent little shits.

Forcing himself to remain calm, he walked slowly to the foot of the stairs. He cleared his throat and tried to sound as firm and forceful as he could. 'You need to clear out. Get away from here. I've reported you to the police. There's a patrol car on its way up from the village right now.'

It had no effect.

They began to sing.

'We are the guisers. The guisers. The guisers. We are the guisers. Come to sing a song.'

Multiple voices this time. Out of time and out of tune, like some chaotically dysfunctional choir. Just how many of them were there? He'd been thinking there might be four—the two from last night and the two from this morning. This sounded like a lot more.

Then from behind him.

Tack-tack-tack coming from the living room window.

Then, from farther along the corridor.

Tack-tack-tack on the back door by the kitchen.

Tack-tack-tack on the kitchen window.

'We are the guisers. The guisers. The guisers…'

The jarring song came at him from all sides.

They had the cottage surrounded.

He pressed his hands to his ears.

'Shut up!' he screamed at them. 'Just shut up and get the hell out of here. The police are coming. You're going to be in big trouble.'

Tack-tack-tack.

Tack-tack-tack.

Tack-tack-tack.

Jack refused to open the front door. Instead, he headed upstairs. He'd throw open the bedroom window and give them a good bawling out. When he reached the window, he found that the mist had thickened again.

He could make out dozens of forms within the swirling miasma, all dressed in costumes that were outlandish, oversized, slightly worn, and grimy. Somehow, they sensed they were being watched

18

and began to dart and dodge around the driveway as if they were playing an impromptu game of tag. And just beyond this blur of rapid movement, out by the gate, stood the tall indistinct figure he had assumed was an adult the previous night.

Jack pushed the window wide. The dampness of the mist seeped into the room, causing him to shiver. 'Hey, you!' he called to the figure. 'This is out of order. Get your kids under control. What kind of person are you to let them run wild like this?'

The rushing around in the driveway came to an immediate halt. Their masked faces looked up as one at the window. They began to sing, in terrible, thunderous unison. 'We are the guisers. The guisers. The guisers. We are the guisers. Come to sing a song.'

Unable to contain his anger, Jack grabbed a vase from the dresser and hurled it with all his might at the figure by the gate. It hit the gatepost and shattered. The kids started to squeal like piglets—the pitch so high it stabbed like stiletto blades in his ears and almost brought him to his knees.

Once the squealing had stopped and he'd pulled himself together, he looked outside again.

They were nowhere to be seen. The driveway was empty and silent within the creeping fronds of mist. The figure at the gate no longer brooded there.

Hands shaking, Jack pulled the window shut.

#

Should he phone Sarah again? What impression would she get of him? Some big city hotshot up from London, pathetically spooked by the antics of a bunch of mischievous kids. But the fact was, he was most definitely spooked. Shaken to the core. Hands trembling. Sweat around his collar. The most unsettling thing of all was the presence of an adult, observing, possibly even directing the mischief. That suggested to Jack a malevolent intent. Something deliberate and spiteful. The bump on his head throbbed like a portent of worse to come.

He decided not to make the call. He'd wait for Sarah's cousin. Kenny, wasn't it? Something to do with mountain rescue. As soon as he heard him pull into the drive, he'd go out there and recount what had happened. He'd show him the shattered pieces of the vase and his wounded head as proof of what he was saying. He was going to have to pay for the vase. House rules. Breakages had to be paid for. He hoped it wasn't an heirloom or an expensive antique.

Kenny would know the value.

He might also have sufficient local knowledge to know who was behind this. If he didn't, they could drive around for a bit. If the kids were back on the hillside among the trees, seeing him in a vehicle with an official livery like that of mountain rescue might be enough to get them to knock it on the head. But what about the adult? Or maybe it was a teenager, some aspiring little thug, exerting a bad influence on the local youth. Probably a drug dealer to boot.

Jack began to feel a lot better, less tensed up and anxious.

Rationalise it. That was the thing to do.

Then a sound that froze him to the spot—

Tack. Tack. Tack.

He forced his legs to walk him to the door, and when he peered through the spyhole, he found that the lanky child in the rabbit costume was back, this time accompanied by a smaller child in a black and white cat costume that sagged a little around its skinny shoulders. It also wore a plastic mask. This one depicting Tom from *Tom and Jerry*.

'Go away,' Jack growled from behind the closed door. 'Get out of here. Tell your little stone-throwing friends that I've reported them to the police. There's a patrol car on its way up here as we speak.'

Tom and Bugs turned their heads to look at each other.

With a synchronised nod, they began to sing.

'We are the guisers. The guisers. The guisers…'

It felt to a Jack like an insect scuttling around in his inner ear.

'Just go!' he yelled. 'I'm not interested. Go bother someone else.'

The song finished and the pair did an unbidden encore—faster, louder, higher pitched. 'We are the guisers. The guisers. The guisers. We are the guisers. Come to sing a song.'

Jack lurched back from the door. 'You want something? Is that it? If I give you something, you'll go?'

He'd bought a pack of four Mars bars to snack on during his long drive. Nothing beats a little sugar boost when you are struggling with driver fatigue. But he'd only eaten two. He ran to the kitchen to fetch them while Tom and Bugs repeated the song over and over, getting more frenetic with each rendition. When he reached the door again, he crouched down and pushed both Mars bars through the letterbox.

'There!' he called over the din of their caterwauling. 'Satisfied? Now shut up and get off my driveway.'

Tom and Bugs reached down and picked up the Mars bars. Jack watched as they held them up to their faces, turned them over and over in their hands, subjected them to intense scrutiny. When they pulled their masks back over the tops of their heads, he gasped and jumped back from the spyhole.

What the hell was this? Masks beneath masks?

Tom had a pink little piggy face, squat nose, black beady eyes, pointed ears that flopped limply to the side of the head. Bugs looked like one of those ugly, hairless cats that peculiar people were fond of.

Jack blinked. His imagination had to be playing tricks on him.

Ever so cautiously, he leaned towards the spyhole. If these were secondary masks, they were works of art. They looked so unsettlingly real. Tom's porky snout flared as he sniffed at the Mars bar. The slits of Bugs' nostrils quivered and trembled. Then, in unison, they both bit down on the prizes, tiny, pointed teeth tearing away chunks of chocolate, wrapper and all. They chowed down sloppily. Tom grunted. Bugs mewled. They turned and headed for the gate, skipping with glee.

The adult, or teenager, appeared from nowhere, and Jack gasped with surprise. But he kept his eye to the spyhole, wanting to see who was behind this. No such luck. Another mask. This one was a ram's head—elongated face, eyes like onyx, horns spiralling on the sides of his head. Tom and Bugs proffered their Mars bars, and he snatched at them greedily and crammed them both into his mouth. Then he looked straight at the door, as if he could see Jack hiding behind it, bowed his head, and bleated a grotesque thank you.

#

He sat at the kitchen table, hands shaking. The guisers—Sarah had said they come disguised as something else, but what a convoluted way to get your hands on a couple of chocolate bars. Those were elaborate masks, not the cheap kind from behind the counter of a

High Street fancy-dress shop. They were more like the type of prosthetics a special effects artist would devise for a movie. And were chocolate bars all they were after? He been warned not to encourage them, or he'd never get rid of them. What had he done? Would they be back for more? What more might they expect from him?

The bump on his head pulsed and throbbed.

He decided to phone Sarah. He wouldn't tell her what had just happened. He'd just ask if she'd spoken to her cousin. Ask if he should expect him to pull into the drive any time soon. Just being in the company of someone, even for a little while, would settle his mind—help rationalise the crazy notions nagging at him. Then he could get on with finishing his presentation.

He picked up his phone. No signal. He tried the cottage's landline. No dialling tone either. Just a high-pitched whining through the receiver. Could it be the weather affecting the reception? Outside the sky was darkening, monstrous boiling clouds rolling in. It looked like snow might be on the way. A feeling of dread fell over him. Heavy snow risked making the road up from the village impassable.

Then, *tap-tap-tap* on the door.

They were back.

Something snapped inside of him. This was the last straw. He wasn't going to be intimidated by a bunch of kids, no matter how ingenious and unsettling their prank was. *Tap-tap-tap* they went, and Jack went crashing along the corridor, forcefully grabbed the handle, unlocked the latch and hauled the door open.

It was not two of them he found on the doorstep. Nor four. Nor even six. It was a dense heaving mass of them, filling the driveway and bleeding out through the gate to the road. The lanky cat-like ones. The squat piggy ones. All of them in shabbily pulled together costumes and all unmasked, staring expectantly at him, as if they were waiting to be invited in.

They began to sing their jarring serenade.

'We are the guisers. The guisers. The guisers.'

Jack moved to shut the door, but they swarmed, advancing like a crashing wave, funnelling through the door and into the corridor. For a moment he stood there with all the futility of Canute before the tide. Then, all at once, he was being dragged along. He found himself wedged as they flowed forward and fanned out into the kitchen. This close, he could tell for sure that the cat heads and pig heads were not masks. They were living flesh, gleaming with beads of sweat, tainted by pockmarks and imperfections, no visible seams at the neck.

They kept coming, cramming every inch of the kitchen, crushing him. The mildewed stench of their costumes made him gag. Those closest to the cupboards began yanking them open and grabbing at whatever they could lay their hands on. They tore packaging with their needle-like teeth. Barley and split lentils went rattling over the worktops. Porridge oats were scooped from a shredded cardboard box and crammed into waiting mouths. A jar of raspberry jam was smashed and its contents licked from the jagged shards. Fronds of flour floated lazily in the air like smoke on a battlefield. A cacophony of grunting and mewling filled the cottage.

Jack found himself jostled this way and that, feet barely touching the ground, neck awkwardly twisted by the pressure of the crush. He tried to free himself, wriggling and attempting to shoulder his way to the kitchen door. But they were packed too densely, constantly shifting and wrong-footing him. Then, without warning, they were on the move again, flowing tightly back along the corridor, taking him with them.

He was carried out of the cottage and onto the gravel of the driveway. It was already getting dark. He remembered now that it was the solstice. The shortest day. Snow was falling in fat marshmallow flakes, brewing up a blizzard, already settling on the mountain road and weighing down the branches of the conifers. He wasn't dressed for such inclement weather. Had it not been for the warmth of the bodies crushing in on him and driving him forward, he would have been shivering.

Out onto the road the horde took him, feet almost floating above the gravel. He wanted to scream out loud but couldn't make a sound. This would be a good time for Sarah's cousin to come hurtling along the road like cavalry, he thought. Scatter these creatures. Release me from their clutches.

By the time they had dragged him past the ruins of the old cottage, it dawned on him that Sarah's cousin wasn't going to show up. There probably was no cousin. It occurred to him that Sarah Monroe was herself a guiser of a different sort. Given his situation, he felt he was more than entitled to a healthy amount of paranoia. Sarah was clearly one thing posing as another. Her remote cottage advertised on Airbnb was a lure. How many others had taken the bait over the years? How many times had she spun her line about not encouraging the guisers if they chapped on the door, when her true intent was to deliver you into their clutches? She smiled and disguised herself as the friendly hostess while all the time angling you into position to be stabbed in the back. He saw it all, laid out in his head in form of a PowerPoint, with slides and bullets. The Airbnb ad, showing a price slightly lower than similar accommodation in the area. But not so low it might cause any undue alarm. The isolated location. The warnings about the guisers, clearly designed to entice curiosity rather than discourage it. There would be no cars coming round the corner any time soon. This was how Sarah and the other villagers kept the guisers away from their own doors.

Present an outsider as a sacrificial lamb.

In a fit of anger, he tried to break free, but it was hopeless. The cat things and pig things just closed in tighter and quickened their pace, mewling and grunting in gleeful celebration of their captured prize. The snow was thickening now. He felt it clumping on his head and shoulders, but his arms were pressed too tightly to his sides to be able to shake it off. Through the haze of it, he could see the ram-headed one walking slightly ahead of the main cluster like a drum major leading some outlandish Yuletide procession.

Then he came to an abrupt halt.

The cat things and the pig things dissipated around Jack, forming a ragged semi-circle behind him. Ram-head stepped to one side. In the road ahead stood five horses with riders. They were unlike any horse or rider Jack had ever seen before. The horses were almost skeletal—leathery flesh stretched tight against white bone. They had black lips and yellow teeth. Huffs of billowing vapour gushed from their nostrils as they shook their straggly manes free of the snow.

But it was the terrible countenance of the riders that truly caused Jack's heart to race and his legs to tremble so much he fell to his knees. They looked like gigantic birds of prey, clawed feet in the stirrups, clawed hands holding the reigns, black beaks curved like scimitars. The one in the centre, flanked on either side by her entourage, was surely their Queen. Jack could feel the raw sexual energy she exuded, almost taste the musky tang of it in the cold air. He was disgusted at his inability to fight back his arousal.

She wore a cloak of glossy black feathers—or were they actual wings? He could no longer tell reality from fantasy. He half expected to see gigantic wings unfurl and spread behind her. Purple fronds of plumage crested her head, waving in the icy breeze, and he could see no sign of ears. But from the way she cocked her head, he could tell she was savouring every faltering breath he inhaled. At first, he thought she wore an emerald breastplate, but the more he studied her, the more he realised she was naked from the waist up. The green appearance of her voluptuous breasts was due to the ancient layers of moss and lichen that clung to them like mildewed linen. Ivy entwined her curvatious hips, creeping up her belly and abdomen to weave itself among the feathers and greenery. She was both flora and fauna.

His nerves tingled at the very notion of being in the presence of something not entirely of his world. Over a sharply hooked beak, that may or may not have been part of a mask, she stared at him, and he found her malevolence erotic. His pulse thumped a tattoo inside his head. A grotesquely delicious tremble juddered through him. He was hers in that instance. Completely and unequivocally. He wanted to rut with her like a wanton beast, but what she would do with him, he could not begin to imagine.

It seemed to take for ever for those dark eyelids to blink.

'Please—if I have somehow offended you, I am truly sorry.'

The Queen looked him up and down, and he felt embarrassed, knowing she could noticed his throbbing erection.

Then she threw back her head and the muscles of her narrow feathery neck contracted. 'Caw! Caw! Caw!'

'Caw! Caw! Caw!' joined her entourage.

'We are the guisers. The guisers. The guisers,' sang the pig things and cat things, swaying from side to side.

Ram-head bleated and bowed dramatically to his Queen.

A chair appeared and was passed over the seething crowd of beasts. There were intricate carvings on the back and arms, and the cushion was of faded velvet. It was set before him and he was forced to sit, wrists lashed to the arms, ankles lashed to the legs. He was hoisted high and the snow lashed his face.

The Queen pulled the reigns of her skeletal steed and turned it. Her entourage followed suit. Ram-head fell in behind.

From somewhere on the mountainside came the mournful skirl of bagpipes.

Then a snare drum began to beat a tattoo that mimicked his pulse.

Tat-tat. Rata-tat-tat.

The procession set off again.

'We are the guisers,' sang the pig things and cat things. 'The guisers. The guisers.'

Jack realised why the sound of it was so awful. The words were in a language their mouths felt uncomfortable with. They were merely impersonating the structure and intonation. It was a mimicry of something they had heard—part of their disguise. Nevertheless, they were singing it joyously. They were celebrating their prize. Jack was the treat in return for the tricks they had played.

It was fully dark now. Solstice. The shortest day. Snow falling thick and fast. After today, the light would commence its slow creep back towards summer. That was why the guisers were returning from whence they had come—and Jack was going with them. He knew instinctively that once they had reached the summit of the winding mountain road, they would pass into another realm. Who knew what new nightmares awaited him there?

The chair soared and dipped as it was passed from shoulder to shoulder.

'We are the guisers,' came the keening refrain. 'The guisers. The guisers.'

Finding his voice at last, Jack screamed.

THE HOUSE ON THE BLUFF
Edward Lodi

'It's only a spider,' Uncle Jared shouted. 'Stop your blubbering.' He grabbed Brianna by the shoulders and shook her.

True—it was only a spider, and not a big one at that. But ten-year-old Brianna was terrified. She sobbed hysterically as the spider, dangling from a rafter on a gossamer thread, descended slowly toward her head.

'Don't kill it!' Uncle Jared snapped at Amanda.

Amanda withdrew her hand. 'Spiders eat bugs,' the old man explained. He took hold of the gossamer thread and let the spider fall into his cupped hand, then carried it over to a work bench, shook it into a jar, and replaced the lid, which had holes punched through it. 'The bigger they are, the more bugs they eat. Bugs are our worst enemies.'

Ignoring the silently weeping Brianna, he led Amanda to a dark corner of the cellar, where a large wooden bin rested on the floor. He lifted the lid.

'See? I breed 'em. Big spiders.'

Amanda stared into the bin, which was divided into compartments, each containing a web and a big black spider in its center—bigger than any spiders she had ever seen.

'You afraid of 'em?'

Amanda shook her head. 'Maybe just a little,' she confessed.

'Someday I'll have the biggest spiders of all,' Uncle Jared boasted. 'And if you're a good little girl—he cast a scornful glance toward her cousin, Brianna—I'll let you watch me feed 'em. They like their food alive. They wrap it in a woven sack, then come back when they're hungry and suck the juices from it.'

'May I watch you feed one now, Uncle Jared?'

The old man smiled. 'Why of course, Amanda. Fetch me that jar from the work bench, the one with the fat caterpillars inside.'

When Amanda returned with the jar, Uncle Jared selected the plumpest caterpillar he could find and dropped it into one of the compartments. 'See how the web vibrates? That tells the spider it has a visitor.'

Amanda watched fascinated as the caterpillar struggled to free itself, to no avail. The spider rapidly approached and immediately set about binding the insect in a sort of cocoon—but not the sort from which the caterpillar would ever emerge as a butterfly.

#

Amanda had hoped to get at least as far as Belfast before nightfall, but a flat tire on Interstate 95, followed by a wrong turn off of Route One, put the kibosh on that plan. It was nearly midnight by the time she turned onto the last of the nexus of unpaved roads that twisted through a forest of old-growth conifers, ending at a remote bluff on an even remoter inlet of Penobscot Bay, where the old, decaying house stood overlooking the vast North Atlantic.

The letter from Uncle Jared had taken her by surprise: Uncle Jared—actually her great-uncle—whom she hadn't seen in over a decade, not since she was a child, when her parents were alive, and then only on a dozen or so occasions. She remembered him as ancient even then, walking with a stoop, tufts of white hair hanging over his forehead, with a hook nose and gold-rimmed spectacles which persisted in sliding onto it, and which he repeatedly pushed back into place with a gnarled finger—to her child's mind the spitting image of Ebenezer Scrooge.

Why, after all these years of no communication whatsoever, had he deeded the house over to her, retaining for himself only a life estate, which she understood to mean that he had the right to remain in the house as long as he chose to, i.e., for the rest of his life, however long—at his advanced age—that might be. Or something to that effect. She hadn't yet consulted a lawyer and had no idea what her responsibilities regarding the old heap might be. Was she legally liable for its upkeep?

Amanda wrote to the old man but received no reply.

As a freelance writer with no pressing deadlines, there was nothing to prevent her from packing a suitcase and setting out from Boston to visit Uncle Jared in person. She'd chosen a sunny day in late October for the excursion. If nothing else, it was an excuse to take on the role of leaf peeper and enjoy the fall foliage along the way.

The foliage had proved spectacular. But driving along unlit, unpaved roads through a dense forest of towering conifers on a moonless night was like driving through a tunnel with no light at the end. As she remembered it, the old mansion, built by a retired sea captain in the mid nineteenth century, remained much as it had a century and a half ago: without electricity, without running water, without phone service. The difference between then and now was that the house had fallen into disrepair and there were no servants.

When at last she reached the end of the road, she pulled onto the circular drive in front of the house, next to a beat-up Ford sedan she assumed was Uncle Jared's. The house lay in total darkness. In a second letter, posted a week ago, she'd announced the date of her planned visit. But of course there was no mail delivery here. Had he gone to the post office recently? Probably not. He was, after all, a recluse.

Amanda sat in the car with the headlights lighting up the portico of the three-story structure looming before her like an abandoned hulk adrift in a sea of darkness. The actual sea lay just a few hundred yards beyond where she was parked. Reluctant to abandon the security of the car, she sat with the motor running and the doors locked. What should be her next move? Sound the horn? She needn't worry about disturbing the neighbors. There were none, not for miles.

She gave two short toots, and waited. After five minutes with no response, she sounded the horn again, this time a single, much longer blast.

Nothing. Maybe the old man was deaf. The sensible thing would be to backtrack and find a motel near Belfast, where she could comfortably spend what was left of the night before returning in the light of day.

On second thought, was it sensible? Hardly. She was tired. After a grueling day of mishap followed by misstep, she had finally arrived

29

at her destination, and damned if she was about to turn around now. Grabbing a flashlight from the glove compartment, she killed the engine and stepped out into the night—to be reminded by a stiff off-shore breeze that she was in Maine, at the end of October, standing on an exposed bluff at the ocean's edge. Like an amorous corpse, the breeze seized her body and probed it with icy fingers.

She regretted having packed her jacket at the bottom of her suitcase, now resting in the trunk of the car.

She followed the beam cast by the flashlight across the gravel-packed driveway to the steps leading up to the portico. The steps creaked under her feet, but held firm. The flooring on the portico, too, felt solid. The old pile Uncle Jared had saddled her with might not be in such a sad state of repair after all.

She ignored the elaborate brass knocker shaped like a dolphin, which the retired sea captain, having made his fortune in the Old China Trade, had attached to the oak door. Instead, she tried the latch. It yielded. Not surprisingly, Uncle Jared, like most folks living in remote areas of rural Maine, had not bothered to lock it.

Edging the door forward, she stepped over the threshold into a dark so absolute she might have stepped into a mine shaft. She hesitated, then swept the beam around the hall. The space was much as she remembered it from childhood: almost devoid of furnishings, the paneling discolored and cracked, dust (more of it now) everywhere. The passage to the left, she recalled, led to the kitchen, scullery, storeroom, and dining room, that to the right to the double parlors, study, library, and sun room.

She directed her beam at the grand staircase opposite the door. When she was a little girl, standing for the first time where she stood now, the stairway with its ornate newel posts seemed like a portal to fairyland. What wonders lay beyond? The round tops of the newel posts were carved globes depicting the world as it was known in the early nineteen hundreds. The globes had fascinated her, as had the wall coverings in the various rooms, with nautical themes, or scenes of tropical isles, or remote mountains, or deserts: places which, like in *Alice Through the Looking Glass*, she might enter and have adventures of her very own.

Now the old dark house seemed to threaten, as if, breaking a taboo, she'd entered a hostile world, one that owed more to Dante Alighieri than to Lewis Carroll.

Her uncle's bedroom and the guest rooms were upstairs. What now? Stand at the foot of the stairs and shout out her presence? But—if the old man hadn't responded to her horn blast, would yelling up the staircase wake him? Probably not. He might not even be home. The Ford parked on the circular drive might not be his. Or he might have purchased a newer car. Or someone might have picked him up, for whatever reason. He might have wandered off into the woods.

Or, the thought crowded into her mind, he might be upstairs in his bed, dead.

She should go upstairs and see. He may have suffered a stroke and be lying there paralyzed, helpless, unable to move or speak. But what if she came upon his rotting corpse? Could she bear the shock? The horror? Under normal circumstances perhaps. But alone, after midnight, in an old dark house miles from the nearest habitation?

She was no coward. Even so—

If he were dead, perhaps for days, wouldn't there be a stench in the house? Maybe not. Not if his bedroom door was tightly closed. Besides, the house was cold—like a morgue. The temperature at night this time of year often fell below freezing. Decay under such conditions would progress slowly, if at all.

So—what were her choices? Leave and drive off into the night? Remain on the ground floor and attempt sleep? (Fat chance of that.) Or go upstairs and confront whatever was there?

She went upstairs.

She mounted the stairs slowly, one step at a time, pausing after each, alert to the silence. A preternatural silence—as if the house was holding its breath. And yet, Uncle Jared wasn't up there, she felt certain of that. The house smelt wrong. The air was stale. There were no lingering odors of fires having been lit, of smoldering embers, of food having been cooked, coffee prepared and poured.

After reaching the landing, where the stairs took an abrupt turn, she hastened up the remaining flight. At the head, she paused.

Uncle Jared's bedroom was to the left. As a child, though her family's visits were few, she had on each occasion explored the house from top to bottom. For her, wandering through the rooms had been like exploring a castle. Was that why he had deeded the house to her? Because she had loved it so? Or was it because she had not been terrified, like her cousin Brianna, of his pets, the spiders he seemed obsessed with? A brave little girl he had called her, had patted her head, had given her sweet treats on the sly.

She went to the room she remembered as his and opened the door. The cold that greeted her was the cold of the grave—a grave, however, which contained no body, dead or alive. The four-poster bed was empty, though it had been slept in and remained unmade. Nothing odd there. Would a man as old as Uncle Jared bother to make his bed every day?

She left the room, closed the door behind her, and made her way two doors down the hallway, to the room that had been hers when, in the halcyon days of childhood, she had come to visit with her parents. The door was not locked. She opened it and shone her beam around the room, at the walls, at the bed and night stand, at the floor. A thick layer of dust lay over everything. She would not be spending the night in this bed. Nor in any bed for that matter.

She went downstairs to the kitchen, where she came upon a half dozen hurricane lamps in a cupboard, along with matches and a fresh box of candles. She removed the candle stub from one of the lamps and attached a new one. She touched a lighted match to the candle wick and switched her flashlight off.

Holding the lamp before her, she took an inventory of what the kitchen had on hand. She was pleased to discover a wood-burning stove with logs piled neatly in a corner and ample kindling, including old newspapers and magazines stored in a cardboard box. There was a dry sink and an old wooden bucket next to it. The well, she recalled, was outside in the back. The scullery contained flour, sugar, coffee, powdered milk, pasta, salt, pepper, and a variety of spices, along with canned goods. The bread in the bread box was stale. Butter and cheese, she knew, and perhaps eggs, would be suspended in a watertight container in the well. She was sure to find vegetables in the root cellar.

If she chose to remain in the house—her house, now—she would not lack for food or drink. If memory served, Uncle Jared kept an ample supply of wine in the basement.

Uncle Jared. Where was he? Something wasn't right. Tomorrow she'd make a thorough search of the house from top to bottom, just to be sure, then contact the state police on her cell phone.

She built a fire in the stove. Guided by the hurricane lamp, she went outside and retrieved her suitcase. She made a second trip for the sleeping bag she always kept in the trunk of the car. She stretched the bag out on the floor in front of the stove, snuffed out the candle, and snuggled in.

She lay in the dark listening to the empty house and heard sounds she hadn't noticed before: the wind sighing through the chimneys, a branch clawing at a window, boards creaking from expansion or contraction—as if the house, satisfied that she posed no threat, had resumed its normal breathing.

In the wee hours, as the fire died down and the stove grew cold, she fell into a fitful sleep.

When she woke, her body stiff from lying on the flag-paved floor, light was streaming in through the windows above the sink. The first order of the day, after rekindling the fire, was to answer a call from nature. The breeze nipped at her ears and nose as she made her way to the outhouse, accessible through a back door. The narrow wood structure, like a rotting coffin upended, listed to one side, a caricature of The Leaning Tower of Pisa.

Before taking up permanent residence, she would tear down the one-seater and in its place install a self-composting toilet, warm and cozy, within the house itself. The wood-burning stove would remain, but for heating only. She would buy a gas stove and have tanks of propane trucked in.

Famished, she fetched water from the well and found submerged below the surface the water-tight box in which Uncle Jared stored butter, cheese, and eggs—two dozen. The bright October sun, hunkering low in the sky, did little to warm the air. Like a malicious sprite, the wind from the ocean nipped at her nose and ears and numbed her fingers. She hurried inside, lugging the wooden bucket, and immediately returned for the eggs, butter, and cheese. When the stove was hot enough, she boiled water for coffee, cooked up an omelet, and fried slices of the stale bread in a cast-iron pan.

The next order of the day, after she piled the dirty dishes into the sink, was to search for Uncle Jared—not that she expected to find him. She began with the pull-down ladder leading to the attic. She poked her head through the opening and swept the flashlight beam around. Dust everywhere, no sign of anyone having been there in years. She found the same more or less true for the servants' rooms on the third floor and the guests' bedrooms on the second. No sign of the old man in any of the rooms on the first floor. That left the basement.

The door leading to it was off the scullery.

She hesitated before opening it. Uncle Jared had spent hours every day in the basement. The stairs leading down were steep. He was old. Old people easily lose their balance. What if she found him at the bottom, sprawled on the dirt floor, dead. She should have checked the basement first. Why hadn't she?

Now, the flashlight in her left hand, her right poised on the latch, she thought she knew the answer: she was afraid. To go down there. Of what she might find.

Then, remembering her cousin Brianna, who was terrified of spiders, terrified of everything for that matter, her resolve stiffened and she yanked the door open. Enough light filtered in from the windows set high in the basement walls for her to see, without resorting to the flashlight, what lay at the foot of the stairs: nothing.

Exhaling—she had been holding her breath—she went down the wooden steps. With luck, she would find the root cellar well stocked with potatoes, turnips, winter squash, and whatnot. And an ample supply of wine in the rack against the wall. She would feel no compunction drinking it. If Uncle Jared complained—*where* was the old man?—she would replace whatever wine she drank, and then some. The brownstone townhouse in Boston's Back Bay where her family had lived for generations, and which she now owned, would fetch a high price in today's market, giving her plenty of money to restore the old sea captain's mansion to its former glory.

She began her exploration of the basement. Root cellar and wine rack lived up to her expectation. A sardonic smile distorted her lips when she came upon the work bench where Uncle Jared had stored live insects in jars to feed to his pet spiders. The jars were still there, but the insects inside were all dead. It appeared the old man hadn't attended to them for some time.

With nothing to eat, having to fend for themselves, the spiders were probably dead, too. Maybe they fed on each other. Spiders were known for doing just that. Why not take a peek and see for herself?

She directed the flashlight toward the corner where Uncle Jared stored the large wooden bin in which he kept his pets. It was still there—but without the lid covering it. The lid lay on the floor to one side. Had he abandoned his project of breeding "the biggest spiders of all"? Surely the task of supplying the spiders with insects to eat, especially in the winter months, must have proved onerous for someone his age.

She approached the bin and peered in. It was empty.

She decided she'd seen enough. It was time to select a bottle of merlot or pinot noir to have with dinner and then contact the state police on her cell phone and voice her concern over her uncle's disappearance.

As she turned to the stairs, the beam fell upon a far corner of the basement which she'd neglected to inspect. There was something odd there, something hanging from one of the rough-hewn rafters. As she approached it, she saw what she took to be a burlap sack—with huge black objects adhering to it.

When she drew closer, the objects began to shift about.

The realization came as a shock. The black things adhering to the sack were spiders. Huge spiders, hairy, their bloated bodies the size of baseballs. And the sack—not burlap, after all—was shaped like a human being.

She'd found Uncle Jared.

Then, as she shrank back in horror, the spiders found her.

THE CHOIR
Kev Harrison

Carl unlocked his front door and walked into the pitch-blackness of the apartment. Tiny scratches skittering across the wooden floor made him pause. From out of the darkness, Sookie, his cat, emerged to nuzzle his ankles.

'Hey girl. Hungry?' he said, crouching to rub the tufts on the side of her face.

She mewed in reply, and he went to the kitchen, grabbing a can of cat food and racing her to the food bowl. He stroked her as she tucked in, before moving back to the doorway. He watched her eat for a while, her tail a question mark.

Then he noticed the singing.

It sounded choral—certainly a number of voices—but muffled, indecipherable. A sort of drone. As for the style, it was difficult to tell. Carl was well-versed in most genres, but this was unusual. Too loose to be classical, he thought perhaps it had some elements of folk. Somehow, he sensed it was *old*.

He looked at his watch, frowning. A quarter to midnight. It *was* Friday, but it still seemed a bit much. He returned to the lounge, peering out the ninth-story window, looking for lights, some sign of a party. The street was dark, the amber glow of sodium lights like halos cast aside by saints. He pulled open the balcony door and went out, Sookie sprinting between his legs, bounding onto the flower boxes.

'Shhh!' Carl petted her absent-mindedly while straining to figure out where the sound was coming from. It seemed so quiet on the balcony. He scooped Sookie in his arms and went back inside, closing the door.

The music immediately grew louder.

'Fucking weird.'

He wandered toward the bedroom. As he crossed the threshold, the volume increased. He shoved the heavy window open and strained his ears.

The volume diminished.

He slammed the window shut, sat on the edge of the bed. Let the music wash over him. Instrumentation remained obscured in the sea of voices. He picked out males and females, deep bass tones, layered with tenors and altos, odd high notes peaking over the drone. There were words, but either he could not perceive them or they were from a language alien to him.

Carl retrieved his phone from his pocket and called Margarida. The phone buzzed twice before she picked up. 'Hey! I'm driving,' she said, her smile transmitted through her voice.

'Where to? Here?' Carl laid back on the bed.

'No, to see my *other* lover. Of course, there. I'll be about ten minutes.'

There was a moment of silence.

'You okay?' The warmth in her tone replaced by concern.

'Me? Yeah…well, someone's playing music. But, like, *really* loud. And…weird…like a choir. Chanting. Or something.'

Mellowness returned to Margarida's voice as she giggled. 'Probably a *festa*. You should know how it is this time of year. It's after midnight. They'll shut up soon.'

'They'd better!'

'Eight minutes. Love you.'

The phone clicked off and Carl placed it on his bedside table. His eyelids felt heavy. He allowed them to droop, then close.

The music roared to life. The voices grew, as if coming from inside his mind. The low notes throbbed in his skull. Patterns formed against the blackness of his eyelids, like undulating plasma in a lava lamp. Colours faded in and out from the nothingness.

The music stopped.

Not at the end of the piece or even the bar. It simply ceased.

The room was silent.

He sat up and tapped his phone screen. The display read *0:09*. He walked to the lounge. Sookie looked up from her basket. Nothing.

The apartment was absolutely silent. He sat in his comfy chair, in front of the fireplace, gazing into the distance.

The clunk of the door's heavy locking mechanism snapped him out of his trance.

'Where's this loud, party music, then?' Margarida said, stepping out of her shoes and striding over to plant a kiss on Carl's lips.

'It's gone. It just stopped about seven or eight minutes ago.'

'I told you.' Margarida's smile lit up her face, while Carl's remained impassive. 'Are you sure you're okay?' She batted her eyelids playfully.

'Think so, yeah. It was just so…strange.'

'Shall we get off to bed? I'm up before eight tomorrow.'

#

The next day was easier. No afterwork dinner meeting, so Carl was home not long after seven. The apartment was silent but for the muted hum of traffic on the coast road below, snaking from Lisbon through the seaside towns and villages toward Sintra. He fed the cat, then set about rustling something up for dinner before Margarida got home.

A bottle of wine was open on the table when she entered an hour later, and dinner was in the process of being served.

'Hey, how was your day?' Carl asked, ladling sauce onto pasta, then sprinkling cheese over the top. Margarida's response was somewhere between a sigh and a grunt. 'Wine's on the table—go!' he said and finished plating up the second dish. They ate, then settled in for an evening of binge-watching a low-budget Portuguese urban fantasy series about a house built on an interdimensional faultline. The dishes had been cast into the sink to be dealt with the next day.

'One more episode?' Margarida said, fumbling for the remote just after eleven. Carl nudged it towards her.

'Sure. Hang on…do you hear that?' He stood, cocked his head.

'Nope. Wait…oh yeah…the music.' Margarida got to her feet, displeasing Sookie, who'd been happily nestled in her sweatshirt. 'It's odd. Is it the same as yesterday?' Carl held up his palm to shush her, then nodded. He gestured for her to follow him, leading the way into the bedroom.

Just like the day before, the droning music was more vivid, as though coming from some hidden corner of the room itself. Margarida marched to the window and opened it. 'It must be from one of these buildings out—' She stopped, a puzzled expression painted on her face. 'It's quieter with the window *open*. Doesn't make any sense.'

'That's what I was telling you.' Carl sat on the edge of the bed, then laid back, head nestling just below the pillow. 'Lie with me for a moment. And close your eyes.'

Margarida stretched out beside him.

'I appreciate the gesture, but this music and its satanic ritual vibe doesn't really put me in the mood.' Carl thumped her playfully on the arm. She closed her eyes. '*O meu deus*,' she whispered. She bolted upright. 'What *is* that?'

Carl sat up, too. 'It's different. Louder than yesterday.' He placed his arm around her—pulled her close. 'It's so unusual, though. Don't you think?'

'I don't like it. I could see—something—reacting to the sounds.' She shivered, then stood and paced into the living room. 'It's much quieter in here,' she called out.

Carl joined her. 'Let's watch another episode. Loud. Until it stops.'

When the show was finished, at around half past midnight, the music was already gone.

#

Carl's phone buzzed on his desk. Margarida. He tapped the screen.

Hey love. Completely forgot I have a weekend away, up north. Some sales bullshit. The director gets us drunk then makes a pass at one of the interns. I'll be back Sunday. Sorry. xx

Though he would miss Margarida, a weekend alone wasn't such a bad thing. He had sketches to finish, housework to do.

Then there was the music.

At first, it had been unsettling—the difficulty in locating where it was coming from, the bizarre, almost hymnal tone of it. But then he'd felt something. Those shapes forming and fading behind his eyelids. There was something more there. As though it were communicating something. Margarida's reaction had only confirmed as much. He hit reply.

Don't worry about me, love. I'll just get a takeaway and have some me time. Have fun. x

#

Shards of sunlight poured in through the balcony doors when Carl arrived home around eight. He fed Sookie, simultaneously scrolling through his pizza delivery app to appease his grumbling stomach. He settled on a Neapolitan. His stomach grumbled at the thought of anchovies, capers, and mozzarella. He pulled a beer from the fridge, uncapped it, took a sip, then moved to the spare room to sit at the desk. He powered up his laptop and loaded the photo of the lighthouse he'd been sketching.

Absorbed in the sketch, he teased out textures, only occasionally taking a swig of beer or looking up to admire Sookie shifting between napping positions and stretches. The room was quiet, the scratching of pencil on paper the only sound.

The music began much as it had previously, in mid-phrase. An organ in full flow, breathing minor chords with unsettling tones. He noted the time. 10:48. He scribbled it on a scrap of paper before stashing his sketch in the desk drawer.

He took Sookie in his arms and carried her with him into the bedroom. Again, the music was louder there—the voices more present. The language remained a mystery to him. It had nothing in common with English or the smatterings of French, German and Portuguese he was familiar with. Sookie struggled to break free. He tried to restrain her, soothe her with his voice, but she squeezed herself loose and swiped, a single claw tracing a red line across Carl's cheek. 'Ow, fuck! Go on then.'

He went into the ensuite and inspected the scratch. Fine globules of blood seeped from it. He wiped it with a tissue and returned to the bedroom.

Lying on the bed, staring at the ceiling, he allowed the music to envelop him. The choir chanted its enigmatic song. He closed his eyes and swam in it, strings and wind instruments carrying him like a current.

In a burst of inspiration, he sat up and reached over to Margarida's side of the bed. He unfastened the scarf she kept tied around the bedpost and wrapped it around his head. The darkness was deeper—the music more intense now. He lay back and tuned into the music, booming drums—perhaps timpani—marking the beat like thunder.

As he focused, shapes swirled behind his eyelids, ethereal yet solid, shifting in shape and colour as their dance played out. From the abstract forms, familiar lines began to appear; faces became fully formed, stable. The eyes were vacant, without focus, but the lips moved. Carl concentrated on them as hard as he could, watching them form the words of the hymn and confirming this was a language he had no knowledge of whatsoever.

Still, there was a message. Something was starting. It was something he was being included in. *An invitation.*

The music stopped and his mind went blank. Startled, he sat up. 0:09, his watch reported. The exact moment it had cut out on the first evening.

He dashed to the spare room and took his sketching pencil and the scrap of paper.

Then, elbow on the desk, he rested his head on his hand and stared at the numbers.

His phone buzzed.

'Margarida, it's late. You've arrived?'

'Yeah. I'm in the hotel now. We went straight to the big dinner after check-in. Traffic was a nightmare. What have you been doing?'

'Sketching. That lighthouse we visited up the coast the other week. And…'

The line crackled, carving up the silence. Voices murmured unintelligibly at the other end.

'Is someone there with you?' Carl swallowed to ease the sudden dryness in his mouth.

'Here? No. Of course not, no. Anyway, you were saying, *and*—'

'And the music came back.'

'Carl, I told you. I don't like it. I don't think you should—'

'I listened to all of it. As soon as it started, I went to the room and blindfolded myself so I could listen more intently.'

Margarida blew out a long breath.

'Don't be angry with me. I just want to understand it—figure out where it's coming from. What it means, you know?' He paused, waiting for encouragement. But none was forthcoming. 'It stopped at the same time. The *exact* same time. Nine minutes after midnight. But this time I was waiting for it. The flat was quiet. I got the start time down, too. Ten forty-eight.'

'Eighty-one minutes,' said Margarida, softly.

'What?'

'The music was playing for eighty-one minutes. Ten forty-eight to nine after midnight. Nine squared. It's all nines.'

'What does that mean?'

'How should I know? Probably nothing, to be honest. Look, Carl, it's late. I'm going to get some sleep. I'll call tomorrow, yeah?'

He paused for a moment, listening carefully to the movements at the other end of the line. 'Sleep well, babe.'

#

The following morning, Carl sat at the table, sipping coffee and waiting for his laptop to boot. Once on, he opened a browser window, typed "9", and hit enter. The screen refreshed, displaying an endless series of results, from 9gag memes to IMDB entries for short films and albums called "9".

He took a long swig of coffee and clicked in the address bar. He typed "nine number" and hit return. This time, the results were more focused. From an article entitled "why is nine a magic number?" to various numerology pages. He was about to close the window when he noticed the text in one preview:

...nine is often referred to as the number of wisdom and initiation.

He felt his pulse quicken. His eyes were drawn to that word.

Initiation.

He clicked the link.

The screen lit up with a rainbow of colour and symbols from a range of religions, old and new. Crammed into a poorly laid out text box was what he was looking for. After the part about initiation and wisdom, it went on to describe nine as a magical number. Three-fold the number three, itself a number associated with power and magic since at least the days of the Babylonian civilisation. It also explained nine was the last number in its series before the next "harmony", identified as ten.

Carl saved the page, then scoured the glowing, new age imagery to find a search box. Finding it, he typed "eighty-one" and hit enter. The list of references was extensive—from some relating it to a symbol of the individual in the nirvana world, to its place in Chinese philosophy as the number of perfection and the completion of life. Others claimed it as the magical counterpart of the moon. It was ingrained in a catalogue of mythologies.

Carl favourited this page too, then tapped "back". His eyes lingered on the word "initiation". He cast his mind back to the night before and the unshakeable feeling that something was beginning—that it had been an invitation—*an invocation*.

Whoever was playing the music, wherever it was coming from, they were reaching out to him—calling him to join them.

He glanced at his watch. 'Shit! I'm late for work.'

He slammed the laptop closed, grabbed his keys and left.

#

Dense fog had rolled in off the ocean by nightfall. After getting home, Carl slid a pizza into the oven, reminding himself Margarida being away was not an excuse for his diet to go to shit. He fed Sookie, who'd refused to sleep at the end of the bed since the music had begun. He curled up on the sofa, switched on the TV at low volume, found a relatively mindless comedy, and turned on the subtitles. He tried to watch, but his eyes were soon drawn to the window. The warm glow of hidden streetlights painted spheres of colour against the fog.

When the oven timer beeped, he fetched his dinner, poured himself a glass of water, and sat at the table. Hands and jaws worked in mechanical unison, making short work of the pizza while he stared out at the shrouded world outside.

His phone shuddered to life. On the screen, was a picture of Margarida, taken on the cliffs on the other side of the river, sunlight bringing the red in her hair to vivid life. Below the photo, the time—22:45. Tension spread through his muscles, white noise a cacophony in his ears. He was paralysed, unable to decide whether to answer or not.

His hand jutted forward, lifted the phone to his ear. 'H-hello?'

'Carl? Are you okay?'

'Yeah. Yeah, I'm fine. Fine. How are you?'

'Carl, your breathing's all over the place. What's going on?'

'It's nothing. I was…in the kitchen. Anyway, tell me about your day.' Carl glanced at his watch. 22:46. He walked into the bedroom, stretched out on the bed.

'Okay, well, that's why I'm calling. Well, also to say hi.' She laughed uncomfortably and he waited for her to continue. 'The whole team up here is a mess. They want me to stay on for a few more days and establish some of the processes from our Lisbon office.'

'When will you be back?' Carl sat up and reached for the scarf he'd been using as a blindfold.

'They said Friday at the absolute latest. And I'll get a bunch of lieu time for all the stopover crap. I'm sorry.'

'You won't be here on the ninth day?'

Margarida coughed. 'Carl, it's the sixteenth today.'

'I didn't mean—it doesn't matter. Okay, well, tell me when you know more precisely, okay?'

'Are you sure you're alright? I can tell them I can't stay. Reschedule—'

'I'm fine. Listen, I have to go. I love you.' Carl hung up before she could reply. The time burned into his retinas from the display: 22:47. He quickly tied the blindfold and laid back.

He felt the hair stand on his forearms as he waited. Only the muted sound of his breathing piercing the silence. The now-familiar drone began mid-melody.

As though it were always *playing.*

He allowed himself to be drawn in, his heart rate slowing as he descended into a near-trance. He stifled his burgeoning anticipation as he waited for the shapes to form in his mind.

Time had already become a long-forgotten concept when the first swirls emerged from the darkness, tails trailing like comets, writhing as faces gradually took shape. As before, they were expressionless, eye sockets vacant indentations, mouths moving in sync with the non-words of the song.

'I accept your invitation. I wish to share in your wisdom.' Carl had no idea whether he uttered the words aloud or within the vision. A ripple moved through the faces, spreading out into the gloom. The volume intensified.

A response.

'How do I do it? H-how can I be initiated?' This time he was certain he had used his physical voice.

The faces drew closer, the rawness of the vacant space where their eyes ought to have been unnerving him.

He flinched.

The music stopped abruptly.

He sat up and tapped his phone's screen. 0:09. His chest heaved. He stood and hurried to the kitchen, poured himself a glass of water and drank thirstily, liquid spilling down his chin. Exhaustion crashed over him. His fingers lost their grip and the glass tumbled to the tiled floor, shattering. Sookie stood at the doorway to the kitchen, ears pinned back.

'Stay out of here. This is dangerous,' Carl said, shooing her with his hand. She backed off and he took the dustpan and brush from a cupboard. He scooped up the glass and carried it to the bin. He watched the shards tumble down into the bag, jangling together in their own disharmonious music.

Turning around, he spotted one large chunk he'd somehow missed. He crouched, pressed his fingertip to the sharp edge until a drop of blood beaded and fell to the floor. He allowed his eyes to linger on the point for a moment, at how the light from the fluorescent tubes above bounced from the jagged surface. He tossed it into the bin and went to bed.

#

Carl left work early. He'd been skittish all day, unable to shake his mental rendition of the droning music. His boss had accepted a story about a forgotten dental appointment and excused him. He went home via the supermarket.

After he arrived, he fed Sookie early and got down to slicing steak and vegetables for a stir-fry. He worked methodically, sorting the ingredients into neat piles, before quickly frying them off in the wok. He added a slather of oyster sauce, then a handful of noodles.

Sookie sat nearby as he ate, licking her lips as he moved strips of beef from the plate to his mouth. He finished his meal, then fussed her. She sniffed his hand, then nuzzled against him. 'Why don't you come to my room anymore, girl?' Carl asked.

She purred.

He spent more than an hour stroking her. He hummed the strange music almost inaudibly, a sense of dread saturating him more with every passing moment. Just before ten, he scooped up the dishes and went to the kitchen. He began to scrub but felt twitchy. He shook his head, focussed on the task.

He finished and moved toward the door, fingers lingering on the light switch. He turned his head, eyes drawn to the bin. He stalked back across the kitchen, taking off the lid and foraging among carrot peel and onion skin. He felt the rough surface of the glass shard from the night before. He fished it out and held it between his thumb and forefinger. He traced the point of it across his fingertip.

Sharp enough.

He stood and ran the hot tap, cleaning the fragment, then shaking it dry. He turned off the light, headed to the bedroom, and lay down on the bed. He checked the time. Eleven minutes. He grasped the glass and held it in front of his face. Slowly moved it closer to his right eye. His vision blurred, divided the fragment in two.

Carl felt the gelatinous membrane of his eyeball with his fingertips and shivered. He drew the glass away and sat up, bile scorching his throat. He went to the ensuite and dropped the broken glass into the bin. The clang as it closed was greeted by the first notes of the drone.

He leapt across the bed and laid back, scrunching his eyes shut. The tone seemed deeper. It seemed to carry more menace, but that could have been his imagination. His heart thumped, unnervingly off-beat next to the choir. He focussed on his breathing. On calming himself. On becoming one with the music again.

He began to relax, the swirling shapes forming behind his eyes, colours deeper than usual. When the faces began to take shape, they were grotesque. Lacerated at irregular angles, their lips chapped, mouths tongueless.

They spat their cryptic verses, saliva rolling down their chins. Carl no longer felt drawn to an initiation. This was pure spite. A warning.

A threat.

As the features moved closer, hollow eye sockets glowed fiercely red. He quivered, as though falling in a dream, and came to.

The music was gone. Eighty-one minutes had passed in an instant.

Carl brought a fingertip to his eye and touched the moist outer layer. He had angered them. They had shown him the path to their wisdom. And he had cowered from it.

He knew what had to be done.

He hurried to the kitchen and rifled through the cupboard beneath the sink. He grasped the bottle of bleach and a pack of disposable cloths. He held up the bottle and read the warnings on the rear.

Under no circumstances bring into contact with eyes. Use in a well-ventilated area.

He pulled on a pair of rubber gloves and fumbled to remove a cloth from the packaging. He held it over the sink and doused it with the milky fluid. Fumes assaulted his nose and throat, making his eyes water.

He placed the bottle to one side and held the cloth at arm's length for a moment.

'Fuck it,' he said and brought the dripping cloth to his wide-open eyes. He rubbed it in, ignoring the unbearable burning. Liquid streamed down his cheeks, a pungent cocktail of tears, residual bleach, and eye jelly.

He pulled the cloth away and dropped it into the sink, straining to hold his eyes open against the fire consuming them. His vision was gone—no more than a haze of burning red. He smiled through the agony, but shock soon settled in. His body began to convulse. His legs gave way. He reached out with his hands and lowered himself to the cold, tiled floor. He was going to pass out.

He dragged himself to the front door of the apartment, reached up to the key and crawled out onto the landing. There, he lay on his back, one forearm covering his liquefying eyes, and groped for his phone. He pulled it from his pocket and held the power and volume buttons, initiating an emergency call.

'What is your emergency?' came the voice at the other end of the line.

'There's been a—an accident. I need an ambulance.'

Carl gave his address and hung up.

#

The doctors wasted little time confirming what he had assumed—permanent loss of vision. He tuned out as they explained the options open to him, the processes for obtaining a stick, a guide dog, and counselling.

'We will, of course, have to keep you here until your next of kin returns, for your own safety,' said the doctor, wrapping up. Carl swallowed.

'I—I can't. My girlfriend is in the north. I need to be at home by—what day is it?'

'It's Wednesday, Mister Adams. You were sedated while the trauma was reduced.'

'I need to be home by tomorrow. Margarida won't be back until Friday. If I'm not at home tomorrow night—' The words died in his mouth.

'Mr Adams, there was an indication of self-harm in the…accident. We are unable to release you without a psychological eval—'

'I'll do it—whatever you need, but I just *have to* be home by tomorrow.'

'Very well then. I'll send up someone from the evaluation team.'

#

The psychologist made no secret of her disbelief, as Carl ran through his version of how the "accident" had happened. He remained calm throughout, answering her questions thoughtfully and in-depth, doing his best impression of a normal, relaxed individual. Understanding Margarida would be home on Friday morning, she reluctantly agreed to sign off his release on Thursday afternoon.

As night fell in the hospital ward, the constant chatter of staff, patients, and visitors died down until the place was quiet. Monotone beeps from various monitoring stations and patients stirring as their pain kept them from sleep were the only remaining sounds.

The music's absence was stark in Carl's ears. He struggled to remember the melody. He could manage an approximation of the percussive vocal sounds, but here he was sealed off from it. There could be no initiation from his hospital bed

He reached for the remote attached to his bed and increased the dose of painkillers in his line. He imagined the clouding saline of the drip, his mind superimposing onto it the coloured swirls of that *other place*. He was painting liquid patterns in his mind when sleep snatched him in its jaws.

#

The ambulance crew checked the door number twice before unlocking Carl's flat and wheeling him inside. Sookie ran and hid, before emerging and complaining once she realised the coast was clear. The ambulance crew lifted Carl onto the bed, then one of them hurried off to feed the cat.

Even after they'd left, Sookie was still unwilling to enter the bedroom. Carl lay motionless for what seemed a lifetime, footsteps from the apartment above carrying a new clarity, appearing more vivid than ever before. The scratching of Sookie's claws on the floorboards of the lounge provided a detailed map of her whereabouts. Tired of this humdrum soundtrack, he called out to his phone, asking for the time.

'22:42'.

Almost.

When the drone began, triumphal notes from horns or trumpets sounded in the mix. The swirling masses appeared in his mind, morphing rapidly into faces whose eyes were black voids and whose mouths spilled forth harmonious voices.

Carl felt himself levitate; whether only in this mental world or the physical, he had no way of knowing.

He nodded. He was ready.

The music increased in intensity. The faces drew closer. His skin tingled with electricity, and something burned painfully at his core. Then he was there, among them. The choir surrounded him. He examined them all, their faces beautiful yet frightening, bereft of eyes. He brought his immaterial hands up to his own face. He trembled and pressed with his fingers, finding nothing but an indentation where the organs ought to have been.

'But how can I see you all? How is it—?'

The music stopped. The faces ghosted away like smoke. Darkness closed in, until there was nothing but silent space.

'Hello?!' Carl shouted. 'Is anyone here? Help me!'

#

Margarida arrived late on Friday and greeted the cat. She put the post on the coffee table. 'Carl?' There was no reply. She walked through to the bedroom. Carl's keys, wallet, and phone lay on the bedside table. She pulled up the window blind and looked down to see his car parked in his usual spot. His trainers, work shoes, and slippers were all lined up at the front door.

I wonder where he's gone?

She perched on the arm of the sofa.

Music began to play, a choir energetically chanting words she couldn't understand. Among them, there was a familiar timbre.

RUBY'S SYZYGY
Matthew R. Davis

Twelve years had passed since *that night* at the Royal Show, and Ruby had always insisted she would never return—but no, Kyall had to have his way, had to throw Jax in her face and play the guilt card: *every little boy should get to see the Show, Rubes. Come on! It'll be okay. You're with us.* And sure enough, the day was rife with ill omens from the start. Jax threw a hissy fit in the car, they had to stand in line for twenty minutes to buy tickets, and the ominously overcast afternoon sky threatened to piss on their parade at any second. When they reached the box office, the dude behind the window took one look at them—Ruby's slumped shoulders and dull gaze, Kyall's neck tattoos and defensive bonhomie, Jax's crumb-spotted lips turning downward to threaten another impending tantrum—and charged them the cheapest rate without even asking if they had any concessions. He probably thought he was doing a nice thing, a random act of kindness for a family down on their luck, but to Ruby, it stank of pity—and she'd had enough of that to last a lifetime.

Why? Because twelve years ago, she'd gone to the Royal Show and ridden the ghost train straight to hell. And now here she was again, revisiting the site of *that night* with a man who thought trauma was due no more gravity and longevity than a bad head cold.

The long queue outside the showgrounds only hinted at the teeming throng within its walls. Kyall held Jax close as they shuffled through the gauntlet of ticket scanners at the gate, and Ruby used them as human shields against the crowds pouring in and out around them. Gods, *the people*—she almost choked at the overwhelming array of faces and colours and voices and odours. To be surrounded by so many and seen by none was to understand one's place in the world, to grasp the insignificance of being: a soul was a single grain of sand on an endless barren beach. Her lessons on this subject had begun during her previous visit to the Show.

Beyond the gate, the entry passage opened up on their right for the dog show pavilion, gaped ahead like a throat for public toilets, and narrowed to a bottleneck on the left where it led into the showgrounds proper. Kyall led them toward the heart of the Show, and Ruby dragged her feet like a woman headed for the gallows. She tried to ignore the stifling cacophony of the crowd until she finally burst into the open, or rather the walls fell away and left her penned only by heaving flesh beneath an unforgiving sky.

The fairgrounds spread out before them like a greasy feast. A two-storey pirate ride loomed on the left, festooned with painted doubloons and mounted by hook-handed corsairs who looked suspiciously similar to Johnny Depp. It was the first stop in a tour of large attractions along the boundary wall; smaller, equally noisy set-ups flanked new arrivals on the right, creating a sideshow alley of lurid spectacles. Ruby stared down this dazzling gullet and then turned toward the exhibition hall instead, hoping her family would follow, but her path was cut off by a train of laughing tweens swinging showbags and Kyall strode on without even noticing her attempt to escape.

Into the mouth of the Show, then, alongside her partner and son—or else on her own, abandoned and easy prey.

The nightmare lives in your head now, not out there.

The Show couldn't hurt her again. It was simply a chore. Something to be endured for the gratification of others.

She hurried to catch up. Kyall was pointing out the sights to Jax, who stared blankly at everything like a moron so numbed by constant stimuli that nothing made an impression any more—or perhaps he was overloaded and shutting down already. Ruby wished she could, shrugging deeper into her old camouflage jacket as a row of clown heads turned their gaping mouths and painted eyes to her in welcome, as a belligerent barker beckoned her to try her luck at a WILD WEST SHOOTOUT. Each stall seemed to be playing a different tune, broadcasting a different distorted voice urging punters to step up and take a shot, and if their combined cacophony wasn't enough, their myriad colours that overwhelmed the eye were—the yellows and purples of tarpaulin backdrops, the blues and reds and greens of stuffed toys hung up in ranks like dead ducks at a Chinese restaurant, the hypnotic flicker patterns of rainbow-like enticing lights. The air was thick with the competing scents of sweat, perfume, vape smoke, fairy floss, machine oil, and roasting meat.

Ruby's eyes flinched away from the scintillating sideshows, but the crowd was no less a visual delirium. Teenage boys disdainful of the attractions they felt they'd outgrown, seeking validation in the currency of laughter at their inappropriate humour; elderly couples who had been coming to the Show for decades, their delight slowly crushed under the increasing weight of commercialised ritual; harried mothers like herself pushing heavy prams loaded down with plastic trinkets as fathers took phone photos of the surrounding spectacle. Large African-Australian families clutching cartoon franchise showbags, troupes of childlike Chinese uni students linked arm-in-arm like a spilled Barrel of Monkeys, suburban white two-point-fours wearing *Star Wars* merch and workout gear the way Bible Belt Christians wore guns and crosses. Girls in mum jeans, boys in mullets, non-binary folx in both—turbans and niqabs and balloons and bubbles and bogans and goth babes, oh my!

A younger Ruby would have taken in this boundless diversity with boggling eyes and an open mind begging for more. The Ruby who walked these showgrounds now, a survivor and mother at the ripe old age of twenty-four, could love it only in an abstract sense. This sight was beautiful and essential, yes, but she'd long since been changed for the worse on a fundamental level. The things that had once brought her joy now seemed trivial and insulting. At half this age, she'd wanted to see and know it all…and then Ender had granted that wish, made her realise how catastrophically stupid she'd been to ever make it.

Not that name. Not here.

As if in response to her thinking it, a chorus of girlish screams rang out nearby. Ruby flinched and turned to see they came from a nearby ride, ROCK N ROLL REVOLUTIONS, where pods shaped like the trunks of 1950s Cadillacs spun around on a floor that dipped and tilted in a way that made her feel sick just watching. The screams rang out from a dozen youthful throats and echoed around the metal cage of the ride, and though they held no true terror, Ruby was chilled. Given her unique experience, it took very little imagination to put those shrieks into a darker context.

Ironically, no screams rang out from the ride that soon loomed on their left, because the SPOOKY SIN HOUSE was the crappiest ghost train Ruby had ever seen. Two storeys high, it was the hackiest, lowest-common-denominator marker of fear imaginable. A large skull was mounted atop it, a glass jewel in a plastic crown, flashing its red LED eyes in time to a pre-recorded maniacal laugh; an incredibly fake giant spider clung to the front wall, and the faux-stone frontage was garnished with hoary headstones, splashes of too-bright blood, and grasping skeletal hands. Ruby, a fan of horror films at ten and an addict at fifteen, regarded such lack of imagination as a cardinal sin—but then this ride was supposed to provide gentle shocks for children, not traumatise all comers. She could all too easily imagine the details of a true terror trip: hot hands in the dark that refuse to let go, the sharp chill of a razor's edge pressed to soft flesh, the unmistakable and sickening stench of mortal corruption, the pitiless smile of someone who knows no remorse and no boundaries, the deepest black of a crack that runs through the shell of the world—

Fingers clutched at her arm. Ruby jerked, sucking in breath for a scream that never came.

'Whoa, whoa.' Kyall let go and held his hands up. 'Take it easy, Rubes. What's with you today?'

'Seriously?'

Her voice pitched sharp and high, and Kyall winced and gestured at her to keep it down—good partners played it cool, good mothers didn't cause a scene in public. Ruby took some little comfort in the fact that she was neither and ignored his warning.

'You know how I feel about this fucking place! You know *why*. And you made me come anyway.'

'Yeah, well, it's not all about *you*.' Kyall reached down to pat Jax's head, and the child looked up at her with wide wet eyes as if cued to do so. 'It's about our boy, ay? So pull your head out of your arse. Jax is hungry, let's go get some grub.'

Ruby stared at them, the man who'd put a bun in her oven and the doughy boy that had resulted, and she couldn't have felt further removed from the life they represented. They might have walked out of the nearby ALIEN ABDUCTION ride—or maybe she had. So much empty space separated her from them, and yet they were drawn together in alignment. The three of them made for a sad and tawdry syzygy indeed.

No. Don't go there. That's one of his *words.*

'Snap out of it,' Kyall said, clicking his fingers in her face and sighing like a busy parent saddled with an addle-brained child. 'Let's go, Rubes.'

This is the carnival, she thought, *we're all fucking rubes here*, and said nothing. That was the easiest course of action, because Kyall got irritable when he didn't understand her allusions. She bit her tongue and followed her family through the hubbub and *hoi-polloi*, passing by a dozen busy food trucks until Jax finally decided what he wanted to eat, and once she even put her hand on his shoulder like a loving parent.

The Show now offered a broader spread of treats than Ruby remembered from her last visit—charcoal meat and vegan salsa, chips on a stick and pizza, souvlaki and sushi—but Jax plumped for the fairground standard. Kyall ordered them Dagwood dogs, deep-fried sausages on sticks with their battered ends daubed in sauce like they'd been thrust into open wounds, and Ruby had to settle for a meatless cheeseburger. As the day's designated card-and-cash carrier, she was obliged to stump up for the meal. The cost was more hair-raising than any of the rides she could see pivoting and flinging their steel arms into the sky.

'Jesus, they charge like wounded bulls around here, don't they?' Kyall twirled his sauce-dipped corndog like a matador's bloodied banderilla and shook his head, accepting one more kick in the balls from a life comprised largely of just such. 'Oh, well. What can you do? The Show is like a rite of passage, ay.'

Ruby glanced sharply at him, but he didn't seem to realise he'd said anything particularly profound or provocative. She blinked him away and sank her teeth into the cheeseburger instead. She hadn't realised how hungry she was, her appetite long since sublimated along with her emotions, and she'd skipped breakfast in order to get the unruly Jax prepped for his visit to the Show. She was halfway done before she stopped to taste what she was eating—halfway done before she saw through the camouflage of tomato and mayonnaise and recognised the texture of meat in her mouth.

Her stomach revolted at once. Ruby turned away and spat a wet chunk of burger patty on the bitumen path, narrowly avoiding a passing man in a DONT DOG THE BOYS shirt who proceeded to curse her manners in a colourful fashion. Kyall bristled and replied in kind, and the pair bickered like scruffy little roosters as the man walked away, neither feeling the need to test their toughness in actual combat. Once his sparring partner had disappeared into the crowd and nearby eyes had turned away from the impromptu spectacle, Kyall flicked his distasteful gaze between Ruby and the unsightly splatter of her regurgitated burger.

'What the hell are you doing?'

She brandished the half-eaten bun at him. 'There's fucking *meat* in this!'

'Well, don't look at me! You heard me order a veggie burger.'

She had. This was something she couldn't lay at his feet, unlike the wodge of unchewed meat she now unseated from the back of her teeth and spat on the ground.

'Jesus! I'd go and ask for a refund, but you've made a right scene now, Rubes.'

Kyall couldn't understand why anyone would ever spurn meat, and Ruby had never explained her own reasons to him. There was so much she hadn't told Kyall about her years in the shadows, so much he would never accept. Sometimes she was tempted to share every vile detail and see if that drove him away; he'd certainly take Jax with him, and the ghastly relief she felt at that thought made the idea appallingly attractive. Imagine how Kyall would feel about the mouth that kissed him when it had to and sucked him when he asked, the mouth that spoke the names of he and his son, if he knew the things it had been forced to do in the past—if he could see the obscene images that sprang into Ruby's mind when she experienced the flavour and texture of meat.

Too late now. It's in me. The sin is done.

She could feel that bolus of burger sitting heavy in her queasy gut. At least the meat was cooked and presumably came from a cow— two points that had rarely applied in her time with Ender.

And there was that name again, inescapable—a shadow that fell over her at all hours and could be chased away by nothing, not medication, nor the passing of time, nor all the garish lights and spectacles the Royal Show had to offer. 'Pull your head out of your arse,' Kyall had told her, a typically insensitive remark, but in a way, he was not inaccurate. Her mind always felt like it was trapped somewhere dark and humid, her senses muted and muffled, held captive in a place few people could ever imagine going.

'Are you at least going to pick that shit up?' he asked.

Ruby looked down at the mess she'd spat on the ground and couldn't bring herself to touch it. The mound of half-chewed flesh brought too many memories creeping up to the glass that separated her now from her then. She shook her head in reflexive denial.

'Classy, Rubes.'

Fuck you, she didn't say. She turned on her heel and walked ten metres to the nearest bin, tossed in the remains of her non-veggie burger, and wiped juicy fingers on her skirt with distaste.

From here, she could observe Kyall and Jax at a distance. They chewed their Dagwood dogs like cud, waiting to be poked back into motion to continue their circuit of the concourse, and she felt a familiar urge to just turn tail and flee—to hurry through the crowds back to the gate, out onto the road, to the car, and from there to fucking anywhere but here. And for the hundredth time, she didn't do that. She stayed put, her feet glued to the ground, surrounded by sixty thousand souls and yet all alone under the barren grey expanse of the moody sky.

Jesus, what was she even doing here? Her last visit to the Show had been the beginning of an ordeal worse than she'd ever imagined possible, a doorway into darkness so thick it choked her still—and even disregarding that, everything about this gaudy ritual was overblown and overpriced, each timeworn experience homogenised to the hilt, every stall set up to gouge consumers until they bled. Kyall had called it a rite of passage, but which passage was he talking about—the kind he'd accused her of using to house her own head? The games were facile, the food was undercooked, and the entertainments were as hollow as her own heart. If this was what passed for monumental in the mainstream, then her younger self had been right in veering toward the underground.

Ah, but little Ruby could not have known the depths that lurked beneath the subcultures she had begun exploring as she entered puberty. If punk and goth and their ilk were underground, the scene to which Ender had introduced her was downright chthonic, and where some scenes traded in exclusivity, that one was so rarefied that few even suspected its existence. It was the cutting edge in a very literal sense, and only the darkest of thrill-seekers would dare its shadows—them, and those like her who were dragged there kicking and screaming.

Ruby had seen and felt and done things far outside the shallow arc of common understanding, and while she had eventually returned from the darkness, she'd left an essential part of herself behind. Her sanity, perhaps; her ability to truly feel anything, certainly. The extremes hadn't just blunted her senses, they'd cauterised them. Usually that was for the best, as Ruby's worst memories were like salted blades drawn across raw nerves, but sometimes, she was so starved of sensation that she would have done anything just to feel that intensity of emotion one more time. Even if it was the terror, the agony, the soul-sickening self-loathing she had lived through between the ages of twelve and fifteen.

As if summoned, the young Ruby walked into view. Only no, of course it wasn't her—just a girl about the age she'd been back then, who looked a little like she once had. This child wore a ridiculous pink Stetson with cheap diamante dressing bought from one of the Show's most popular stalls, but her tights were striped white and black like cartoon spiderlegs, protruding from under a black denim pinafore that had been artfully frayed and arrayed with declamatory badges and patches: Gunship, rainbow pride, Misfits, an open book, *Stranger Things*. This echo of young Ruby was alone, the way she had been twelve years ago, and the urge to approach her was strong—maybe this time advice could be given, an innocence saved. But Ruby did nothing, said nothing, as the girl disappeared back into the swarming mass. That young woman would never have any inkling of the nightmare that lurked below the world's surface; so few did, and never happily, not even those who sought it with blood in their teeth and hell in their hearts.

Her eyes flicked back to Kyall and Jax. Her partner was looking at her with an expectant tilt of his head, which triggered her anxious feet into motion. She cut through the crowd like a commanded child, wondering at the ways her trauma puppeteered her through this bland drama people thought of as life. After all she'd been through, she was at the beck and call of these guys?

They're as much your captors as Ender ever was.

A blander pair of jailers could not be imagined. Kyall wore a black *Sons of Anarchy* singlet despite the cool weather, keen to show off his toned biceps and uninspired tattoos; more ink crawled up his throat to meet the habitual stubble there, the word JAX nestled prominently in his clavicle notch. That was typical of his shoot-first, realise-it's-your-foot-later style of thinking—despite presenting as the tabloid ideal of a drug user and often treated as such, he rarely took anything stronger than caffeine and held down a long-term job in a furniture warehouse. He believed this drudge work, along with his dysfunctional young family, was the best he could expect from life, and so he never tried for or even dreamed of more. Four-year-old Jax, his heir to this mustn't-grumble life, already resembled his father in so many ways, from the blonde hair that would darken to honey at puberty to the entitled pout that appeared when things didn't go his way. While Ruby loathed those aspects of Kyall in her son, she'd never stepped in to take a firmer hand in his parenting, and that was on her—but was it her fault that the parts she'd need to be a good mother had been stolen from her and left to rot in the dark?

Ruby had lost three years to Ender's nightmare, and the girl who returned to the ordinary world was not the one who'd disappeared from it. This young woman was diffident to the point of apathy, addicted to horror movies despite her counsellors' warnings of trigger effects, and entirely incapable of healthy emotion. She could still experience the mechanical functions of humanity—terror, sickness, anxiety, arousal, intoxication—and after a couple of years cloistered in her mother's house, shut off from a world that might hand her back to Ender and his like at any moment, she'd unleashed them without a thought for the consequences. And why not? Her mother had died, her only true tether to the world severed—a raw, visceral pain like a knife scraping flesh from bone. That death had hurt, but it had also been welcome. Alone in its aftermath, Ruby had flung herself headlong at life in search of more, and it mattered little whether it was agony or ecstasy.

She'd been a virgin before her abduction. In its aftermath, she'd shunned any and all intimacy—even if imaginary, until the fantasies that should have been safe had stopped savagely turning on her. Ruby had known many lovers in the turbulent time following her mother's death, though *love* had never once shown its face to her, and she'd embraced each fuck with a reckless disregard for consequence. Ultimately, it was Kyall's child who caught and took root in her, and while she'd planned to remove the inconvenience, he'd convinced her to start a family with him instead. Why not? She didn't really care what happened to her anyway, and Kyall's many flaws didn't extend to domestic violence or outright misogyny. Besides, motherhood offered new extremes of emotion and experience—the diverse intensities of pregnancy, the tearing agony of childbirth, perhaps even an all-encompassing love that would spark her heart back to life. Imagine that, not just survival but *happiness*, the ultimate *fuck you* to Ender and everything he'd inflicted upon her. A victory.

But it didn't come, not any of it—not the love, not the happiness, certainly no sense that she'd won. Sometimes something stillborn stirred in her heart when she looked at Jax, but more often than not, she just felt nothing—or worse, a pitiless contempt that bordered on violence. For *this* she had endured nausea and bloating, a compromised pelvic floor and a pouchy belly that wouldn't go away? He was just one more bleating bag of bones the world didn't need, a doomed homunculus of his deadshit father. Yes, Jax was a part of her, but what was *she*? A kidnap victim haunted by the things she had seen and done, reduced by trauma to a pale imitation of humanity unable to live properly or even love. With her as his mother, the kid never had a chance. Only shit came from shit.

'Let's go, Rubes,' Kyall said when she reached him, after what felt like a long trudge through a baying crowd to the gallows. 'There's heaps more to see, and we need to get done before it starts to rain.'

Ruby glanced up at the indecisive sky, occluded by shifting shades of grey, and felt her mood reflected across the surface of the world. She spoke without thinking.

'Why are we doing this?'

'Ay?' Kyall's brow furrowed, and Jax's followed suit. 'What do you mean?'

'You know I'm no good. Why did you want a family with me? Why do you want me to stay?'

Kyall rolled his eyes. He'd always dodged deep questions as if innately suspicious of introspection, and she didn't expect that to change now.

'Because I love you,' he said, not meeting her eyes. 'Dickhead. Can we just get on with it now?'

Ruby was certain he simply could not love her, though he probably believed he did. But he didn't want someone who burned in his soul like a strange dream, lent him fanciful ambitions, inspired scraps of poesy and heart-song. He wanted someone to dump his mundane needs and obligations onto, someone to hold his hand in public and his dick in private, someone to wash his clothes and feed his child and keep his humble house in order. Someone to agree and commiserate when he spoke, to discharge her duties without complaint or betrayal, to be buried beside him as the ultimate testament to a life adequately lived.

Maybe he should've just stayed home with his mother and bought a dog instead, rubbing the odd one out into a sock instead of Ruby's disinterested cunt. She wasn't unique and essential to him, just a quick drunken shack-up who'd caught pregnant and activated his latent sense of obligation. Kyall couldn't name her childhood best friend or primary school, any of her favourite songs or previous lovers, anything that made her different from the other women he'd cleft and left. He knew what had happened to her as a girl but never wanted to hear the details, always wanted to push that horror away and not think about it—it was inconvenient and irrelevant to his life, might as well have been a childhood accident that had left no visible scars.

Ruby opened her mouth to ask the question of the day, the one whose answer might just pull the trigger on her exit: *Why did you insist on bringing me to the Royal Show when you know I was once abducted from here and spent three years in the blackest pits of hell?* But Kyall had already turned away and was leading Jax toward the noisome farm animal pavilion.

If she just stood here and didn't move, maybe he would leave her and never return.

Just like Ender.

And again, as if provoked by her thinking that name, came the keening chorus of screaming girls from the ROCK N ROLL REVOLUTIONS ride. Maybe if she went on it, she could scream too. Maybe that would shake something loose, dislodge her shackles at last. Return her to the person she used to be, like that stripey-legged echo she'd seen a few minutes back.

Yeah, and maybe if you just stand here until night falls, you can fade away into the shadows and cease to exist. Get a grip! This is it now—just this. And you know what? It's a better deal than you deserve. So suck it up, princess.

This is as good as it gets.

Ruby loosed a disconsolate sigh, the sound swallowed up by a laughing child on her left and the DODGEM DELIRIUM ride on her right, and trailed after her family.

The animal pavilion was no less abrasive than the maelstrom outside. Ruby's lip curled at the people cooing at the captives, at the ignorant livestock who allowed themselves to be caged—her contempt all the deeper for understanding she was no better than the sheep who stared blankly back at her, just as tame and manipulated as they. The ripe smell of beasts at bay was nauseating—too many graphic memories came to mind at the stench of shit and unwashed flesh, and again she remembered the taste and feel of meat in her mouth. The idea of sinking her teeth into these creatures was disgusting, but she'd partaken of worse. She looked at Jax, soft and laden with baby fat, and threw up in her mouth.

Kyall glanced over, alerted by the sound she made as she swallowed the sick back down, but saw no need to speak until they left the pavilion and returned to the cooler air outside.

'You okay?'

'No! Of course I'm not!' Ruby saw Jax flinch at her tone, and somewhere inside her a sick grin opened up like a stab wound. 'Do you think I really want to be here?'

'Oh, that's lovely. What, you don't want to be with Jax while he gets to see his first Show? Jesus, Rubes.'

'Why do you always do that? Why do you weaponise our child? You might as well pick it up and beat me over the head with it.'

Kyall scowled. '*It*?'

'You know what I mean.'

'Look, I get that this place has bad memories for you, okay? But that was so long ago. Get over it, Rubes, because life goes on. All that bad shit—it's over.'

He grabbed Jax's hand and led him away past the merry-go-round carousel. Ruby stared after him and thought: *No. You don't get it, you fucking idiot. It's not long gone and it's not done. How could it EVER actually be OVER?*

When evil events ended, something else was required to shut them away: closure. And like so many of her fellow survivors, Ruby had struggled in vain to find it. Some kidnapped kids were relatively lucky and got to see their captors arrested and put on trial—put in jail. Even those who didn't, but who escaped through their own efforts, got that boost from exercising their agency and taking control of the situation.

Ruby had not been so lucky. She hadn't escaped, and her kidnapper had not been caught. One day he'd just left her, stranded in the middle of nowhere to make her own way. After everything he'd put her through—the humiliating abuse and the rivers of blood and the living, screaming dark—Ender had just fucked off and abandoned her like a toy in which he no longer found any interest. Abhorrent as he was, he'd been the only constant in her life for three years, and then he was gone without a single whispered word of explanation. Ruby had spent the last decade going around in circles like the kids on the nearby carousel, gripping the mane of her trauma with fingers too confused and terrified to let go, dreading the moment when the music stopped and she had to face what came after.

She looked into the painted eyes of the pole-mounted carousel animals—those vacant horses and ostriches and elephants—and saw the blank gaze of the dead. They were doomed to turn the same circle time and time again, just like her. She'd danced this loop alone, without her mother, without even Ender's cruel attentions to mark the time. Maybe it was better to have company on this ride after all.

Ruby hurried after the boys until she walked once more by Kyall's side. He glanced at her with an indulgent smile and his fingers crept into hers, accepting an apology he assumed she meant to give. She squeezed back in reflexive irritation until he winced and tightened his own grip to assert dominance. It reminded her of *that night*, the way Ender's hand had captured hers in the darkness, and the memory stunned her into docility until Jax brought them to a halt outside a face-painting stall and Kyall let his hold slip.

'What do you want, mate? A tiger? Spider-Man?'

Jax pointed to a mask that might have been a vampire or a zombie—white powder, blackened eyes, a drool of crimson at the lips.

'Well, all right then, little man. It's your first Show, it's your choice.' Kyall turned to her, expectant. 'It's twenty bucks, Rubes.'

She absently fished out a note and passed it to him, staring at the design Jax wanted to wear. The red lips mesmerised her, tried to pull her back into nights she could never forget. Her son would look like a leering corpse. Why would he taunt her like that? Had Kyall put him up to this?

Oh, this was stupid. *They* were stupid. Why was she even tolerating this vapid tripe? Her son wanted to play dead, and his ignorance of the horrible truth was as insulting as Kyall's refusal to even consider it. If they knew death as intimately as she—frank and foul and forever—they would never dare to mock it like this.

She hated them then, deeply and violently, and at once, she realised this was the only way they would ever make her truly *feel*. No love, no pride, no joy—just contempt and disgust. They would hold her down and cut her up with the blunt blades of their mundanity, slowly defacing her with all the idiot patience of plain water dripping onto stone, and sharing their lives would kill her as surely as sharing Ender's nightmare journey to its depraved conclusion.

Ender. *Ender.* He could at least have shown her mercy at the end and slit her throat, bashed her head in, carved her into pretty little joints to take away and share with the shadows. But his final cruelty had been exquisite—allowing her to live, and yet never know why. Exposing her to the great and terrible Show deep beneath the surface of all things, and then leaving her to limp through a life an inch deep and dull.

Truly, nothing matters. Not even this.

The face-painter directed Jax to sit on a stool before him, and the boy did so, finally quiet and still the way she had begged him to be all day. The man's brush dabbed at his boldest colour, swift stabs that left his instrument stained red, and Ruby flinched as if it were hers. The words were out before she even knew she was going to speak.

'I have to go.'

'Huh?' Kyall turned to her, one eye on his phone as he checked a message. 'Go where?'

Where indeed? Ruby blinked. He turned back to his text, trusting—not in her, but in her obedience to the rules of the world. She needn't think too hard.

'I need to go to the toilet.' Yes, that was believable, but an awful farewell; even as she seethed with loathing, she knew they deserved better. 'Be well. Be happy. Keep an eye on him, okay?'

'Of course. Someone has to.'

That might have been a blunt barb, but Ruby barely felt it. Kyall was still messaging, ignorant of the irony in his statement, and that made it all the easier to turn away. She glanced at Jax, who grinned as a wet red brush danced across his lips, and then she fled without another word.

She had no idea where the nearest toilet might be, nor any intention of going there. She had no need to relieve herself, and even if she had, she'd honed her bladder control during her time with Ender, through long days and nights locked in black basements or handcuffed to cooling meat or, once, buried alive in a cardboard box. No, Ruby was cutting herself free at last, and with barely a pang as the remaining threads parted. The terror of freedom was exhilarating.

No more would she be expected to care about who was on *The Masked Singer* or whether Port Power won the match this week or the love lives of Kyall's deadbeat friends or what his fucking parents thought of her dubious motherhood skills; no more would she be required to rinse shit from shorts or semen from skin. No more pretending to be someone she maybe once could have been—now it was time, finally, to discover what she really was.

For a moment, she allowed herself to know the honest hurt Kyall and Jax would experience because of her abandonment. She understood all too well how it felt to cope with such a confusing lack of closure, and her own pain ached in sympathetic resonance. But then that fell away into the dark and it was just her now, only her, ready to align herself with her perverted past and her undetermined future—the syzygy of Ruby. She had the cards and the cash and the car, enough to get her rolling down the road.

Only, where would she go?

She knew something lay ahead of her, something monumental—there had to be, after all she'd been put through, all she'd seen in those shadows beneath the skin of the world. After years of closing in on herself like a frayed flower, she was wide open and receiving, ready to bask in a black sun. She'd fought the abyss in her past, seeking to deny it, when it was the only thing that had ever turned her inside out and exposed her to the extremes of sensation. If that was all she could hope for—if this was what Ender's lessons in suffering and humiliation and complicity had been intended to convey—then perhaps it was time to stop pretending there had ever been any other options.

She hurried through the crowd, hands in the pockets of her camouflage jacket, and she didn't look back. She didn't even look forward. Her feet followed a rhythm only they could hear and took her where she needed to go.

Red letters burned down at her from on high: SPOOKY SIN HOUSE. Yes, why not? She'd come full circle today, so riding the ghost train made perfect sense. Ruby joined the queue for the ticket box and let her mind roam back a dozen years.

The ride *that night* had been TUNNEL OF BLOOD. It had been smaller but just as shitty as this one. Ruby had split off from the friends she'd come with—they'd wanted to follow some boys from school around the showgrounds, ignoring everything the fair had to offer—and she'd bought herself a solo seat on the ghost train, feeling alone and unseen, ready to be swallowed alive by the shadows. The interior of the ride had been dim, all the better to frighten punters and hide the obvious artifice around every bend—that way consumers couldn't see the strands of fishing line dangling from above to drag through their hair, couldn't see the struts and power leads behind the spring-loaded cackling corpses. Even at twelve, Ruby knew the hustle, but she accepted the artifice and opened herself to the dark.

She'd been halfway through the ride when the power shut down and the lights went out, leaving her stranded amidst Styrofoam gravestones aboard a lifeless car. For a moment, she'd wondered if this was a part of the trip, but the cry of the fire alarm had sent her pulse racing faster than any fake fright had.

And then a shadow had bloated toward her, pouring through a crack in the world, and she'd felt Ender's hand taking hers for the first time.

A much warmer hand brushed hers now, and she flinched away as she snapped back into the present. Just some passing kid, a toddler waddling after her distracted family—why, someone could have snatched her and been away into the crowd for long seconds before the parents had any inkling she was even gone. The girl turned back and saw her watching; Ruby was expecting a sneer or maybe a scream, but instead, the kid grinned. She lifted a plastic wand to her lips and, with a long, wet breath, sent a stream of bubbles dancing through the air toward her witness.

Ruby turned on the spot, fascinated, as the fragile globes clustered around her and disappeared into nothingness like discarded thoughts. Through one bulging bubble, she saw a pink Stetson a few places behind her in the ticket queue, and below that, a familiar face. The girl in the black pinafore and spider-striped leggings—the echo of her youth. For a moment, Ruby felt as though she were in two places at once, but then the last bubble popped, and so did her thin-skinned fantasy.

She bought a ticket from a young woman dressed up in witchy clichés, and then she was joining the shorter line for the cars. This close to the ride, she could differentiate its playlist from the cacophony that surrounded it; the stomping beat of "Dragula" gave way to HorrorPops' psychobilly rag, and then a brusque mummy waved her into a little car with room for two on its bench seat. When "Walk Like a Zombie" crossfaded with "Cemetery Girl", the car jerked to life, the doors of the SPOOKY SIN HOUSE lurched open, and Ruby rolled forward into the darkness.

Her hands gripped the safety bar with rigor mortis strength. If the Show was one big trigger waiting to be pulled, then here was the hammer. She barely even noticed the sheeted ghost that popped up through the floor like a jack-in-the-box as years peeled away and shed from her like dead skin. She was twelve again and deep in the guts of the TUNNEL OF BLOOD, only this time she knew exactly what was coming for her. All at once, her lie to Kyall became a truth; she needed a bathroom, and soon.

Cackling spirits flew by and disturbed her hair. Skeletons danced through hidden doors, their jaws jouncing out of time with a triggered recording of lunatic laughter. Then she was dazzled by multi-coloured lights that raced across the black walls as her car hit a ramp and inched its way up an incline. Another door flew open, and she saw the silhouette of a dangling spider—or maybe it was a twitching hand—in time to duck beneath it before the car popped back out into the open air.

For five seconds, she trundled along the second storey at the front of the ride, allowing her an elevated view of the showgrounds. She could see the dense crowd seething and feeding below, sixty thousand souls gathered beneath a darkening afternoon sky as the lit-up Ferris wheel rose above them like a giant pagan icon. Then she rolled through another door, back into the darkness, and a man in a glow-in-the-dark skull mask lunged half-heartedly past the front of her car.

Ruby's past-born fear had largely worn off by now, replaced by disappointment at the tawdry nature of the ride. She'd expected nothing more, really, but then…she had. She'd thought to receive a message here, some truer direction to follow now that she'd jumped the tracks laid down for her. Instead, she was again party to a pointless rehash of the past—for wasn't Jax just that of Kyall? She might as well go back to them, pretend she'd never intended to abandon them without explanation the way Ender had deserted her.

No. No going back now.

She'd thought there might be danger here, something to provoke the deeper feelings she'd been unable to express for so long. Well, if there was, perhaps it was only what she'd brought in with her.

The car whined down a ramp and returned to ground level. The ride would be over in another minute. Ruby glanced around and saw that she was rolling slowly through a fake cemetery, its crooked headstones wreathed in dry ice, and she shivered at last. This scene resembled very closely the one inside TUNNEL OF BLOOD—so much so that she expected the lights to go out any moment.

This was as close as she was going to get.

Without thinking, she stood up and leaped out of the car. She hit the fog-shrouded ground and stepped away from the tracks, slipped quickly through the gravestones until she reached the edge of the chamber. Hoping there weren't any ectoplasmic employees lurking nearby to spot her folly and report her, she found a place where the walls interleaved to allow access to the areas behind and slipped between them. Here she could see the metal struts that held up the fake mossy-stone walls, could see the den of cords snaking across the floor to power the lights and the dry ice machine, could stand out of view for a moment and try to understand why this action felt so right.

Ender must have done something very much like this. He'd had his escape planned in every detail—a knife held out of sight in her armpit as he hustled her along the wall behind the rides, an order for her to cough as if she'd inhaled smoke, a quick departure through the busy and distracted gate staff for a concerned father and his stunned daughter. Had he spotted her beforehand and lain in wait for her, or had she been a random selection? He'd never revealed his motivations on *that night*, had never shared anything with her that wasn't degrading or disgusting. She hadn't seen him as a man, not in the sense that her father or her teachers had been men; to her, Ender was a deep crack in the shell of the world, and when he'd stood close behind her or pressed her body to the floor, she'd felt a cosmic chill blowing through him from some darker place. Some of the things he'd shown her beggared belief, and not just in their amoral obscenity.

The tracks clanked as another car made its way into the cheap cemetery, this one holding two giggling teens, and Ruby made sure she was out of sight. It was while she pressed herself against the unglamorous back side of the wall that she noticed the red box mounted on it nearby. There must have been smoke detectors all through the ride, but there were also manual triggers in case of emergency. The fire alarm was only an arm's length away, right next to a junction box that controlled the electricity.

Her feet followed fate and stepped into line with these two elements, creating an inevitable alignment.

Ruby peered around the wall and saw the car disappear through a flap of fabric, its occupants too busy making out to notice their surroundings. How long before the ride attendants realised that her car should not be empty, before she was discovered lurking back here like some haunted-house hopeful auditioning for a position?

69

Would she have enough time to understand why she was here in the first place?

Dry ice hissed from unseen nozzles, and distant canned laughter rang out through the structure, and Ruby awaited revelation.

The next car held a single occupant, and when she saw who it was, she knew it couldn't have been anyone else. Pink Stetson, badges punched through her pinafore—it was the echo of herself. The girl who might have been her, and who, if she made it to the other end of this ride, might go on to be the woman Ruby should have been.

In a blade-cold moment, everything became clear.

The intensity of the horror Ender had inflicted upon her wasn't just what made her who she was—it was all she could be, and it was the only way she would ever truly feel again. She understood now why her kidnapper hadn't simply killed her; he'd known that his torments would haunt her until she faced them, embraced them, *became* them. All this time, she'd been waiting to find her way back into the shadows—not to be claimed and devoured, but to be welcomed and enthroned. Ender was just the beginning.

Ruby watched closely as the girl's car trundled down the track through the gravestones, one hand resting on the junction box. She waited for just the right moment, when three bodies would come into perfect alignment: the girl, herself, and the shadow she could feel swelling behind her. *Syzygy.* Finally, the word felt right, and she understood why Ender had used it so often.

Now.

It was a simple matter of two beats—*click*, and both the power and the lights cut out, leaving the car stranded as its occupant let out a cry of genuine fright—*click*, and the fire alarm took up its banshee wail. Just like last time, just like *that night*. A chill blew through her, as if a fresh crack had opened in the shell of the world.

Ruby slipped swift as spreading smoke through the deeper dark and closed in on the girl in the car, reaching out to take her hand for the first time.

HUMUS
Sam Dawson

You just don't know where you are with Morris dancers, he decided. You spend your life thinking you know about them and then they surprise you. Mark's heart had sunk when he'd arrived at the pub after a hot, three-mile, deliberately thirst-inducing walk, only to find them noisily jigging about in the car park. And then, as he mourned the loss of a quiet summer pint in the heart of the countryside, they had tricked him.

They'd actually been quite *interesting*.

He had inadvertently stumbled into a mini-festival, with teams from around the country. They'd confounded his expectations, of people in white leaping about, hitting sticks. That had been true of the first few sets. But then there were a surprising number of variations on a theme: a green goth troupe; an all-woman one with a strong Amazon warrior vibe; an imaginatively folk-horror inspired lot; a Wicker Man-martial arts-Capoeira sort of mashup; dancing orcs, even a steampunk side who wore so much metal they couldn't really manage the jumping up and down very well.

It appeared that Morris dancing had evolved. The fact that he was the only one in the audience who hadn't known this made him feel even more like an outsider, the city boy recovering out here in the countryside, the bird with a wounded wing.

Even his appearance, he suspected, gave him away—a fidgetiness, the crew cut, the fact that at thirty-six he was still nervously gym-lean when he could have legitimately relaxed into having a little pot belly and swapped his trainers and London-bought clothes (which looked unintentionally trendy here) for comfy old slacks and sandals.

The dance troupes had brought their followers with them and it took a while to get served, but although busy, the landlord made an effort to remember his name and ask how he was. Mark wondered if the question was as simple as it appeared—wondered how much the locals knew about him and his history. How he had intervened in an incident in London before the armed police arrived, when most other bystanders had run or filmed it on their phones. How the resulting physical scars had begun to heal, the mental ones less so.

They say there are no secrets in villages. So how much did they know? Maybe that his employer, the London Ambulance Service, had given him three months' leave to recover, rest, and recuperate, along with a glowing reference that led to a job offer from their county equivalent here.

What Mark hoped they didn't know was that he wasn't sure he could make it—that in an area with virtually no public transport, he was scared to get on his Ducati motorbike, unnerved by crowds but unhappy alone, frightened daily at what could happen next. He tried not to imagine fanatics with knives duct-taped to their hands suddenly emerging here among the innocent spectators. Cold sweat pricked his skin. His T-shirt began to stick to him.

He attempted to let the entertainment distract him. The MC was introducing the next act. He had come with one of the Gloucestershire teams and his accent was so pleasingly rounded it resembled a chuckle, and his laughter, when it came, the sound of apples rolling into a barrel.

'...dancing a story you may not know. A local legend, of someone you wouldn't want to meet walking home from the pub at night. The Green Man with red on his teeth, the John Barleycorn who wouldn't die,' there was a drum roll, '...The Floppy Man!'

A dancer called out a Viagra joke, but the announcer was ready for it: 'You're probably right, Bobby Rogers, and if I see him I'll tell him you'll lend him yours,' which got a supportive laugh from the crowd.

The accordionist struck up a jauntily traditional tune and began to sing:

'Harken fellow, pay heed maid,
He steps near with silent tread.

Born of rot, born of earth,
Born beneath the yew tree's girth.

Being of corruption, not beast nor man,
Best ye flee while still ye can.

Has no bones, has no face,
He'll steal thine with one embrace.

Has no eyes, cannot see, has no ears, cannot hear,
Yet he'll find thee through thy fear.

Harken fellow, pay heed maid,
He's here NOW with silent tread.'

As the song finished, two performers walked onto the green, dragging a dummy behind them. It was dressed vaguely like a Bonfire Night Guy: stuffed coat with raised collar, old trousers, shapeless hat, a face made of eyeless sacking.

A half broom handle had been run through the sleeves and coat back, stopping at each elbow. It raised the shoulders high and left the lower arms dangling oddly free. The hands were fashioned from branches. The legs hung limply, and trailed across the ground. For Mark, it brought back an unpleasant memory of two bouncers at a Brixton nightclub ejecting some poor punter they'd nearly crippled. There was the same lolling head, limp arms, and lifeless legs. An all-over bonelessness.

But then the figure jumped up and free from the others. It wasn't a dummy, after all; it was a third dancer. There was an intake of breath and a quick round of applause from the watchers. Theatrically, the other two turned their backs, hunching and urgently covering their heads, as the figure ran to each in turn, kicking his legs loosely up from the knee and flicking his drooping arms in vain at their protected faces.

Then, feigning curiosity, one of the dancers let his hands drop. It was immediately on him, hands flying for the face but this time making contact and holding it, as though the twigs had taken root in the other's flesh. The victim, vainly trying to tear away, sank slowly to his knees, hunching over, while the other stood taller, more upright, as though draining something (Life? Bones? Identity?) from him.

Then he disengaged, turned and lolloped off, reluctantly followed a minute later by his prey, now transformed into one like his attacker: disjointed, shambling, an unboned disciple of a new and faceless master. But no, not faceless anymore. There had been some sleight of hand, a swap, and the victim now wore a face of eerily featureless white muslin, while The Floppy Man's was painted with the features he had stolen from the other man, twisted into an expression of cruel triumph.

A child in the audience cried.

There was more clapping and then a rush for the bar. Mark decided to leave. Pale and perspiring, he was still experiencing visions of that London attack transposed to this peaceful scene. He felt he was radiating distress and otherness, and that everyone would notice. He could smell his own sweat now, bitter with an undertone of fear. As he prepared to rise, at the limit of his vision, out past the churchyard, he saw a figure, blurred and rippled by heat haze. It was slowly turning a tilted head, as though sniffing the air.

No one else had noticed. They were heading into the pub or milling around the performers, but its voyeuristic air held Mark's attention. Slowly, the silhouetted head swivelled towards him, past him, then too rapidly back again, as if sensing that he was its only observer. Contact was made.

It lasted only seconds, then the figure moved off with a strange lack of rigidity that was not unlike the spectacle he had just seen acted out. The spell broke. Disbelievingly, Mark noticed the sharpness of his breathing, the tingle of adrenaline, his readiness for fight or flight.

He decided to stay for another drink after all. Maybe two.

Against expectations, he slept well that night, back at the tiny cottage that had been found for him to use during his leave. They'd warned him that it had few creature comforts, but they were only half right. It had no comforts, but plenty of creatures: rats in the garden, mice under the floorboards, pigeons in the attic. The one thing it did have going for it was its location beside the road to the village, with sweeping fields around and behind it, leading up to fine woodland at the very top of the slope.

If Mark couldn't always impose discipline and control on his mental state, he could on his physical one. Drink was for weekends, exercise for weekdays. He had started by running almost every day and had now settled down to four times a week, always timing himself, aiming to go just a little farther, a little faster each time.

When exercising, he looked younger than he was, partly because of a tension that showed in the way he held himself, born of London's new no-go zones and his former daily grind of grime, gangs, and gun crime. Someone looking at Mark was likely to see what he did not; an ordinary-looking bloke, tallish, light on his feet. But still holding himself too ready for a metropolitan provocation, an insult or emergency.

But he was far from the capital now. The banks of the footpath that ran behind his house were high with tall grasses that split the day's fading sun into long, honeyed beams alive with slow-gliding seeds and faster midge clouds. Every so often, the vegetation parted, giving him a view of unharvested wheatfields, meadows, and farms.

He liked to sit at the path's end, at the very top of the hill behind his house, where the woods began. He would sometimes climb into the branches of a tree and perch and kick his legs lazily. Only when the insects became too persistent would he head back. He took pleasure in the subtle differences that that last, occasional, unreal light of the day gave to everything, washing out its colours, yet making it all look deeper, more profound, in that rare artist's gold.

Odd though, he thought there'd been a scarecrow in that field when he'd passed. Nothing there now.

The next day he noticed a smell. Faint, but distinctive. It wasn't an animal one. It couldn't be foxes or what looked to be the bloody great dog he'd seen far down the lane, snuffling its way along the ditch in the direction of his house.

No, it was more like vegetable decay. Humus, compost, leaf mould, the odours of the stored and gone-bad apples he and his dad had cleared from his grandad's garden shed after he died, its air sodden with a brew of rot and fermenting juices, full of piles and piles of fruit with fungus-grown, brown-spotted skins rupturing and parting to release the frothy saps within.

The day after that run was when he began to think he was being stalked.

By an animal, or someone behaving as one. A shape glimpsed briefly in the grasses, close to the ground, seeking a scent. His, he suspected.

Which meant, he told himself, he really was going mad. Surrendering to a paranoia generated by past events which was being given some utterly fanciful form by his unfamiliar surroundings.

The resulting nervousness had one positive side effect. It edged out any worries about riding his motorbike, which he used to get to the weekly appointment with his psychotherapist. There, feeling like a fool, he shared his suspicions. Which she, perhaps not unnaturally, completely misunderstood, and suggested increasing the dose of his Citalopram to better tackle the anxiety, just at a time when he was easing himself off it.

Telling her was a pointless exercise, really. To explain he would have to admit that he felt he was being followed. And she, naturally, would see this as his neurosis giving a physical form to his pre-existing anxieties. He wondered if he should go to the local pub instead and risk derision by asking if there was an animal loose.

At least, he *hoped* it was an animal…

He kept a watchful eye out when cleaning the Ducati the next day. It was surprising how sneakily you could monitor your surroundings by peeking over the fuel tank while kneeling and supposedly fiddling with the engine. The smell was slightly stronger, but he had decided that it might be down to a farmer spraying his fields.

He went indoors for his usual struggle with rural broadband and a desultory attempt to find something worth watching on TV. From time to time, he'd head upstairs and stand well back from a window, covertly scanning the countryside.

Because now he had a theory. There was another alternative. That some of the locals were having a laugh at the expense of the outsider. Trying to spook him. Allowing themselves to be seen fleetingly and for an instant, a little nearer to him each time, mimicking a hunt by scent. This, he decided, would be fine with him, because they'd have to show themselves up close sooner or later. One of the things that had saved him from the life of petty crime that was the fate of several of his schoolmates was a nearby boxing gym. It had turned him away from street delinquency and into a gifted amateur boxer.

He knew he was like a tightly-wound spring at the moment. If someone wanted to push him till that spring snapped, they'd have to accept the consequences.

Mano a mano. Face to face.

That evening, he pulled on his new trainers and his old, once black but now grey sparring tracksuit and ran again. And it was fine. Smellier outside, yes, but fine. Until, suddenly, it wasn't. Up at the fringe of the woods. He became sure he was being watched. Instinct kicked in. Edginess crystallised into threat.

Because there were no rational grounds for the feeling, he refused to look back. That would be an admission of fear. Only at the bottom of the hill, when he was almost home, did he glance behind him.

It rose from below the trees. Impossible to say if it had been crouching low to the ground or was part of it—if it had formed itself up from the forest floor, up there where the woods began.

The Floppy Man. It was in silhouette, part of the greater semicircle that was the hill against the twilight sky. Its legs stayed bent back on themselves, and it pulled a little on them, as if uprooting them fully from the soil. The arms dragged behind the body, the hands, all twisted roots, trailing. The head lay flat on the chest in a way that should only be possible with a broken neck.

Then it jerked up to look at him and took three faltering, unnatural steps. And ran. Horribly.

It was an eighth of a mile from the woods to the house. It took it less than a minute.

Mark dropped into a boxer's crouch. Head down, fists protecting his face.

Then it was on him. Fear charged his body with strength. He threw an uppercut—always the least expected punch, the one that, done right, can snap an opponent's head back so hard that he's out before he even hits the floor.

His fist sank into the figure, his momentum and the thing's speed carrying him shoulder deep into it and its spongy form—warm with vegetable decay, worm-ridden, maggot-squirming, gassy with rot and sap.

He pulled free, his body pumping adrenaline and energy, his mind unused in the sudden sure reflexes of pure survival. His hands went undirected to a nearby garden rake. The first wild swing tore the creature's stomach apart. The next knocked aside its flailing arms just as they reached for his now unshielded face.

Blow after blow, the thing was ripped apart, flung aside and scattered, the wretched rotten clothes shredded, the foolish floppy hat blown away on the breeze.

When the fight was over and won, the overdrawn balance of his body took over and he sank, dizzy and shaking, to he ground, his clothes chill with ice sweat, his face wet from unnoticed, hot tears.

Then, above his breathing, he heard the rustling of a light draught that was sweeping the soil and straw together, and he realised that like calls to like, that earth abides, that nature…endures.

Instantly, he was on his feet. He vaulted the fence into the road and ran. Risked a glance back. Nothing behind him. Ran faster still.

But was that something on the other side of the hedge, moving parallel to him and not far behind? Did it jump unnaturally high over the walls between the fields, crumple low on landing, then spring up impossibly quickly?

For the sake of speed, he looked straight ahead, ignoring the shape he thought he glimpsed flitting almost alongside then dropping behind as he put on even more pace, his trainers slapping on the road.

He was winning.

Finally, when The Floppy Man tired of the game, it leapt high into the air, effortlessly vaulting the trees, and landed facing him, its rooted hands outstretched, ready to receive his face.

Mark never had time to stop. He certainly never had time to scream.

#

In the back of the Range Rover, the five-year-old girl on the way back from the weekend gymkhana began to whimper uncontrollably. Her mother tried to soothe her with logic and sweet reason. But even a little girl's grasp of the world and its workings includes the fact that a scarecrow in a field dressed in new trainers and a washed-out grey tracksuit does not turn a face as featureless as an egg to sniff the air, before moving inexpertly off on unpractised legs.

And what kind of legs were ever meant to bend *that* way at the knee?

QUESTIONS A MAN OUGHT NOT TO ASK
Elizabeth Broadbent

When he walked into Brewster's, old men in Vietnam vet ballcaps turned from their sausage and eggs. He took a seat at the counter and flipped his mug. Though we pretended to ignore him, we watched, and the diner at the back of the convenience store seemed too quiet as Shirley poured his coffee. 'Whatchu want?' she asked.

'The special.' He wore ratty jeans and a thermal shirt, but his winter hat looked expensive, and his boots seemed made for hiking. Our men were hard-muscled and rough-palmed with hard work. He was slim and soft-handed.

At least he didn't ask for cream and sugar.

I sipped my own bitter-black coffee from the other end of the counter.

Shirley dropped a plate of biscuits and gravy on his paper placemat. 'You passing through?' she asked.

He shook his head. 'I'm staying at the Gaston Motel,' he replied, and didn't add, 'twenty miles and a world away.' 'I'm hoping to get to know some folks and hear some stories.'

She snorted. 'We ain't got no stories in Lower Congaree.'

He gave her a tiny smile. 'I doubt that.'

She ripped his scribbled bill from her pad and turned away.

Those stupid students came up from the university every so often. 'Tell me your local legends,' they'd say, or, 'I heard you believe in root medicine—do you have healers here?' They brought dumbass questions, questions a man ought not to ask. My stomach turned. 'Forget the biscuits,' I called. 'Just put the coffee on my tab.'

Shirley didn't glance up. 'Don't you worry 'bout it, Ella Lee.'

I shivered down the street to a little house behind Hopkin's General Store. Dixie's baby wanted to come too soon. 'I'll bring you some things tomorrow,' I told her, and laid my hands on her belly. He was thumb-sucking and opinionated already. I had to sweet-talk him: Stay there for your mama. Just a little while longer, please?

I straightened and gave Dixie that smile she wanted. 'He'll stay put till I come again.'

'He?' She grinned like spring had come early. Clint wanted a junior.

I nodded.

Outside, I hugged myself, fast-walking before my toes went numb despite my wool socks and old boots. I had to get back home—Dixie needed her things. Shirley's leg was hurting again. Mattie's back was acting up with this cold snap, and if I could manage something for Sue Ellen's migraines, she'd knit me some gloves. I never could knit. Mama always said I dropped stitches like the devil dropped cusswords.

Anyway, my babies would be getting lonely.

I stepped around the puddle next to my truck, hopped into the driver's seat, and turned my key. The engine cranked and died.

Goddammit.

'Can I help you?' That damn student peered at me. He wasn't bad-looking with those dark eyes and that shoulder-length hair meant for pulling. They'd call him names over that hair. I liked it.

'Can *you* help *me*?' I snorted like Shirley. 'I doubt it.'

'It's either a dead battery or your starter. If you're unlucky, it's your alternator. Can I take a look?'

He might've worn fancy wool gloves, but he sounded like any man in Lower Congaree. I nodded at my Ford. 'Go ahead, city boy.'

He stuck his head under her hood and poked around. 'Your battery kicked the bucket. I can jump you, but it'll die again. Or I can take you to the hardware store, show you which to get, and put in the new one.' He went quiet, like he'd said too much. 'I mean, if you want.'

Not a bad offer, and it would save me from paying Dale down at the garage. 'Pick out the battery, jump me, then follow me home and change it out?' I asked. 'I'll make you something hot to eat.' Then maybe something else. Maybe.

He nodded. 'I'm Henry Jenkins.'

'Ella Lee Merle. I'm halfway down Lost John Road—you'll have to follow me.'

He carried the battery. I let him do it, then played helpless while he jumped my Ford. Before Henry hooked up the positive clamp, he handed me those fancy gloves. I could've glared. I could've said I wasn't cold. My fingers were numb, and I pulled them on.

Our roads wove around the edges of blackwater swamp. They twisted like phone cords, and I didn't go slow. Henry kept on my tail, then wound down my unpaved drive like he'd learned it long ago. 'Fun ride,' he said, popping out of his shiny Pontiac Firebird.

'You're a good driver.' I had to hand him that.

He didn't seem to hear. Instead, he gazed at the bare-branched cypress and tupelo surrounding the swamp. My babies watched him. 'You have a lot of crows up here.'

'Mmm-hmm.' They probably wondered who the hell he was, too.

Henry shivered, even though he wasn't cold in that fluffy new coat. 'Crows always scared me.'

'Why's that?'

'They're carrion eaters.'

I shook my head—the lies they told about my babies. 'Believe me, they'd rather not. If you change out that battery, I'll heat up some soup. That okay with you?'

He was already popping my hood. 'Sounds great.'

I was good to him in that kitchen—vegetable soup, warm bread, sweet tea, and hot coffee. Lunch was finished when he knocked. When I opened the door, he looked, then looked away. I should've expected it. Instead of a ratty winter coat, I wore soft jeans, a tight T-shirt, and a snuggly flannel that belonged to my daddy once. Henry hung his own coat. He had some muscle to his chest, and his arms weren't the sticks I'd imagined.

Lunch was small talk, stupid things. He liked my soup. He was up from Carolina's anthropology department to collect folktales. No one had any luck in this area, and he thought he'd try. He'd grown up in Charlotte. His daddy was a mechanic, which explained why a soft-handed grad student could tell a dead battery from a faulty starter.

'What do you do?' he asked.

'Oh, I stay over here and keep to myself,' I told him.

'No boyfriend?' He smiled when he said it.

'Why?' I asked, sweet as my tea. 'You auditioning?'

Henry had white, even teeth someone had paid a lot of money for. 'Maybe. You're too pretty to stay here all alone with those crows.'

'You think so?' No one had called me pretty in a long time. The ones who had didn't have his long, dark hair, and while they might've fixed a roof tile or banged a loose chair together, they'd expected plenty of cooing over it.

'With that blonde hair and blue eyes? You're definitely too pretty to sit here in this swamp alone,' Henry said.

I could've used any of those Lanier or McAllister boys, but they expected coddling, even from me. More than that, I'd come up with them. We'd climbed trees, lost teeth, and picked blackberries together; they belonged to Mattie or Sue Ellen or Dale. They belonged to Lower Congaree.

Henry didn't belong to us.

I pursed my lips. He couldn't stop looking. 'I like it here,' I told him, then stood and walked toward my room. Thank the Lord Mama had taught me to make my bed every morning. 'You coming?' I called.

Henry's chair scraped the floor. 'Yes, ma'am.'

I liked that boy already.

#

'That was unexpected.' Henry sounded uncertain. We lay under my grandmother's quilt while I combed my fingers through his hair, shiny as a girl's.

'Mmmm.' He didn't need answers.

'It was nice, don't get me wrong.' He paused. 'I mean, much more than nice. Just unexpected. God, my professors would kill me.'

I cuddled closer. He was warm under that quilt, and it was good to be warm. That cold snap seeped into a person's bones. 'Those stupid old men are a world away,' I said. 'Forget them.'

His hand slipped down the small of my back. 'I forgot to, um, ask. Exactly how old are you?' He chewed his lip.

I tapped that pouty lip, like my mama did to me. 'Stop. You'll chap it. I'm old enough to buy liquor and not much more.'

'That's young to be living all alone. I guess you got this place from your parents?'

'From my mama, when she died.' My chest hurt.

'What about your father?'

I kissed his nose and said it fast so I never had to say it again. 'My daddy died the day I was born, during a hurricane.' Hurricane Denise was a big one, but it was supposed to make landfall at the North Carolina border. It turned, slammed Charleston, and tore straight up the state to Lower Congaree, like Mama said it would. Her labor started as that storm hit. She'd brought plenty of babies into the world, and she knew when she began to bleed out. Daddy refused to watch her die. 'Take me instead,' he told her. 'Save the baby.' He knew Mama could. She said no, but Daddy had made his choice. In the morning, Dale and Preston Hewitt found him dead in the front yard. 'My daddy's name was Lee Evans,' I told Henry. 'That's why I'm Ella Lee.'

'You have your mother's last name, then.' Henry pulled me closer.

I nodded. 'We do that in my family.'

'Why?'

Men and their questions. 'We just do. You as good a mechanic as you say?'

He shrugged, which meant yes.

'I'll talk to Dale tomorrow. He's looking for a man and if you want to fit into Lower Congaree, that's the best way to do it.'

Henry pulled back a little. 'You think so?'

I nodded.

Then I kicked him out.

In the morning, we met at the diner, and everyone pretended not to watch as we sat together at the counter. 'You pick up a straggler, Ella Lee?' Shirley asked when we turned our mugs.

I made a sound that could've meant yes and could've meant no.

She eyeballed Henry. 'I guess you want the special again.'

He nodded. 'Yes, ma'am.'

I knew better than to talk to Henry with everyone listening, and he was smart enough not to talk to me. But Shirley asked, 'You want this check separate or together?'

'Together,' Henry replied, damn him, which told everyone exactly how far we'd gone, and exactly how he felt about it, too. They'd have found out later that morning when I took him to the garage, but that news would've taken time to travel through town. By taking my bill, Henry guaranteed people would talk about nothing but "that student sleeping with Ella Lee".

As we walked out, Lonny Evans—who was the sheriff and my uncle—fixed me with his meanest glare. I threw it right back. When Dale and Preston had found my daddy, they called him.

'Why'd you have to go and do that?' I asked Henry as the store's cowbell clanged behind us. I resisted smacking him. They'd see from the window and talk about that, too.

'What?' Henry's eyebrows met.

'Buy me breakfast.'

'I thought it was the right thing to do?'

'You think that won't go all over town in a minute?'

Henry didn't look at me. 'I guess it will.'

'Did you think it would give you some sort of leg up?' I asked. 'Use me like that again, and we'll run you out of town so fast your head'll spin.'

That shut him up. As we trudged toward the garage, cold crept through my coat. 'I didn't mean it that way,' Henry finally told me.

'Like hell you didn't.'

I still took him to Dale, and I had to talk fast, but he said he'd try Henry for the day. Once he agreed, I smiled and gave him a small bag. 'I know your hands get dry, working out here in this cold all day,' I told him.

'That's sweet of you, Ella Lee,' he said, and we had a deal.

With Henry settled, I hiked around Lower Congaree all morning, my hands going numb between houses. Dixie's baby had stayed settled—restless, she said, but settled. I visited Mattie, then Sue Ellen, who promised me a pair of gloves.

Shirley was wiping down the counter when I showed my face at Brewster's again. 'I have something for you,' I said.

She took the bag I handed her. 'You brought that boy in this morning.'

I made another sound that didn't mean anything.

'You sure you want to mess around with that?' Her eyes were beady as a chicken's.

'You sure you want to mess around in my business?'

She opened her mouth, then shut it.

'Uh-huh,' I said. 'That's right.'

#

'How'd it go?' I asked Henry that night. Dark had already dropped, but he found my house without trouble.

'Dale said he'd hire me if I wanted a job.' He started to sit.

I shook my head. 'Not on my kitchen chair. You get in that shower first. I'll have dinner ready when you get out.'

He looked at his feet. 'You didn't have to make me dinner or have me over here again. I don't want you to feel—'

'I wanted to. And you wanted to come. So get your ass in that shower, then come eat my chicken.' I turned away. I didn't say, 'This house gets lonely with only my babies for company. My bed'll be warm tonight, and it'll be good to wake up with someone in the morning.'

'That murder of crows was watching when I came in,' he said at dinner.

I made another one of those sounds. Later, I pulled his hair.

Henry kept working at the garage. He complained about paying the Gaston Motel for a room he wasn't using, and I told him to move everything to my place. 'I don't want to impose,' he said.

'It's not imposing.' I gave him a sweet smile.

He moved in.

Of course, his questions started. I did most of my work while he was at the garage, but some things needed moonlight. 'What were you doing last night, Ella Lee?' Henry asked one morning. 'I woke up and you were gone. I thought maybe you were in the bathroom, but you didn't come back.'

'I had things to do.' I poured his coffee, then my own.

'What kind of things need done in the middle of the night?' He squinted at me.

I kissed his forehead. 'Things you don't need to worry about.'

Once in a while, Henry made some noise about those stories. 'Worry about that later,' I said. 'You need to get to know folks better before they'll talk to you.'

85

He passed me his cigarette. He'd started smoking Dale's Pall Malls, then buying packs of his own. I drew my arms close as I dragged on it, and he tucked me under his arm. 'If you'd let me smoke in the house—' he started.

'Nope.' I took another puff. 'No cigarettes in the house, and anyway, I like you hugging me.'

Once, I found him tugging at my root cellar door. 'What's this?' he asked.

'Herbs,' I said. 'I dry stuff in there.'

That seemed enough for Henry, especially when I kissed him. 'Come inside,' I told him. 'I need warming up.'

'God, those crows again. You have to find a way to keep them out,' Henry said as he followed me back to the house. My babies glared from their tree. One flapped angrily.

'They live here, same as you, and don't say things like that, Henry Jenkins.' I rubbed my hands together.

He gave them a look, then shivered in his fluffy coat. 'It's like they're judging me.'

'They do when you say things like that.' I pushed the door open and slipped inside, then poured myself a cup of coffee, partly to warm my fingers around the mug.

He snorted. 'Crows can't understand people.'

I sat in a kitchen chair my daddy had built for Mama. 'Planning on leaving?'

He opened his mouth, shut it, and then finally managed, 'I wasn't planning on it anytime soon, but if you want me to, I'll—'

'I didn't say I wanted you to. I'd rather you didn't. But if you're staying here, you don't talk bad about those crows.' I got up to stir the stew. Henry played with his placemat.

He asked too many questions, but he didn't sit on his ass while I cleaned up. He helped. He showed up with little presents from the general store—stupid things, like cards or candy bars. He'd give me the last cigarette in his pack. I'd brought him there for a reason, but that's not why I kept him.

My mama had told me it happened like that with my daddy. 'I made a plan to bring him here.' She laughed. 'Then I spun around and realized I was in love.'

Clint Junior was a month old when Shirley told me to visit Dixie. 'You need to get over there,' she said as I turned my mug. 'Dixie ain't well.'

'She seemed fine when I ran into her at Hopkin's yesterday.'

Shirley glanced at Henry, then glanced at me. 'You go see her.'

Dixie had two black eyes, and I was gentle when I touched the bruise on her side. 'He didn't break anything,' I said. 'This isn't the first time, is it?'

She stared across the room at a calendar, one that came free from Greene's Feed and Seed. 'First time since the baby came. He said I have to stop nursing him.'

I trudged out to my truck, then mucked back, noticing on my way that the trash was overflowing with beer cans. 'So he's done it before?' I asked as I crouched beside her.

Dixie pressed her lips together and looked at that calendar again.

'Put this on three times a day. It'll help it heal and stop it from hurting,' I told her. 'How often does he do it?'

She must've known I wouldn't stop asking. 'Maybe once or twice a week, but never where anyone can see. Do you have anything to dry me up?'

'I'll take care of it,' I said as I straightened up. 'Don't forget that salve.'

She nodded. 'Thank you, Ella Lee. God bless you.'

Henry came home wide-eyed that night. His lip was chapped from chewing it. 'I had to take the wrecker out to get Clint Booker's truck,' he said. 'He slammed it into a tupelo and went into a drainage ditch. The sheriff and the coroner were there.' He shuddered. 'Ella Lee, I told you crows were carrion-eaters. They took out his eyes. Why the hell he had his windows open in weather like this, I'll never know. Those crows were still hanging around in the trees, like they were waiting for more.'

'Did you get his truck out okay?' I kissed his head.

'We did, but—'

'Good, because his wife doesn't have another.' I tapped his lip. 'Don't nibble like that. You chapped your lip up. Let me get you something for that.' I opened my extra pantry and rooted something out.

Henry smeared his lips and didn't speak till we sat down to dinner. 'You have something for everything, don't you, Ella Lee?'

I tucked some of that pretty hair behind his ear. 'Sometimes.'

'The sheriff was there. Isn't he your uncle? He hates my ass. He keeps asking when I'm planning on leaving.'

'He never liked my mama,' I said.

'Why not?'

'He just didn't.' I gave him another biscuit. 'You know how folks get.'

Dixie's bruises hadn't faded before the funeral, and makeup caked around her eyes. Henry held my hand as we said we were sorry about Clint. Her mama hugged me around Clint Junior. 'Didn't you see Dixie the morning Clint died?' Henry asked as we drove down Lost John Road.

'Yeah.' Damn Shirley for talking when he could hear. 'She wasn't feeling well. I sat with her for a while.'

'What was wrong with her?'

'Sad, mostly,' I said, and it wasn't a lie. 'You know how some women get after they have a baby, especially when their husbands drink too much.'

He didn't answer. I took his hand and squeezed it.

Goddamn him for noticing. My stomach flipped and my toes curled in my black church shoes. He had to stop asking questions, because he wouldn't like the answers.

By the time the swamp went green with spring, Henry sat with the younger men at the diner and hit the Roadhouse with them every night. He said they teased him for keeping it to one beer. 'But they say they'd run their asses down the road if they had you waiting for 'em, too,' he told me.

I'd've seethed over that, but when we were thirteen, I'd knocked Randy out of an oak tree and kissed him afterward. At fourteen, I tricked Darryl into a thicket of poison ivy, then made it up to him in the back of his daddy's pickup. Dalton and I lost it together, and I still smiled over it. We remembered each other's lost teeth and broken arms and bee stings. They were mine. They were Lower Congaree.

'I've got to get started on those stories,' Henry said one night while we snuggled under warm blankets. 'I'll lose my funding if I don't.'

'Hush. I need to tell you something.' I'd held her close for weeks, told her stories, and sang her into staying. 'You'll either be real happy or real mad.'

He quieted. Henry might leave, or he might stick around. One way or another, Lower Congaree would catch fire with gossip. I prayed he wouldn't go, this man who brought me cookies, kissed my cheek, and held my hand when we walked into Brewster's.

He turned enough to slip a hand onto my belly. 'Right there,' he whispered.

I nodded.

Henry took a leave of absence from Carolina.

#

Like all men's fights, it was stupid from one end to the other. Randy started on Dalton. Dalton started on Randy. Randy got angry, and Dalton got angrier, and they took it outside. They began with punches, then Randy picked up a broken bottle. Dalton pulled out his Bowie knife. Maybe he forgot Randy had his concealed carry. Maybe he'd drunk himself dumb enough to think Randy wouldn't use it.

It only took two shots. Dalton's blood pooled in the hot summer dust. 'Tell Ella Lee,' he said as red trickled from his mouth.

Henry saw it, start to finish. He sped up down the road and held me while I cried. The child wept inside me.

'Why'd Dalton want someone to tell you?' he asked as he rubbed my back up and down, up and down. His shoulder was wet with my tears.

'Don't you worry about it,' I managed between sobs.

'You can tell me, Ella Lee.'

My sobs stopped fast. 'Don't ask questions,' I said, and walked out back. My babies saw my tears. I lifted my arms to them and whispered words Henry could never hear. They rose into dark as black as their wings.

A cop found Randy dead in the jail's exercise yard. Heart attack, said the coroner, maybe a stroke. Randy's eyes and tongue were missing.

That's how Sheriff Evans told it down at the diner, with me sitting right there. Our eyes met. My daddy's choice hung between us. He hated me for it, but he was blood, and blood was untouchable.

Henry whirled. 'What'd you say?'

Sheriff Evans glanced at him. 'We found him with a murder of crows. They didn't leave till we took his body away. You remember it happened with Clint Booker. Dale's father, too. Ella Lee here, it happened with her daddy when we found him after that hurricane.'

People shifted in their chairs. No one said much of anything after that. I couldn't finish my breakfast, and Henry told Dale he didn't feel well. The baby fluttered as Henry followed me home. He got out of his city-boy car and trailed into the house after me.

I waited. It was coming as sure as a summer storm. I could almost smell the ozone. The hairs on my neck rose, and our child kicked hard.

'I came up here looking for stories.' Henry's voice shook. 'You know them all.'

I didn't speak.

'You don't go sit with women. That root cellar's not for cooking.'

He'd always asked questions, and he hated my babies. I should have known it would happen one day.

'You're the wise woman or the healer or the folk magician. Whatever they call you.' Henry took a step back. 'You're the witch.'

I stared him down. 'Don't you call me a goddamn witch.'

'They all know it. You wanted me because I didn't.' He wrapped his arms around himself, despite the heat. 'You killed Randy because he killed Dalton. You killed Clint because he beat up Dixie. Those crows out there'—he pointed toward the trees my babies loved—'tore out their eyes.'

Damn my uncle to hell, because I couldn't send him there.

Henry gestured at my belly. 'And that's the next one.'

'Maybe that's why I liked you at first. You didn't know.' He'd caught me, and I couldn't hand him anything but the truth. 'But it's more now.'

'How do I know you didn't make me fall in love with you? It's fake. You made me feel this way.'

'No.' My voice caught. 'Henry, I would never do that. Anything you feel is yours.'

His boots slid on my wooden floor as he backed up again. 'If I leave, you'll set your crows on me. I'm trapped here. I'm like a goddamn princess in a tower, and I fathered a psychopath.'

I tried to take his hand. He jerked back. 'No, it's not like that. I help—'

'You kill people. You decide who dies.'

'They deserved it!' I shouted, and my babies rustled in their tree. 'Henry, please.' Our daughter kicked and punched. 'Stop. I never did anything to you. I never made you stay, and I never made you fall in love with me. I could've, and I didn't. Someone here has to help people. Someone has to keep order—'

'That's not how it works!'

'That's how it works here, and it's always worked that way.' My voice dropped low. 'You came here for stories? That's your story, Henry. It's different out here in the swamp, and it always will be.'

'Now that I know, you'll never let me leave.' He turned and walked out—walked straight to those trees.

I sucked in a hard breath. They hated him because he'd always hated them. 'Don't!' I yelled, but it was too late. Henry held out his arms like Christ on the cross. Still as stone, they burst suddenly to life, like they'd waited for that moment, like they'd known it would come, and they'd only bided their time.

Henry disappeared behind beating black wings.

I screamed. Deep in my belly, our child screamed with me.

MARJORIE
Meg Belviso

Mama was going to have a baby. That, Papa explained to Elsie, was why she had not come down to breakfast and why Elsie was not allowed to enter Mama's bedroom even after Mrs Platt, the housekeeper, made sure Elsie had washed all the butter and jam from her hands. When she saw Mama again, Elsie would have a new brother or sister, better even than her baby doll, Marjorie, who closed her eyes when laid down flat.

That was three days ago and Elsie had seen no baby yet. She had heard no baby crying in Mama's room either. When Papa finally called her into his laboratory, she knew something unexpected had occurred, because Elsie was never permitted in Papa's laboratory.

Things had gone wrong, Papa explained, and plans had changed. The baby had died and so had Mama. 'But,' Papa said, 'you will have a new doll.' He took Elsie's hand and led her toward the back of the room. Despite her disappointment, confusion, and a strange numbness in her limbs, her eyes roamed the forbidden space. The walls were covered with shelves full of copper bowls and glass bottles, and skulls whose eye-sockets seemed to flicker under the lamps.

Papa led her to a large machine whose purpose Elsie could not immediately guess. There was a belt on one side, wrapped around large gears, that fed itself into a hulking contraption of iron and copper with dials, wires, globes, and what looked like tiny lightning rods sticking out of the top. Elsie knew, without being told, that she mustn't touch anything. She didn't want to anyway. It was an ugly machine.

'I've been working on this since before you were born,' Papa said.

When he bent down to her level, Elsie saw that his cheeks were dark with the beginnings of a beard and there were shadows under his eyes. 'I tried to capture your mother's soul, but the trauma of the birth, or death—or perhaps the mature soul, being more used to the body, having been kept apart from its maker for so long—perhaps the more mature soul is able to resist the lure...'

He trailed off, lost in his own thoughts. Elsie was used to Papa doing that, and to not understanding anything he was saying.

'Be that as it may,' said Papa, catching her attention again, 'your mother is in heaven but your baby sister's soul is here with us.'

Papa led Elsie to the far end of the machine, where there was a bassinet. He reached in and lifted out not a new doll at all, but Elsie's own baby doll, Marjorie. Elsie had been searching for Marjorie since yesterday. She hadn't thought of asking Papa where she was. He had never showed any interest in dolls before.

'What do you think of that?' he asked, placing Marjorie carefully in her arms.

Elsie peeled back the cotton blanket in which the porcelain baby was wrapped, and as she did, the doll moved.

Elsie froze. When she looked up at her father, he was smiling in a way he had never smiled at her—he was smiling at the doll. 'It's no trick, my dear,' he said, tickling the doll's cheek with his finger. 'I caught the *anima*—the soul—and placed it here, in the doll. It's never been done, not ever, not until now.'

Elsie stared at the doll and the doll stared back, despite the fact that she was lying down and her eyes were meant to be closed in that position. Elsie had never had such a doll before. Nobody had.

The doll lifted a porcelain hand and wrapped one of Elsie's curls around her finger.

'She's all mine?' asked Elsie, not daring to believe it.

'You must bring it to me when I need it for my studies, and, of course, when I present it to anyone from the society,' her father said. 'But it seems to need something like a mother. Something like, but not exactly. It's too much of a distraction to keep in here all the time. It needs someone to quiet it when it starts making noise. You're a big girl now. You should do just fine.'

'Oh yes,' Elsie said eagerly. 'I'm very good at dolls. I'll feed her and change her diapers and sing to her when she's sad.'

Mama used to sing to Elsie when she wasn't feeling well, and she would never do that again. Mama would never do anything again. She had left her all alone. But Elsie had Marjorie to think about now.

'I'll take good care of her,' she promised solemnly. 'I swear.'

#

Papa referred to the soul inside the doll as "the anima" but Elsie still called her Marjorie. It was Elsie who was always with her. She had always taken very good care of her doll, but Marjorie ensouled required more attention. She cried incessantly. She cried until Elsie lifted a silver spoon to her mouth and cried until Elsie unwrapped and rewrapped her in a diaper. She cried until Elsie picked her up and sang. She cried until Elsie was exhausted.

'What a lucky girl you are!' Mrs Platt said when she came upon Elsie dozing on the divan with Marjorie in her arms. 'I never had such a doll when I was a girl.'

'Yes,' Elsie said, waking with a start. 'I'm a very lucky girl and Marjorie is a beautiful doll.'

When Elsie's friends came over for a tea party, she kept Marjorie's bassinet where they could all see her.

'My Barbara doesn't cry at all,' Elsie's friend Florence said, bouncing her own doll on her knee. 'She used to, but something happened to her voice box mechanism. I think my brother broke it on purpose.'

'I wish my Sara cried,' said Deirdre, looking sulkily at the brand-new doll she'd just received for her birthday. 'It isn't fair. Elsie always has the best toys.'

'Elsie's mother is dead,' Florence replied severely. 'She needs toys to soothe her heart because she has no one else.'

Marjorie let out a wail in her bassinet and Elsie proudly took her out to pretend-feed her. She was the best doll, all the girls agreed. She did all the things real babies did. And she didn't stop when you were tired of playing with her either.

Long after midnight, patiently holding another empty bottle to Marjorie's lips, Elsie imagined Deirdre sleeping, tucked into her bed, with her brand-new, quiet doll lying silently beside her.

Sometimes the men in Papa's society came to see his machine. On these occasions, Elsie would be called to bring Marjorie to the parlor.

'Examine it closely, gentleman,' Papa said. 'There's not a gear or mechanism inside her. It's an ordinary doll, animated completely by a genuine, discarnate human soul.'

'My God.'

'I wouldn't have believed it.'

'You'll be a standout in the annals for generations.'

'You'll bring it to the conference in San Francisco, of course?'

'Does it communicate, Edward?' a man with a monocle asked. 'Has the soul spoken of the other realms from which it came?'

Marjorie had begun to speak, though Elsie hadn't mentioned it to Papa because she wasn't sure how to describe it. It had started during her late-night feedings. When Marjorie finished a pretend bottle, she often let out a satisfied, almost guttural, burp, which Elsie didn't like. More recently, she had begun burping unexpectedly in her crib at night. These burps, in the past few days, had begun to be followed by a muttering sound, like an old man having a puzzling dream. Then, last night, the muttering stopped and Marjorie said her name: 'Elsie.'

Elsie had always liked her name, but not when spoken in Marjorie's deep, course voice, nothing like how Elsie would have expected a little sister to talk. She tried to go back to sleep, but every time she was about to doze off, she heard her name again, coming from the crib. By the time the sun rose, Elsie had wrapped her head in the blanket and decided that the only thing worse than hearing Marjorie say her name was the dread of waiting for her to say it.

'She says my name,' Elsie said to Papa's friends. 'She says it all night long.'

The bundle in Papa's arms twisted ever so slightly and Elsie knew Marjorie had turned to look at her.

'Is that all?' asked the man with the monocle, disappointed.

'The anima depends on my daughter for its simpler needs,' Papa explained. 'I'm sure it's but a matter of time before it communicates something of value.'

The men clinked their glasses in an encouraging toast as Mrs Platt led Elsie and Marjorie out of the study.

Marjorie began to talk a lot after that, but Elsie had no idea if any of it was important because she didn't understand much of it—yet.

The doll was especially noisy at night. It was difficult to sleep with Marjorie constantly crying and muttering. Perhaps lack of sleep was the reason for the whispering noises in Elsie's head. It started softly, so softly that Elsie couldn't say for sure when it started, then became so constant she sometimes stopped noticing it at all. Eventually, though, the whispering became louder, like the buzz of some angry machine. It made it difficult to sleep even when Marjorie was pretending to, and when she did sleep, Elsie dreamed she was trapped in a cramped room with curved walls and woke up furious at everyone and everything. Mrs Platt said that Elsie was becoming unpleasant and reminded her that cross little girls didn't have friends and didn't get to choose which jam they were served at breakfast.

One rainy morning, when the anima had finished its bottle, Elsie took the opportunity to walk outside. Papa didn't like her to walk outside with Marjorie. He was afraid she might attract attention, that people would ask questions and Elsie would not answer them correctly. So Elsie left Marjorie in her crib, took an umbrella from the stand by the door, and went outside alone.

She walked to the park. The wind was wet and her feet squelched in the mud, but she felt better than she had in months. The buzzing in her head decreased considerably. She knew there was no one at home to change Marjorie's diapers or pretend to feed her, but Elsie had begun to suspect Marjorie didn't actually need those things. They were just a way of getting and keeping Elsie's attention. When Elsie gave her a bottle, Marjorie fixed her blue glass eyes on Elsie's and pinched the skin on Elsie's wrist with her cool, smooth doll fingers. When Elsie sang her lullabies, Marjorie stuck Elsie's finger into her brittle doll mouth and chewed on it.

All this time, Elsie had been waiting for Marjorie to become the little girl Papa said she was meant to be, but she seemed to becoming less like a little girl every day. Was it possible, she thought, stopping short in the mud, that Papa was wrong—that he was the fool Marjorie so obviously thought he was?

At the thought of returning to those blue glass eyes and cool fingers, Elsie's stomach turned and she threw up in a gutter. She wondered what would happen if she never went home at all. What if some kind person took her to an orphanage where there were no toys or dolls or fathers? She imagined herself in a shabby gray uniform, eating gruel at a long table with her hair in tight braids, contented with all of it if only she could be left alone.

But Papa said Marjorie needed her. And Papa would find her. They didn't just accept girls in orphanages without looking for their parents first. Besides, Elsie was a mother now, or something like one. She couldn't just leave Marjorie alone to be questioned and prodded by Papa and his friends. What would Elsie's own Mama think of that?

When she did come home, Papa was very angry.

'Where have you been?' he demanded. Mrs Platt stood just behind him, frowning. 'The anima has been crying for hours. I've been unable to work at all and neither has Mrs Platt! What were you thinking, leaving it alone and abandoning your responsibilities?'

'I'm sorry, Papa,' Elsie said. After all, it was true. Marjorie was her responsibility. Even if it was Papa who was preparing to take a lot of credit for her. As Elsie climbed the stairs back to her room, the buzzing returned and chased all other thoughts from her head.

She didn't leave Marjorie's side for three days. Mrs Platt brought her meals to her room. Papa no longer allowed her to visit with friends, assuming Elsie had gone to the park that day to see them. He didn't want to lose any more time before his society's conference.

Marjorie seemed to understand that she had caused some trouble. She forgave Elsie for leaving her alone and began to let her sleep more often, even stroking her hair and gurgling something like a song to help her rest like Mama used to do when Elsie was unwell. Elsie wondered what things would have been like if Papa thought he'd caught Mama's soul instead of a dead infant's.

Papa had no idea what he'd actually captured with his infernal machine. He would have appreciated that if he'd taken care of Marjorie himself. Or if Elsie hadn't begun lying about Marjorie's behavior, about the growls and grunts, the teacups hovering in the air. Or what Marjorie really thought about Marjorie's father. None of Elsie's friends' little sisters hated their fathers as purely and gleefully as Marjorie hated Papa. It was fun sharing these secrets with Marjorie. Mama had always said Papa was intelligent, but he was, in fact, quite easily fooled.

It was easier to understand these things when Marjorie was being quiet and nice. Whatever lived behind the doll's rosy, porcelain face knew things. She knew much more than father. And it was with Elsie that she chose to share her knowledge. At night, in dreams, she took Elsie flying on thick, leathery wings over yawning canyons and endless black seas, until she woke up in tears to find herself back in her bed with Marjorie's hard pink lips pressed against her own.

Some mornings, Elsie didn't bother to get out of bed. She just laid there, carefully watching Marjorie draw pictures on the walls with the colored pencils Elsie had once used to decorate dresses for her paper dolls. Marjorie often muttered while she sketched these shapes. Elsie had no trouble understanding Marjorie now. In fact, often she found herself muttering along with her. Sometimes she was unsure which one of them was speaking at a given moment. In time, Elsie came to understand the powerful symbols on the walls as well, and even how to draw them. And wouldn't Papa have liked to know it all too! But he never would.

In the days leading up to Papa's conference, Mrs Platt regularly escorted Elsie down to the parlor where Papa asked a lot of questions about Marjorie's care, such as how one could tell if she was crying for a bottle or a diaper change or what. The sorts of things he'd had no interest in before. It was hard not to laugh at Papa's questions now, just as it had always been hard for Marjorie, Elsie now understood. The one inside her didn't need bottles or diapers. She needed someone to care for her, and Elsie did that because Elsie had been chosen. While Papa prattled on about electricity, ether, and his ugly machine, Elsie thought about the dark temples where Marjorie had once been worshipped centuries ago and made plans to build something like them again.

On the day before they were to leave for San Francisco, Papa spent the whole day in his lab and Marjorie spent the whole day in Elsie's room, the lower walls of which were covered in Marjorie's beautiful runes, as high up as she and Elsie could reach. It wasn't a temple, but it would do for now.

While Marjorie drew, Elsie dreamed. She dreamed of the canyons, the skies, and the seas she'd come to love. She dreamed herself bursting out of smooth china walls in triumph and the look that would be on Papa's face when he saw what Marjorie could do.

Elsie often muttered during these dreams, which didn't bother Marjorie, who muttered also, but disturbed Mrs Platt profoundly when she brought Elsie lunch, as did the unholy symbols drawn in colored pencils on the walls. She considered telling Elsie's father about them, but how to describe them in a way that wouldn't sound silly? In the evening, Mrs Platt was reluctant to take Elsie her dinner. The moon had risen by the time she forced herself to carry up a light supper and she returned to the kitchen pale and shaky, her face shiny under a sheen of cold sweat. At midnight, when Papa called her to bring him more coffee, Mrs Platt was long gone with no plans to ever return.

Elsie woke from her dreaming just before dawn. She went to Marjorie, lying peacefully in her doll crib. The two looked at each other, glass eye to fibrous eye. The master and the disciple. The goddess and her high priestess. Marjorie lifted her china arms. Elsie lifted a hammer she had stolen from Papa's workshop.

The porcelain made a satisfying crunch when shattered and Marjorie exploded out of it in a burst of stars and whispers.

Papa wasn't happy to discover his housekeeper had left the house, never to return. He would have to pack the anima for travel himself. When his daughter failed to respond to his calls to bring the doll downstairs, he went to her room himself and loudly knocked.

Marjorie answered the door. And she was glorious.

CHILDREN OF BLOOD
Greg Chapman

Kristy ran down the receding tunnel of darkness, desperate to reach the end, but with each step, escape seemed impossible.

She clutched her swollen belly, trying to stifle the stabbing contractions within. Her legs were slick and cold with uterine fluids. There was nothing she could do to stop the baby from coming.

Kristy couldn't have this baby, not ever.

The makeshift prison was a labyrinth of corridors. She turned right down one and tried the countless doors on either side; the first was locked and, as another powerful contraction almost buckled her at the knees, she tried the second, and the third, until finally, a door opened.

The sight on the other side of the door made her cry out. Two women, dressed only in blood-red robes, stood holding hands in an empty room, their eyes closed, but lips moving in whispered prayer. They turned at the sound of Kristy's terrified voice.

'It's time, isn't it, child?' said one of the women, wrinkled and old.

Kristy dropped to her knees as her abdomen bulged, the skin stretching and contorting. The robed women began to chant in time with her agonized screams and the cacophony seemed to conjure a spark of light in the center of the empty space between them.

She collapsed onto her back and screamed again as the baby began to move, as if it was being driven to crawl its way out by some force more palpable than mere biology. The younger of the robed women knelt by Kristy's quivering legs.

'Let the child come,' she told Kristy.

'No…please!'

Behind the women, a coil of viscous smoke slinked from the light and snaked towards Kristy.

'No! Get away!' Kristy said.

But the ritual could not be halted now.

Ghostly fingers crawled along Kristy's thighs, like drops of ice water, closer and closer to her womb. The baby within moved with an even greater sense of urgency. Kristy's back arched in pain as the entity and her unborn child connected. The subsequent jolt of energy shattered the structure of the room, breaking down the walls of reality. She could only scream to the heavens to beg God to save her very soul.

#

Kristy awoke still screaming, covered in a sheen of sweat. Hands touched her in the dark and there was a bevy of voices. Heart racing, it took her eyes a moment to recognize that the women around her were not her enemy, but fellow prisoners.

'Kristy, it's okay,' Diana said. 'It's okay!' Diana stroked Kristy's hair. 'It was just a dream, honey.'

Kristy sat up and Diana offered her a smile, but there was a sliver of recognition there too—and fear.

'It was awful…' Kristy told her.

'So that's all of us then,' another woman said. 'We've all been abducted the same way. We've all had the same dream.'

Kristy and Diana looked to the darkened corner of the cell, to Veronica, the one who had been imprisoned the longest. Veronica stood and walked to them; she was heavily pregnant. They all were.

'What…what does it mean?' Kristy said, finally feeling calm. 'Why do we all have the same dream?'

'The same reason we're all here in the first place,' Veronica said. 'It's all part of their plan.'

Diana rubbed her belly. 'They want our babies,' she said. 'To hurt them.'

Veronica sat on the seat beside Kristy. 'In the dream—did you see the women in the robes? And the ghost?'

Kristy nodded.

'Did the ghost enter you?' Veronica asked.

'Veronica, that's enough,' Diana said.

'Did the ghost go inside you?'

'Yes!' Kristy said, choking back tears. 'It felt like it was going to take the baby.'

Veronica sighed and lifted herself off the seat, pressing a hand to her back. She walked back and sat in the corner.

'It's clear they want the babies for some reason,' Veronica said. 'They can gladly have mine.'

Diana gasped. 'How can you say that about your child?'

'It's not my child!' Veronica snapped back. Despite the shadows, Kristy and Diana could make out the anger in the older woman's eyes. 'I never asked for this child. Now we're just surrogates for some stupid experiment.'

Kristy leaned on Diana to stand. 'I don't know what they want with the babies, but I know that it's evil. We can't let them get the babies. We have to get out of here.'

Veronica chuckled. 'Are you mad? There's no getting out of here.'

A rattle of keys turned their attention to the cell door. Fear filled Kristy's mind and her unborn child kicked at her in response. Two women entered the cell—the crone-like matron, Agatha, and her tall, heavy-set nurse, who the prisoners dubbed "Dolly". Both exuded authority. The old woman pointed to Kristy.

'Take her to the chamber,' she said.

Kristy froze.

'No! Leave her alone!' Diana tried to block Dolly's path, but the big nurse moved her aside with a forearm and then took Kristy by the wrist.

'What are you going to do?' Kristy said.

'It's time to check your progress,' Agatha said. 'It will be quick and painless—if you do as you are told.'

#

The women sat Kristy in a wheelchair and pushed her down the corridor towards a door gleaming with black lacquered paint—a door completely in contrast to the clean white architecture of the rest of the prison.

The door loomed like an open grave and Kristy's heart pounded frantically in her chest. The child in her womb kicked again in anticipation; it seemed to be feeding off of her emotions and this terrified Kristy even more.

Dolly stopped just short of the door and Agatha came forward and pressed her wrinkled hand against its shining surface.

'*Nos ingressum quaerere*,' she said.

Kristy didn't understand exactly what Agatha had said, but she'd heard Latin before; she recalled attending a mass with her mother where the priest had uttered the strange language. It was so long ago, when she was a child—and free; before she was taken by these women and locked away where no one would find her. How she wished to see her mother again, anyone but these horrible people. She fought back tears.

The door opened with a sighing creak of hinges. On the other side shone an amber light emanating from a large hearth in a stone wall. Dolly wheeled Kristy inside towards a flat stone altar in the centre of the room.

'Take off your gown and lie down,' Agatha said as she went to a wooden table, upon which rested a large book and various silver accoutrements.

'What are you going to do to me?' Kristy asked.

Dolly lifted Kristy out of the wheelchair; her face was as hard as the walls around them. 'Do as you are told,' she said. She tore the gown from Kristy's shoulders in one fierce rip, almost pulling her to the floor.

Kristy, naked and terrified, watched Agatha peruse the book.

The old woman about-faced, holding a dagger. Kristy gasped and tried to back away, but Dolly held her to the spot.

'No! Please! Don't hurt me!'

Dolly lifted Kristy onto the altar and the frigid stone surface against her bare skin made her shriek.

'Stop!'

The nurse pinned Kristy's shoulders as the matron held the blade above her abdomen. The sight of the knife edge so close made her scream. She tried to move but she might as well have been a statue; Dolly was so strong. Kristy saw Agatha lift the knife and…

'God, no! Don't!' Kristy begged.

'*Ostende nobis, modo*,' Agatha whispered. She let go of the knife and it floated above Kristy's belly. Then it started to spin, like the needle in a compass.

Kristy gasped for breath as the dagger spun, the steel cutting the air with each turn, just inches above the skin. Then it simply jerked to a halt. She saw Agatha smile, the lines on her face forming a map of madness.

'Yes!' the old woman said. She came to Kristy's side and peered down at her. 'Your child was conceived on November 28, 1994, yes?'

Kristy struggled to understand Agatha's question, to comprehend anything other than fear.

Why would they ask about the year?

'What do you want from me?' Kristy replied, her body trembling.

Agatha plucked the knife from its invisible perch and held it against Kristy's throat. 'November 28! Milwaukee! The child was conceived in a hotel!'

Images of that night bled into her mind; the man at the bar—who'd told her his name was Dale, a salesman; the instant connection between them; the hotel room where they'd made love. Kristy remembered how afterwards they'd been watching television and the news was on every channel; the execution of the "Milwaukee Cannibal".

'Yes! Yes, I remember!' Kristy said as the dagger's edge stung her neck.

Agatha withdrew the knife and placed her hand almost lovingly on Kristy's stomach.

'Good…good,' she said. You're doing well. Soon, your son will be born and the Blood Brethren will grow in number.'

Kristy blinked away tears. 'Please…just let me go!'

Agatha shook her head. 'Impossible. Your place is here; mothers to the chosen.' She looked to Dolly. 'Take her back to the cell with the others.'

Dolly pulled Kristy down from the altar and sat her in the wheelchair.

'What do you want with the baby?' Kristy sobbed.

Dolly strapped her into the chair as Agatha moved to a depression in the rock wall on the other side of the room. She pressed her hand against it and another door opened, rolling upwards with a rumbling of stones.

'Why are you doing this?' Kristy screamed as she was wheeled away.

As the black door closed, Kristy caught a glimpse of two figures talking to Agatha; they were swathed in shadow, but she could make out the forms of a man in a long cloak and top hat and another in the shape of a young boy. The boy stared at her with cold and callous eyes.

The door closed and left Kristy even more in the dark—a darkness that threatened to consume her.

#

'We have to get out of here,' Kristy later told Diana and Veronica in the cell.

'And how do you expect us to do that?' Veronica said, her mouth a thin line of defiance.

'I don't know, but we have to do something because I know for a fact they plan to kill our babies!'

Diana chewed her nails. 'What happened in there—what did they do to you?'

Kristy took a deep breath. 'They…they did some sort of…magic on me.' She saw Veronica straighten to attention. 'They asked me when the baby was conceived.'

'Why?' Diana asked, absently caressing her abdomen.

'I don't know, but they were very interested to know about the date.'

Veronica stepped closer. 'What date did you give them?'

'November 28, why?'

Veronica's eyes widened; Kristy had never seen her afraid until now.

'What is it?' Kristy asked. 'What's wrong?'

Veronica shook her head. 'Nothing.'

'Wait,' Diana said, taking Kristy's hand. 'Did you say November 28?'

Kristy could sense the same anxiety in Diana. 'Yes…' She looked from one woman to the other. 'What's going on?'

Diana bit her lip. 'That's the same date I fell pregnant,' she said.

'You're serious?' Kristy turned to Veronica. She was leaning against the wall, appearing helpless. 'Veronica, what about you? When did you fall pregnant?'

There was a moment's pause, then she said: 'November 28.'

Kristy backed away. 'Hang on, how did you…fall pregnant?'

Veronica turned to frown at her. 'What, are you stupid?'

'Do either of you know a man named Dale?' Kristy asked, pointing to each of them.

'No,' Veronica replied.

Diana shook her head.

Kristy took a deep breath. 'I'm sorry, I don't mean this in a bad way, but…do you know who the fathers of your babies are?'

Veronica pushed off the wall, her fists clenched and Kristy thought she was about to be punched.

'What kind of question is that, bitch?' she said.

Kristy held up her hands. 'I only asked because the father of my baby told me his name was Dale.' Veronica's eyes narrowed, but Kristy went on. 'We met at a bar and I haven't seen him since.'

Diana shuffled towards them. 'I know who the father of my baby is. His name is Alex. He was an old school friend…a crush. We ran into each other at a conference, after almost fifteen years.' She smirked. 'It had been a long time.'

Veronica huffed and went back to the wall. 'Well, isn't that nice,' she said, her voice carrying a hint of sadness.

'Veronica…' Kristy reached out to her. 'I don't mean to pry, but it could be important—'

Veronica whirled around to face her. 'I don't know who the father is because I was raped! Is that what you wanted to hear?' Her face shone with tears.

'Jesus! I'm sorry. I didn't know—'

'No, you didn't, did you?' Veronica snapped. 'I was jumped by someone at a train station. I never saw the fucker's face. I just went home and wallowed in self-pity. Never told the cops…not anyone. Then I realised I was pregnant. I was on my way to an abortion clinic when those bitches out there grabbed me. That was almost nine months ago. I don't know how they knew, but they said they'd been waiting for me.'

The others sat in silence while Veronica sobbed. Kristy's mind

106

raced with fear and confusion about the complexity of Agatha's plans, but there was guilt now too because she'd forced Veronica to reveal a horrible secret. Diana's broken voice drew her back.

'I don't want to have my baby here...' she said holding her belly. 'I don't want them to have him.'

Kristy went to her. 'And they won't—not if we work together.'

Diana wiped her tears away. 'What are we going to do?'

Kristy squeezed her hand. 'They have to come and check up on one of us soon, so all we have to do...is wait.'

#

Dolly unlocked the cell door and found the women forlorn, staring at the floor. She looked back to Agatha for instruction.

'Take the oldest one to the chamber,' the old woman said.

Dolly nodded and pushed the wheelchair into the cell, stopping beside Veronica.

'Get in,' Dolly ordered.

Veronica got to her feet and shuffled towards the chair, but stopped, suddenly doubled over in pain.

'Ohhhh...'

Dolly gave Agatha a panicked stare.

'The child is coming—get her in the chair now!' Agatha said.

Dolly moved to grab Veronica up off the floor; she took her left arm, but failed to see she already had her right clenched into a fist. With a roar, Veronica brought it up hard into Dolly's face, a snap of bone ringing out inside the cell. The big nurse staggered and clutched her face, blood spilling out from between her fingers.

Kristy and Diana took their chance and moved in to kick Dolly while she was down. Veronica brought a knee into the side of the Dolly's face to finish her off. The nurse slumped to the floor, unconscious. All three expectant mothers then turned their attention to the old matron. The crone turned and ran down the corridor, unbelievably sprite for her age.

'Get after her—quick!' Kristy told her friends as she fished around in Dolly's pockets for a set of keys. Veronica and Diana gave chase but Agatha had already reached the black door and pressed her hand to it.

'We can't let her get away!' Veronica said, but Diana's scream stopped her in her tracks. Diana was on all fours, red-faced with pain.

'Oh, God—the baby's coming!'

The black door opened wide just as Kristy and Veronica came to Diana's aid. Agatha stepped aside and let the young boy come through. The hunting knife glinted in his small, yet agile hand.

'You hurt my mother,' the boy said.

Kristy and Veronica looked at each other.

Was he referring to Dolly or Agatha?

'Diana, you have to get up,' Kristy said.

'I…can't!' Her cries became desperate sucking breaths.

The boy tilted his head to let Agatha whisper something in his ear for a moment, but then he strode towards them with a determination well beyond his years.

'You hurt my mother,' he said again.

'Get up, Diana!' Veronica cried.

Kristy and Veronica lifted Diana to her feet, but she was rigid from the contractions. The boy broke into a run, sheer contempt in his gaze. Veronica released her hold on Diana and stepped between the boy and her fellow captors.

'Stop!'

The boy kept coming, lifted his arm and drove the knife into Veronica's chest.

'No!' Kristy screamed.

Her friend fell and blood spurted across the tiled floor. The boy turned his eyes immediately to the remaining women, Veronica's blood mixing with the vicious red grin on his face.

Agatha had turned the boy into a monster. Or had he been born that way? Was that the reason behind all this madness?

Kristy had no time to contemplate such thoughts as the boy stood over the women, ready to bring the knife down again. Kristy and Diana held each other.

'Edward—stop!'

The voice came from the cloaked figure in the doorway. Its face was half-obscured but the outline of its top hat and cloak were unmistakeable. The man beckoned Edward with a gloved hand.

'Bring them to me—their work is not yet done.'

Edward made the women follow the cloaked man and Agatha into the stone chamber.

Veronica's body was limp in the cloaked man's arms, her blood leaving a trail as he carried her to the altar. Edward made Kristy and Diana sit on the floor, and Diana—wracked with contractions—moaned into the dirt.

'Bring me my instruments,' the cloaked man told Agatha once he'd placed Veronica's corpse.

Kristy watched as the old woman handed him a leather bag. He produced a long, thin-bladed knife from with within.

'Will the vessel still be viable?' Agatha asked him.

He removed his top hat and cloak, revealing a black coat and tails beneath. It was if he was on his way to a ball, or a theatre performance, but with the knife in his hand, he might as well have been preparing for surgery. His entire appearance seemed so out of place and time to Kristy—and this terrified her even more.

'All in good time, mother,' he said.

Agatha is his mother? She looks one-hundred years old. Had this horror started with her?

The man tore open Veronica's gown and pressed the knife to her abdomen.

'Stop! Don't!' Kristy cried.

Agatha's son stopped, glancing at Kristy over his shoulder from deep-set eyes.

'Keep them quiet, Gein,' he told the boy.

The boy growled and pointed his own knife at the women. Diana whimpered in Kristy's arms; she didn't know what was going to happen, how to save herself or her friend. Their babies were lost. Kristy flinched as the suited man ran an incision across Veronica's flesh.

'You fucking monsters!'

Edward gripped Kristy by the hair to pull her head back and rest the knife against her throat. She and Diana sobbed as Agatha's son pried open Veronica's womb and withdrew the limp baby.

'Prepare mother,' he told Agatha.

Agatha donned a red robe and uttered more of the strange

language into the chamber. The door to the room opened and Dolly staggered in, half her face covered in blood.

'Mommy!' Edward said, and she embraced him, keeping her vile gaze on the pregnant women.

Agatha's son assessed Veronica's baby, but it was as lifeless as its mother.

'Watch the hosts carefully,' he told Dolly and Edward and they moved around behind the women, pinning their arms and forcing them to witness the unfolding perversity.

In the centre of the room, a spark of light emerged, just like in Kristy's dream. A wisp of ethereal smoke came forth and gathered a humanoid shape. It twisted through the air towards the baby in Agatha's son's arms. It reached for it desperately—only to recoil with a piercing screech. It hovered around the room in a rage, flicking in and out of phase.

'Jeffrey has rejected the vessel!' Agatha moaned.

Her son put the baby down and addressed Dolly and Edward.

'We're running out of time!' he said. 'Bring me the next host!'

Dolly pulled Diana off the floor. Kristy tried to hold on to her friend, but she was pulled back by the boy. Diana was stricken with terror; she thrashed and screamed against her captor's grip—until the macabre surgeon produced a syringe from his bag and plunged it into her arm.

'Leave her alone, you bastards!'

The suited man glared at Kristy and in his eyes she was granted a vision of the pit of hell.

'No! No! Don't take my baby!' Diana screamed as they dragged her to the altar.

'The contractions have intensified,' Agatha said.

Diana was overwhelmed by the urge to push.

'You murderers!' Kristy was powerless beneath the threat of Edward's knife.

Diana pushed as labour took hold and Agatha and Dolly pinned her down. The shrill cry of a newborn reached the chamber's zenith, but there was no joy, only darkness. Agatha's son quickly tied off the umbilical cord, severed it, and then presented it to the apparition waiting impatiently above.

'Please! Don't let it take my baby!' Diana screamed with every last ounce of breath.

The spirit recoiled again, its frustration almost tearing it apart. The surgeon gave the babe to Agatha and paced the chamber, pulling at his hair, roaring obscenities.

Until the ghost shifted in Kristy's direction.

'No…' Kristy said.

'Run! Kristy, run!'

Diana reached out to Kristy from the altar, but her outburst only focused the surgeon's wrath. He ran the edge of his knife across Diana's throat. Her baby boy wailed.

'No! Diana!'

Kristy wrenched free of Edward's grip and made a move for his knife. She grabbed at his wrist, and drove her elbow into his jaw. He yelped and dropped the blade to the dirt. Quickly, Kristy retrieved it and pressed the tip to her belly. Every one of her captors froze; for the first time, she had power over them.

'Stay back or I'll do it—I'll kill it!' she said.

'You will kill yourself,' the suited man told her. He stepped closer, placating her with hands caked in Veronica's blood. Agatha circled in, while Dolly comforted her blubbering son.

'You won't get my baby!' Kristy said.

Agatha let Diana's child suckle at her withered breast. 'Jeffrey must live,' she said, leering. 'His time was cut short.'

Kristy looked to the ghost; its face had a familiarity to it. She'd seen it many times on the television, in the newspapers. The last time she'd seen it was the night she met Dale.'

'Jeffrey…Jeffrey Dahmer…' she could hardly believe the words passing her own lips.

'Yes,' Agatha said. 'A child of blood, just like Edward…' she looked to her own son, the surgeon. 'And my boy, Jacky. All reborn to continue their art. Your child will be Jeffrey's new vessel.'

They came closer and Kristy pushed the tip deeper, drawing a rivulet of blood to ooze into the weave of her gown.

'You will let me go—or I will take him away from you!'

'Put the knife down you filthy whore!' Jacky bellowed. He ran at Kristy and she screamed, instinctively swinging her arm out in a wild arc. The blade caught him across the inside of his arm. A torrent of blood splattered to the dirt and his fine suit soaked up every splash. He staggered about the chamber, sending all the others into a frenzy. Agatha, distracted by her son's torment, never saw Kristy raise the knife until it was too late. The old woman howled as the blade entered her shoulder. Kristy plucked the baby from the crone and ran.

Agatha collided with her son and they both fell into the hearth, the flames engulfing them. Dolly and Edward ran to their aid, but in the panic, the flames spread with a powerful hunger, catching on clothing and flesh in quick succession.

Kristy, with Diana's child in her arms, ran from the chamber, through the black door and down the corridor.

The screams of her captors—of the mothers and sons of blood—followed her at every turn as she ran through the prison.

The threat of the vile cult members somehow appearing to re-capture her drove Kristy on. As smoke began to fill the building, she held Diana's child, promising to keep it safe. She thought of her friends; that she didn't want to end up like them. Didn't she and the children deserve a chance to live?

Kristy turned a corner and found her answer—an elevator. She pressed the button and the doors slid apart. She jumped inside and tried to comfort the baby, letting it suckle at her breast, telling the boy that it would be okay. As the elevator ascended, she prayed it would take them to freedom.

The elevator opened onto a foyer, unused and decrepit. They'd been locked away in an abandoned building—a hospital—for months, but Kristy didn't care once she saw the front door.

A single door that gave way to liberating light. She'd saved her soul and the souls of her unborn child and the child of Diana.

But still, she knew in her heart that no mother with child would ever be safe.

QUIVER
Angelique Fawns

Constable Jill Henderson assumed a shooting stance and nocked an arrow on her bow, slowly drawing it back. She focused on her target, replacing it in her mind with the killer presently confounding her police department. She took a deep breath, ignoring the faint waft of pig manure, and closed her eyes. She paused a moment as the stress left her body, then she released the arrow. A whistle cut through the air, followed by a sharp smack. The arrow had struck the knot of the tree dead-center.

That's what she needed to do to kick-start her career. Solve the rash of murders plaguing her small Canadian town. That would show all those misogynistic assholes. She was the first female officer in Arkadia's not-so-lustrous history, so she had to be like the arrow and make an impact. She blamed her cherubic face and wild curly blonde hair. Who was going to respect Shirley Temple's doppelganger?

She should have been practicing with her gun instead, but she loved the feel of wood and wire. Guns were artless. The cold metal. An unpleasant jolt in your arm. The acrid smell of gunpowder. Archery relaxed her in a way the cacophony of bullets never could.

Dang! Thinking of guns made her think of the meeting yesterday with their four-person department—three older beer-loving men plus her. The whiteboard in the staff room was filled with gruesome photos. Three victims in the last month alone and Arkadia was a tiny town. Each drained of blood, and each with a strange pattern of red marks on the arms and legs.

A rustling in the trees caught her ears and she swung her bow around. A little dog popped out of the bush and barked. It looked like a cross between a pug and a pitbull, but what caught Jill's attention was the red liquid staining her nose. Jill wanted to sling arrows for at least another half an hour. Just ignore the dog—there could be a dozen reasons for the blood on its nose. But a sinking feeling in her gut told her which one was at play.

She sighed, threw her gear back into her Ford Ranger pickup truck, and called the dog. 'Come here, girl. I'm not gonna hurt you.'

The little dog wiggled over and Jill gingerly patted her head while reading the name on the collar.

'Pippen. You *look* like a Pippen. What's on your nose, girl? Have you been hunting in the forest? Did you catch a squirrel or chippie?'

Pippen yapped and trotted into the forest.

Jill sighed and followed. Roots grabbed her ankles as she jogged behind the dog on the pine needles. An errant tree branch scratched her face. Her stomach clenched when she saw Pippen stop a few feet ahead on the path and lick the face of a motionless figure. A middle-aged man dressed in spandex running gear, a fanny pack, and sneakers.

'Chicken and cheese, this doesn't look good,' Jill said to the dog.

She checked for a pulse—nothing. Y-shaped marks mottled his skin. He looked affluent and in good health—except for the being dead part. Blood saturated the ground.

The marks on the new victim were the same as the previous three. Those unfortunate souls had died from exsanguination. Blood leaked from the Y-shaped indents.

She took a few photos with her phone and called it in. She gritted her teeth, determined to stand her ground and take charge of this murder. No more treating her like the token female, good only for taking meeting notes and pouring coffee.

The investigative team and coroner arrived on ATVs with equipment strapped to their backs. Jill approached the coroner, Bill Atkinson, a skinny octogenarian with yellow teeth and a fishing addiction, but he waved her off. The yellow crime scene tape went up quickly.

Inspector Pat Fullerton, in his early thirties and already a master of smarm and smugness, strode over to her. 'Constable, Henderson. Trouble always finds you...or you find it.'

He winked at her and Jill shuddered. Pat was going through his fourth divorce.

'Inspector. I was taking my lunch break when a dog alerted me to the location of the victim. Upon arriving, there was no perpetrator, and the victim was lying on the ground, dead. I'd like to take lead on this investigation.'

Pat took some tobacco chew from a pouch on his gun belt and shoved it into his cheek. He sucked on it and gave her an appraising look. 'Nope.' He spat a stream of black juice into the grass and walked over to Bill Atkinson.

Jill bit the inside of her cheek and tried not to scream. She hated this backward town and the sorry excuse she had for a boss.

She tromped back through the forest to her car, wishing she'd tried to join a bigger police force. Like maybe Toronto. Every rock she kicked; she pretended it was Pat's face. Pippen followed her. When she reached her car, Jill opened the door and Pippen hopped into the back. She stopped at the Arkadian Vet Hospital on the main drag. They agreed to hold Pippen until the jogger's family could claim her.

Jill returned to the cop shop to file some paperwork and found Detective Don Hodge staring at the murder board. The fifty-year-old veteran was the best of the bunch in her opinion. His wife brought donuts every Friday, and Hodge never checked out her butt or made snide remarks under his breath.

'I heard on the radio you found another body.' He took a sip of the tarry brew in his hand.

Jill nodded. 'Male, late-thirties. Was out jogging with his dog.'

Don offered her a cup of coffee from the ancient machine on the Formica table. 'Did the victim have those suction marks? Has the bloodsucking killer struck again?'

Jill wrinkled her nose. 'No to the coffee. But yes, it looks like the same killer.' She studied the murder board with him. 'A homeless man, a young mother, and a prostitute so far. Now a jogger? The perp doesn't seem to have a type.'

'Is Pat letting you take help with the investigation—now that you discovered a victim?'

Jill scowled. 'No.'

Don shrugged.

'I'm off,' Jill said.

She left the cop shop and drove her pickup to a roadhouse bar a few miles from the farm she rented. It was a dark drinking hole known for great food and epic weekend fights.

She sat at the bar and Daisy poured her usual—a half-carafe of mediocre white wine. From the corner of her eye, she saw a bald man with tanned skin, intricate tribal tattoos, and farm-strong muscles. Jill's belly filled with butterflies. She liked her men sexy-ugly. This fellow looked like a cross between Tony Soprano and Jason Momoa, and her hand went up to smooth her wild hair. He shot her a smile and a nod. Electricity raced up her spine. Big lips, a wide mouth, and a hypnotic grin. Yup. Sexy-ugly. He motioned her to his table with a quick tilt of his head. Jill picked up her wine glass and went over.

'Well, well, well, a stranger in Arkadia. I'm Jill.'

The man held out a gloved hand. She took it, thinking it was mighty eccentric for a farmer to wear white silk gloves. In a pub, no less.

'I'm Seth. Pleased to meet you.' He let his hand linger on hers, giving her palm a quick stroke. 'Something so refined in such a rustic place.' He had a slight lisp. Super sexy.

'Seth? As in the god of chaos and storms?' She took her hand back and shoved it between her knees, her nerves tingling.

'And she knows Egyptian mythology. Greek too?'

'A little.'

'You put Aphrodite to shame my dear, but I'm no god. I'm the owner of Witven Pig Farms.'

Jill remembered the waft of manure while she was shooting arrows.

'I was just behind that farm today. Funny I've never seen you around before, I'd remember you.'

'I don't get out much. I usually just stay at home tending my animals and servicing a select clientèle with discerning pork requirements. It's auspicious I ventured out tonight though.'

'What's with the gloves?'

'Just an affectation. Gloves complete an outfit, don't you think?'

Jill shrugged, keeping her tingling hands below the table.

'As a fan of things Greek, I think you'll like this.' Seth gestured at Daisy and she came over a minute later with two shot glasses full of a clear pungent liquid.

'This is ouzo.'

'Thank you.' She tossed back the icy licorice shot. 'Not bad at all. So, I was behind your farm today and I found a jogger who'd been attacked and left for dead. Our coroner said he was drained of blood. Creepy, eh?'

'Oh,' he said.

Jill bit her lip, remembering she shouldn't give out specific details of active crimes. Perhaps this ouzo stuff loosened tongues.

'A man drained of blood? Dark discussion for a night that has been most pleasant so far.' Seth leaned back and crossed his arms. Something dark and unpleasant flashed in his eyes.

'You're right, I came to the bar to stop thinking about it.' Jill put her hands on her hips and stretched her back.

'You should visit my farm tonight. Especially if you are looking for an even more pleasant distraction. Our facilities are state of the art.' Seth sipped his Ouzo.

'You want to show me your etchings? Isn't that the line?'

'I have some really stunning etchings if that's more your style.'

Jill pressed her lips together. For the second time that day, she knew she was about to make a bad choice. She was probably about to follow yet another dog. She tossed back her wine and followed Seth out of the roadhouse. He had a thick, sinuous way of walking.

They climbed into his dark, tinted-window truck. Witven Farms was a five-minute drive. Neither of them said anything but Jill's insides were quivering. The sexual tension was almost unbearable.

It was odd. She wasn't the kind of woman to fall easily for a man...

When they arrived, he parked in front of the big century house and ushered her through ornate wooden doors. Her jaw dropped at the sheer wealth hidden in the brick farmhouse. Expensive wainscoting, high ceilings, stained glass windows, antique furniture, and suspiciously famous paintings on the wall.

Jill slid her boots off at the door. 'Is that an actual Monet? The pork business must be good!'

'It is, but I'm more interested in looking at you right now.'

Seth took her hand and led her upstairs to a bedroom with a big wooden sleigh bed, plush carpeting, and dark wood armoires. He didn't give her much time to admire the décor, winking at her as he turned off the light.

Her stomach flipped. Was this what she wanted? She held her breath as she heard the slithery sound of him removing the white gloves. Desire fought with panic and created a heady cocktail of anticipation within her.

She gasped when his mouth finally fell on hers. She knew she should stop him but why not make three bad decisions in one day? She gave in to his mouth. He sucked at her lips, neck, and stomach. His hands slid over her body, a tickling sensation wherever he touched. He carried her to the bed and undressed her.

#

When Jill woke up a few hours later, a deep languor radiated from her entire body. She slipped out of bed, pulled on her clothes, and stumbled through the dark room to look out the window.

She'd almost forgotten she had murders that needed to be solved. Almost.

She pulled back the thick black curtain and saw that the sun was rising. Its red glow bathed the trees, paddocks, and hay fields. Large black Berkshire sows walked free across the turf. Most conventional pig farms kept their livestock in barns with no access to the outdoors. These pigs had acres of paddocks and were roaming through gardens of vegetables and fruit trees, munching on breakfast.

Smiling to herself, she headed downstairs to get something to drink. The smell of warm coffee filled the room, the brew must be on a timer. In the old-fashioned kitchen, she opened the fridge. Typical bachelor. Almost no food, a few beers, and some bags of— she leaned in closer to get a look—beet juice? Blood? Her own blood froze in her veins.

Seth was standing behind her, dressed in farm overalls. 'Morning, dear.' His voice was filled with gravel.

Startled, she jumped, then forced a smile, like a fridge full of containers of red fluid was no big deal. She noticed he had the white gloves back on.

'Morning. How did you sleep?' Jill wished she hadn't left her purse—and the gun—upstairs.

'Like the dead.' A slow grin spread across his face.

Closing her eyes, she counted to ten—barely able to stop from screaming and dashing towards the door. There was no clear way past Seth.

He poured her a cup of coffee. 'Can I make you breakfast?'

Jill took her coffee and sat at a café table by the window. Little spots on her arms were sore. Terrified of what she would find, she pulled up her sleeves and saw them. Little Y-shaped bites. Her nerves screamed and she knew her face and chest had flushed red. Adrenaline and fear left her shaky. She couldn't trust her legs.

'Why do you always wear gloves?' She forced herself to ask.

Seth pulled off his gloves and raised his hands. There were little suction mouths on each palm. Barely discernible circles of black with dark pink openings that pulsed and sucked.

She wanted to scream, run, maybe even launch herself out the window. But she remained calm. Her weapon and badge were still upstairs.

Seth held his hands up by his ears in a non-threatening manner. 'I would never hurt you.'

She bit her lip. 'Someone is killing innocent civilians and draining them of blood. How do I know it's not you?'

He looked at her thoughtfully, and then came over and stroked her, his suctioning mouth gently rippling down her arm. She shivered but remaincd still. She felt no pain from his palms.

'If I was a killer, you'd be dead already.'

'Unless you like to play with your food.'

Seth removed his hand and sat down opposite her. 'I'm not a cat. But perhaps you can help me prune our bad apples, so to speak. There are a few of us in the area.'

'A few who?'

'Leech people. We need blood, but pig's blood will do.' He nodded at the few Berkshire sows grazing outside his window.

Jill's shoulders relaxed an inch. 'What could I possibly do?'

'Someone with my condition can only die from a sudden injection of salt. The most effective way to deliver the amount of sodium needed is with an arrow. The tip filled with salt.'

Jill remembered the leeches from her childhood shriveling up under mounds of salt prior to being removed.

'What makes you think I can help?'

Seth took a sip from his mug, the blood staining his teeth. 'I've seen you practicing in the woods. You're a very good shot. Sadly, my coordination is a bit lacking.'

'What are you telling me? That you need Buffy the Leech Slayer?'

'That's exactly what I need. You can be my beautiful Buffy. I don't want your co-workers involved. I need discretion in this matter.' Seth walked to the back door and put on boots and gloves. 'I have something to show you. Come.'

Jill thought of her gun upstairs. Could she trust him? She shrugged and finished her coffee. Her curiosity was always stronger than her sense of self-preservation. She rose, walked to the door, and put on her boots. Seth walked out into the sunshine.

There was a lovely trail of stones that led past the paddocks full of black Berkshire pigs she had seen from the window. They walked past the main pig barn and started hiking beside a hay field. The stone path turned to dirt.

Jill's armpits became damp. What if he just didn't want to kill her in his house where she might stain the hardwood?

'Where are you taking me?'

'One more minute. Almost there, dear.'

They walked into a forested area, and Jill gave a quick scream when she saw a black bear. The huge animal was half hidden by a tree.

Seth laughed. 'The bear's not real.'

Jill centered herself and let her brain, rather than her nerves, assess the situation. The bear was realistic, but the paint was chipped in spots. There were also deer, coyotes, and even turkeys. They were probably made of foam, and when she looked closer, she saw they were peppered with small holes.

This was an archery range.

She'd spent enough time on them to recognize the setup. Seth walked to a wooden shed and pulled out two quivers full of wooden arrows with oversized heads. He handed them to Jill. She could see that there were more made of metal in the shed.

'You sure take your archery seriously.' She accepted a bow.

'I wish I was better at it. There were rumors of new arrivals in the area, but they haven't contacted me about blood delivery. I'm assuming they are leaving the leftovers in the forest.'

Her stomach seized. Did he just refer to dead humans as leftovers?

Jill balled her fists and focused on what she understood. She pointed to the oversized arrowheads. 'I assume these are full of salt?'

Seth nodded.

Jill sheathed an arrow and let it fly. It pierced the bear in the center of one eye.

He nodded appreciatively. 'I knew you were good. Let's try something new.'

He retrieved the bow and went back into the shed. He came out with a lethal-looking crossbow and a new quiver full of wooden bolts.

'I've only used a crossbow a handful of times with my dad. This is a beauty.' She took the heavy metal weapon, put her boot into the cocking stirrup, and fluidly pulled the ropes into place while putting a bolt into the barrel groove.

'Why not guns? Couldn't a bullet pierce the heart and be filled with salt?'

Seth shook his head. 'Bullets don't work. Can't deliver enough salt.'

Jill took her stance, feet slightly apart, and lined up her crossbow at the most distant target she could see. There was a turkey sitting on a rock about a hundred yards away. She let the bolt fly and it blew away the foam wattle.

'Wow! The best shooters can usually only score a hit at eighty yards. You have talent, my love.'

Jill let his praise wash over her.

'Beauty, archery skills, and no apparent fear of death.'

She bathed in his compliment, smiling despite herself. 'You don't think I'm afraid of death?'

'You chose a dangerous profession, and you go home with strange men at night. If that's not courting death, what is?'

She felt another wave of disquiet. This man was igniting a flurry of conflicting emotions. Was he shaming her or complimenting her?

'Well, here's your stuff. I got to get to work.' She tried to hand him her weapon, but he shook his head.

'Keep it. You'll need it. We're going hunting for leech folks.' He gazed into her eyes, and saliva welled in her mouth.

She was literally salivating to please him. She spat and gave her own face a little slap.

'You think it's dangerous for me to go home with men like you but you have no qualms at all asking me to hunt down a mutated murderer?'

He grinned, a spark of admiration in his eyes. 'Zero qualms.'

She'd seen her share of vampire movies. Was he *compelling* her?

He strode back down the path. She hurried after him, slipping the crossbow and quiver over her shoulder. When he reached the paddock, he stopped to pat the pink nose of a Tamworth sow at the fence.

'There's something unique about you, Jill.' He kept his eyes down as he pat his pig. 'I noticed you shooting in the forest. When you hunt tonight, I will be protecting you from a distance.'

'I don't need help from a man. Never did.'

Seth spun and pulled his gloves off. Before Jill could protest, he placed his hands on both of her cheeks. The pulsing hands tickled and massaged just under her cheekbones. Jill's brain filled with happiness. Waves of endorphins coursed through her.

The damn man was charming her, but she didn't care. She just wanted his hands to remain on her face. She felt bereft and cold when he dropped them.

He gave her a knowing grin and walked back to his farmhouse.

'Go back upstairs and get your things. I'll drive you to your car.' His voice caressed her.

Jill nodded and smiled. She put the crossbow and quiver into the back of Seth's pickup truck and ran upstairs to grab her purse and jacket. Her gun was still where it was supposed to be.

Her cell phone said it was already 9:00 am. Her shift at the cop shop began in an hour. She hopped into the truck with Seth and he drove her back to the bar.

'Dinner tonight? We can strategize?' Seth had put his gloves back on and stroked her hair. She shivered, half wishing he'd take the gloves off again.

'Sorry, but I have to work. Raincheck?'

He nodded and winked.

Jill transferred the crossbow and quivers to her truck and drove home. Her mouth was dry and she felt hungover. She craved the company of Seth. What had she gotten herself into?

Jill examined the murder board. The location of each killing was marked with white pins on a map. It was clear to her now—the killer was ritualistically hitting all the local forests.

She didn't tell any of her co-workers about her leech man. She thought about it, but then a sharp pain in her forehead silenced her. They'd probably laugh and treat her like a delusional child. She had to solve this herself.

After her shift, she changed into an all-black outfit with a camo jacket and drove to one of the forest tracts that hadn't been hit yet. She'd hunted here with her father and knew the best spot for an ambush. She pulled into the dirt parking lot, took the crossbow and salted bolts, then walked along the path for twenty minutes before cutting into the middle of the forest. Once she'd arrived at the deer stand, she clambered up onto the planks of wood, lay on her belly, and positioned the crossbow so she could keep an eye on the trail.

She remained still as the sky grew darker. Though her body was getting stiff, it was nice to hear the birds. A coyote stopped beneath her tree to mark his territory before slinking off in search of dinner.

Eventually, her patience was rewarded. She saw a figure move behind a bush. A brown mule carrying a slender man dressed in an Australian outback slicker and a cowboy hat came into view. She recognized him as local farrier, Bob Kettle.

She paid close attention to the shadow in the undergrowth and didn't have to wait long. A short and curvy figure slithered out from the other side of the path. Completely dressed in black, the only visible skin on the figure was the pale flesh of outstretched hands and the glistening suction pods.

Jill fired the crossbow.

Her shoulders jerked from the sudden recoil, but the bolt flew true. The woman screamed as she crumpled to the ground. The mule reared up with a bray and bolted down the trail. Bob lost his cowboy hat but managed to cling to the saddle. Jill jumped off the stand and ran to the figure having seizures on the path.

The leech woman was terrifying. The mouths on her hands pulsed as she corkscrewed and writhed on the path. Her body shrank as she

123

dehydrated, the salt doing the trick.

'Take that, you mothersucker!' Jill kicked dirt at the figure.

The leech woman spoke around burbling saliva. 'I'm melting. It burns.' Her mouth shriveled around the words.

Jill dropped to her knee. 'How many of you are there? Why are you killing humans?'

'We will not drink pig's blood any longer. Our time has come!' The woman tried to grab her face.

Jill sent another bolt directly through the leech woman's heart.

Like sand through an hourglass, the woman disappeared. Just a pile of dirt was left on the trail. Jill kicked it into the shrubs.

She smiled, a glow radiating up from her belly. Jill the Leech Slayer. It had a ring to it. Why was she seeking acceptance and approval from those old men at the police station? She could do more outside the badge. Her stomach tightened thinking of Seth's tickling palms and hypnotic eyes. He was probably using some leech magic on her, but damn it felt good. She knew she had a thing for making bad choices, but what had the leech woman said?

Our time has come.

That must mean there were more mutated leech folks hunting humans. There would be other victims if Jill didn't stop them.

She would let Seth make her dinner tonight. Hold the salt. They had plans to make. But first, she was going to practice her archery. She'd always loved the feel of wood and wire, but what she'd been lacking was a purpose.

CAMEO
Deborah Sheldon

Tom sat on the steps of his back veranda, sipped at a beer stubby, and contemplated the urn containing his mother's ashes. He had placed the urn next to him, so it was almost like he and his mother were enjoying the evening air together. The thought provoked an ironic smile.

'Well, here we are,' Tom said to the urn. 'Home sweet home. Now what the hell am I supposed to do with you?'

The speed of events over the past week had disoriented Tom a little, thrown him off-centre. He felt *wobbly* somehow. His mum had died at the nursing home, and the direct cremation provider had picked up her body, arranged the death certificate, burned her promptly, and then scooped the ashes into the cheapest urn Tom could find in the catalogue: a tube of biodegradable paper with a dove motif, $55.00. Tom and his sister Cathy hadn't seen the point of a funeral. While they generally didn't see eye to eye, they had agreed on this.

Tom had picked up the urn that afternoon. Cathy didn't want the remains. But Tom didn't want them either. Cathy had suggested scattering the ashes somewhere, perhaps in a place that had meant something to Mum in life, but that begged the unanswerable question—had *anything* meant something to their mother in all her vitriolic seventy-eight years?

Tom took another sip of beer and said to the urn, 'I ought to flush you down the dunny.'

He tried to laugh at his dumb joke, but tears came to his eyes instead. Oh, it was complicated losing a parent who had apparently despised you from birth. You hated them back, often passionately, yet at the same time, a hurt and bewildered part of you always mourned the mother that could have been, the bond you might have had, if only you had perhaps been a more loveable child, if only the mother—

Tom jolted as if from an electric shock. His teeth snapped together with a loud click.

Across from the veranda, obscuring the back fence he shared with a neighbour, grew a wide stand of silver birch trees. Ordinarily, it was a sight he liked very much. The white and dark papery bark, the vibrant green heart-shaped leaves, and lately in the midst of spring, the brown catkins of pollen that fell at the slightest touch and drifted on the slightest breeze; these were a pleasure to view. But the birch directly opposite Tom showed his mother's face.

A trick of the light, a play of shadow. What else could it be?

The dense foliage was arranged in such a way that his mother's profile leaped out in sharp relief. Her high forehead, snub nose, tight and thin-lipped mouth, that jutting chin that resembled a billiard ball right to the bitter end, despite the cancer eating her down to the marrow. There she was, as if ready to turn and glare at him.

Tom squeezed shut his eyes and pressed fingers into his eyelids.

It had been a long day, that's all.

Picking up the urn. Paying for this last expense with his Visa card. Sensing the hostile judgement of the kid behind the counter as the register dinged its measly $55.00 charge. Tom had felt like telling this kid the truth: that Joy Grace, the deceased, had been a cold-hearted sow who had despised her two children, even while they had turned themselves inside-out for years in an exhausting and futile quest to win her over. *What do you do with a mother like that?* he had wanted to ask this judgemental kid, who no doubt had wonderful parents and took them for granted. *Why would you show respect to the one person who was supposed to love you but refused?*

No. Mum's profile was not in that tree. Tom was just tired.

He opened his eyes and stared at his boots. The strain of the past week had simply got him seeing things. Cathy, with her deadbeat husband and bunch of teenaged kids, had left the fallout of Joy Grace's death to Tom and, in dealing with it, Tom had become worn down by ugly memories. But he was in charge of himself now. If he looked at the silver birch directly opposite him, it would once again simply be a tree.

Bracing, he looked.

His mother's profile was still there. He didn't know what to make of this. He took his beer and the urn inside, closed the curtains, and spent the rest of the night drinking and watching TV until he felt ready for sleep.

#

Bad dreams made him ponder, upon waking, whether he could use a few days to sort through his emotional garbage. He decided over breakfast to take "bereavement leave". As a courier, a contract worker using his own van, he could take time off whenever he wanted; it just meant he'd have less in his pocket that week.

As he rinsed the cereal bowl in the sink, he risked his first glance that morning out the window to check the birch tree. His chest felt clenched with a jittery kind of panic. Yet the foliage was harmless today, once again nothing but leaves. He breathed out slowly and nodded, emboldened. Light and shadows, he told himself, and an active imagination. Grief too. A peculiar, warped kind of grief. Maybe Cathy was grappling with the same kind of shit.

He paused—he and Cathy weren't touchy-feely siblings—but he called her anyway. Of course, she'd be awake. While it was early on a Saturday, her teenaged kids always had weekend activities like basketball or gymnastics or some such. The mobile trilled in his ear.

Tom's mind wandered. When they had been kids, Mum used to kiss him (and Cathy too) in a way that he thought strange. She would grip the hair on the back of his scalp firmly inside a fist, and smack her lips against his forehead so hard that it felt more like a punch than a kiss. Around the time they became teenagers, Joy Grace had stopped kissing them altogether. Why? Had she deemed them too old for sham displays of affection? Or perhaps she had tired of keeping up the charade—

'Tom!'

'G'day, Cathy,' he said. 'Just thought I'd check in.'

'Are the ashes behaving themselves? Not catching fire?'

He laughed, and glanced uneasily at the paper tube by the kettle. The printed doves had wings outstretched against a pale blue background. 'Not yet,' he said. 'I'll let you know.'

There was a long pause.

'It's weird, huh?' Cathy said. 'That she's gone.'

'Yeah.'

'Look, she wasn't *all* bad. She gave us shelter, food, clothes, schooling...orthodontic braces. At least we don't have buck teeth.'

'True.'

'I guess...' Cathy's voice trailed. 'Hooray? We made it? I'm not sure what to...um...'

'I know. Me neither. Listen,' he said, and cleared his throat, knowing now exactly why he'd called his big sister. 'You remember Peanut?'

'The budgerigar? Sure.'

Tom's best friend in primary school had had a father that bred various birds. As a birthday present in grade six, they had given Tom a budgie in a fully furnished cage. Peanut loved music, loved the bells in his cage, loved talking in his croaky little voice, and loved sticking his beaked face into Tom's raspberry-blowing lips. Every morning before school, Tom would replace Peanut's water, top up his seed, and supply him with fresh apple and spinach, while every afternoon after school he'd let the bird fly around his room until dinnertime. Peanut especially liked playing a game that involved sitting on the curtain rail and—

'You actually called me to discuss crap that happened forty years ago?' Cathy said.

'I loved him,' Tom said, louder than he had intended. 'And she killed him.'

'Well, that's debatable—'

'No, I *never* took the cage outside and let him out. No. I did *not*. Joy Grace did it because she accused me of not cleaning his cage properly.'

'Is this helpful, Tom? To your state of mind, I mean?'

'And Peanut flew out and panicked. He didn't know where he was, or what was happening. I was running after him, calling his name, holding out my hand in the hope he'd fly back to my finger. But he was shit-scared, Cathy. He didn't know what the fuck was going on. And he kept flying, to the next tree, and the next tree—'

'Hang on a minute, Tom, just—'

'And then the hawk or the kestrel or whatever the hell it was grabbed Peanut and took him to the top of a telegraph pole, the one outside the Robinson's house. Do you remember?'

'No, I wasn't there. I was at a girlfriend's place, I think, or at the mall—'

'And it ate him. It ate him alive and I saw it. I saw Peanut's green and yellow feathers floating down, covered in his blood. And you know what Mum said as I was crying and screaming?'

'Please don't—'

'She said to me, "Look what you've done."'

Tom's mum had followed him outside and all the way down the street to the base of the telegraph pole. Until she'd spoken, he'd had no idea she was even there. When he turned, he caught her expression of pure exultant pleasure, the glow of triumph in her eyes that seemed to say *Ha, gotcha!* Anger had swept in to join his grief and horror, and the physical sensation raging within his guts was a hot rising tide that threatened in its ferocity to take off his head. In that moment, eleven-year-old Tom could have strangled his mother to death with both hands. And he swore to himself, right there and then, that one day, he would have his revenge. *One day when I'm a grown man, I'll make you suffer.* He saw in Joy Grace's stunned face, in the startled rise of her eyebrows, her recognition of Tom's new resolve, and that made him smile through his tears with clenched, bared teeth.

'Stop it, Tom,' Cathy said.

He passed a trembling hand across his sweating forehead. 'That's what she said. "Look what you've done." As if it'd been my fault.'

Cathy's long exhale down the phone sounded loud as a freight train. 'I've got to go.'

'You don't want to talk about this?'

'Honestly? No, I fucking don't,' she said. 'I don't want to talk about *any* of this. And if you've got a scrap of common sense, you'll let this shit go, and be happy. All right?'

'Oh, all right,' he snapped. 'Just so we're clear—*be happy*. That's your advice?'

'Come on, Tom. You know what I mean.'

'Do I?' he said.

'Happy that she's *gone*.' Cathy sighed again. 'Look, I really gotta go.'

'Yeah, sure,' he said, and hung up.

He tossed the mobile towards the other end of the couch. Swallowing down a sob, he knuckled at his watering eyes and then opened them to his mother's profile—

On the wall. Behind the TV.

Shadows and light, shining through the camellia bush outside and the venetian blind, stamped Joy Grace on the wall like a black-and-white lino cut, an overexposed black-and-white photograph, a chiaroscuro image that looked both dramatic and threatening. The billiard-ball chin brought the vomit to the back of Tom's throat. A light breeze moving through the camellia bush animated his mother, and it looked as if her mouth were moving, as if she were muttering something (*look what you've done*) through tight lips. Lunging, Tom crossed the room and shut the blind. Joy Grace disappeared.

He stared at the wall for a few moments, heart thudding dully in his chest. With a soft groan, he sank back into the couch and balled his hands into fists.

Crazy. He must be going crazy.

From long habit, he tamped down his feelings and regained control. Sniffing, he grabbed his phone and Googled "seeing faces in things". To his surprise, it turned out he was experiencing a common phenomenon called *face pareidolia*. There were plenty of examples in Google Images—a bearded old man in the clouds, a screaming face in a halved capsicum, a house with slitted windows in the attic that resembled a pair of shifty eyes. Perhaps the most famous example was taken in 1976 by the Viking Orbiter, the "Face on Mars" photograph, which was revealed by the higher quality photograph in 2001 to be just an ordinary hill with a few lumps and bumps. Apparently, the human brain is wired to make sense out of random shapes.

Tom felt relieved at first.

Then very, very stupid. He was like those idiots who see the face of Jesus Christ in burnt toast or in the mould on a shower screen, and then spend the rest of their lives in religious fervour. He read on. The illusion of face pareidolia had something to do with the brain's "frontal cortex" and the "posterior visual cortex". But now that Tom had a rational explanation, he didn't care about the details.

He stormed into the kitchen and approached the urn. It was his intention to pick it up, maybe even shake it, but his hand froze as if sensing an invisible aura or forcefield around the paper tube. Blushing, Tom changed his grasping hand movement to an aggressive finger-point, and said, 'This isn't your doing. You have no power over me. None.'

The urn sat there, inert, but it seemed to emanate vibes of a tense and coiled energy that Tom didn't much like. Using a tea towel, he picked up the urn and put it into a kitchen drawer beneath a pile of plastic freezer bags.

#

Tom spent the rest of the weekend drunk. On Monday, the nursing home called. There were a few outstanding charges, and a box of Joy Grace's belongings to pick up. Tom paid the charges over the phone with his Visa card and, after a cold shower, drove to the home some two hours away. It was on the other side of the city in a suburb that featured potholes, cracked footpaths, graffiti, and skulking groups of loitering pedestrians in track pants and hoodies.

The home itself was a two-storey, flat-roofed collection of tired buildings arranged in the shape of a horseshoe. Its forecourt was separated from the car park by a median strip of weeds and dead grass. Tom parked, killed the engine, and admired the blatant vileness.

Some eight years ago, when Mum's cancer and increasing frailty had meant she could no longer take care of herself, he had picked this place because it was the worst of the lot.

He remembered his first tour.

The place had smelled of piss, shit, and some kind of harsh detergent that reminded him of a urinal cake. The walls were scuffed, the old carpet napped. Apart from the bored fat nurse showing him around, Tom spotted only one other staff member, who was trundling a trolley of paper medicine cups that presumably contained pills. Faint cries and moans sounded constantly. When he peered into open doorways, he saw the same sight over and over: a cramped and dark room, a dishevelled person in a bed looking lost and desperate, a sterile environment devoid of photographs, knick-knacks, books, or house plants.

'Where do I sign?' he said to the bored fat nurse, who stopped and turned to him with a questioning look. He chuckled and whispered, 'My mother's a bitch.'

The nurse smiled and nodded. Leaning in conspiratorially, she said, 'We get that a lot. Payback, am I right? No need to answer; that was rhetorical. Okay, let's do the paperwork.'

Now, Tom sat in the car wiping absently at his sweating forehead and staring at the shabby buildings. He didn't want to go in there. Over the phone, he had asked if his mother's belongings could be couriered out instead. *No*, was the answer. *We have to deliver it direct into your hands and get your signature. Company policy.*

Reluctantly, Tom got out of the car. The day had started warm but was cooling off. Strips of grey clouds scudded, but after a cursory glance, he decided to ignore them in case he happened to spot Mum's profile somewhere. Maybe after this final chore, he could put his mother behind him and forget it all, just as Cathy had seemed to suggest.

A lanky, pimply teenage boy in a white tunic led him to Joy Grace's room. The blind was up, the window open, but the room still smelled like mothballs and piss.

Tom had visited infrequently; three times per year. Easter Sunday, her birthday in July, and Christmas Eve, with each visit lasting about fifteen minutes. He had always brought chocolates. Cherry liqueurs. Whether she liked them or not, he didn't know. He did know, however, that Joy Grace hated living there; he could see it in her face, even though she never gave in and complained. Could she see his expression of *Ha, gotcha!* and the glow of triumph in his eyes? Yes, of course. She had asked him only once why he had chosen this god-awful place, and that was on the day he had moved her in. His reply was something he'd been holding inside for a long, long time: 'Be kind to your children, because they choose your nursing home.' He had expected her to look contrite or upset, even angry. Instead, she had narrowed her cold eyes and smiled at him, as if to say *This isn't over yet.*

'Mate?'

Tom started. 'What?'

The lanky, pimply teenage boy held out a cardboard box. 'I said, here it is. Your mother's personal effects.' He rattled the box. 'There's not much.'

'Fine, give it here. Hey, what happened to the nurse who used to work this wing?'

The kid shrugged. 'We've got a high turnover.'

'She was, uh, short and stocky. Brown hair in a bun. Tortoiseshell glasses—'

'Oh, you mean Phillipa?'

'Phillipa! That sounds about right.'

'Yeah, um, I think she died.'

In the car, Tom peeked into the box, moving items aside with the tip of a finger. Among the detritus, some Mills & Boon paperbacks, a smattering of costume jewellery, hair brushes, a lipstick tube that smelled rancid. And a plastic photo album. The small type with plastic sleeves that each hold only two photos back-to-back. He hesitated.

In his hands, the album felt brittle. He opened the creaky cover, flicked through the pages. Square black-and-white snaps. Joy Grace in a psychedelic mini-dress and knee-high boots. Joy Grace and Dad with his Brylcreemed pompadour standing by a blocky car in an unfamiliar driveway. Joy Grace and Dad with their arms about each other's neck, Dad exuberantly kissing her on the cheek. A handful of wedding photographs—on the steps of a church, her in a short white gown, Dad in a suit, old relatives in lumpy coats. Joy Grace in a flowered maternity smock—that would be Cathy, Tom thought. He turned the page. Nothing. He kept turning pages, faster and faster. The rest of the album was also empty.

A hollow feeling started up in his stomach. He remembered Dad in fleeting, half-baked memories. Pushing Tom on a swing. Throwing a plate of bacon and eggs against a wall. Watching a black-and-white bout of wrestling on the TV. Then he'd died of a heart attack when Tom had been, oh, about five years old. Tom contemplated the photo album, weighed it in his hands. Where were the baby photos of Cathy and himself? The rest of Joy Grace's life? Shouldn't there be photos of Cathy's children?

Tom threw the album into the box, turned the ignition key, and reversed out of the car park.

Tom said into the phone, not caring how it sounded, 'She's haunting me.'

Cathy didn't say anything. Nor had she said anything when Tom had described how Joy Grace's profile had revealed itself that afternoon in froth and bubbles on his beer glass.

'Did you hear me?' he said.

'Yeah, I heard you.'

'She's getting closer. Birch tree, lounge room, beer glass. What next?'

Cathy made an exasperated noise. 'You never stopped trying. That's your problem.'

'Never stopped trying what?'

'Even dumping her in that shitty home was just another one of your ploys.'

Tom sat upright on his couch. 'What are you talking about?'

'Putting her in that home was meant to break her, right? Meant to finally crack her shell. So that she'd spill her guts and confess why she'd been such a shithouse mother. Why she'd done such terrible things to us. God, you always wanted *reasons*.'

He didn't answer.

'Tom? You still there?'

'Yeah, but I don't understand—'

'You're fifty-one years old!' she said. 'You don't *need* to understand. Just let it go.'

He scoffed. 'Easy for you to say when *I'm* the one getting haunted.'

There was silence. He tightened his fingers reflexively on the mobile, wiped the slick of sweat from his forehead, and waited, grinding his teeth.

'You're not special, Tom,' Cathy said at last. 'She didn't love you more, or hate you more, whichever one you reckon. We both got a shit deal, and that's all there is to it.'

'Oh yeah? Then why is she haunting *me*?'

'Just throw out the ashes. Don't keep them in the house—'

'Listen,' he said, 'do you remember how she used to kiss us when we were kids?'

Cathy barked out a short laugh. 'That headbutt manoeuvre with her mouth? Sure, I do.'

'She stopped kissing us when we got to high school.'

'Did she?' Cathy sighed. 'Look, I've got to go.'

'Of course, you do. I ought to print that on a T-shirt for your birthday.'

#

He woke up, heart pounding from a bad dream. 12:48 am. A full moon cast just enough light around the curtains to tint the room in shades of black and white. Tom flung off the blankets. Next, he pulled the slicked T-shirt away from his chest and flapped it a few times. His shorts were bunched too, gobbled up around his ball sack. Puffing, face sweating and hot, he straightened his shorts, threw both feet clear of the blankets, and glared up at the ceiling.

Fuck this. Maybe Cathy was right.

Maybe he ought to throw out the ashes.

The only sound was the breeze soughing about the eaves. In a minute or two, Tom's breathing returned to normal. His sweat cooled off. A piss, a drink of water, and then he could settle back into bed and return to sleep.

He became aware of his forearms as the hairs lifted in prickling gooseflesh.

An abrupt shivery sensation travelled in a flash along his body from head to toe, as if fingernails had screeched down a blackboard. The bedroom felt cold all of a sudden. Tom's mouth dried out. His heart began to boom, slowly at first, then faster until he could hear it loud and clear, the pulse concussing against his eardrums as if his body were a kettledrum.

If he happened to look across to the other side of the bed, he knew what he would see.

But he didn't have to look. No reason to look.

Don't look.

He wrenched his head in the other direction towards the bedside table. There lay his mobile phone. He thought about ringing Cathy. But what for? She couldn't help him. Didn't want to help him. Oh, she'd been home that day when Joy Grace had killed Peanut, not at a

135

girlfriend's place or at the mall. No. Cathy had been an uninterested third party who had watched the drama unfold without feeling any need to intervene. Over the years, Peanut had become a symbol, Tom realised, a neat summary of his family relationships, the first thing he would tell a therapist whenever he or she said, *Talk to me about your mother.* And maybe Tom *had* taken the cage outside. So what? Did that justify what Joy Grace had done?

Despite the cold in the bedroom, Tom was sweating afresh. Rivulets ran from his furrowed brow into his hairline. Every nerve fibre in his body screamed in alarm. He didn't want to look across to the other side of the bed. He didn't. But finally, he did.

And there she was.

Joy Grace, her profile sculpted in the furrows and folds of the blankets. One deep-set eye, that snub nose, tight mouth and billiard-ball chin, so close to his left arm that her presence touched the raised hairs on his forearm. It felt like being touched by a huntsman spider.

Tom shrieked, thrashed, leapt, getting up so fast he almost cricked his neck. Gasping, he looked again. Surely, the blankets were now in disarray. Surely, the arrangement that had caused the face pareidolia was destroyed.

But no.

There she was.

Joy Grace wasn't in profile this time. Instead, huddled deep in the bedclothes, she was full-faced, staring with two darkened and malevolent fabric eyes. If Tom paused, if he hesitated for just a moment longer, he knew that the blankets would coil with supernatural tension and throw themselves at him, subsume him, take him by the neck and smother him, throttle him. With a strangled cry, he snatched up the bedclothes in both arms, hauled the flat sheet and blankets from the mattress, and ran from the room.

Down the hallway he raced as the material caught and swirled around his bare feet, trying to trip him. He wrenched open the back door. Staggered to the fire pit. The last time he had used it, he'd smoked and barbecued a pork shoulder. Now, he would smoke and barbecue his mother's ghost. He lifted the grill plate, threw it aside, and stuffed the bedclothes into the pit. A squirt of lighter fluid. A strike of an extra-long match.

The bedclothes caught fire.

He watched, transfixed, the cool breeze nuzzling about his body, freezing the sweat in his armpits and groin. Birds in the nearby birch trees began to fuss and cluck at the disturbance.

The urn.

Tom scrambled into the kitchen, opened the drawer, grabbed the $55.00 biodegradable paper tube with the dove motif, and went outside to hurl the damned thing into the burgeoning, licking flames, to rid himself of Joy Grace for ever. But it turned out he couldn't do it. The urn stuck to his hand like flypaper. Oh, shit. Cathy would have a field day about this failure, he realised. She would mock him. Call him a Mummy's Boy. Wasn't that what she'd called him when they were kids? Derisively, whenever she'd caught him trying to curry Joy Grace's favour? *Mummy's Boy...*

Tom opened his hand. The urn fell into the flames, caught immediately, flared and shone red. He felt a surge of triumphant pride.

But the flames intensified, gathered together into a rising spout, caused him to step back in alarm. The fire grew larger and hotter. The crown of the spout, bright and lambent, began to shed embers. He looked up. Errant breezes took those embers and propelled them in two directions: backwards across the roof and into the gutters that were full of dead leaves from autumn; forwards into the piles of bone-dry pollen that lay in a deep bed beneath the stand of birch trees.

Dozens of spot fires sprang up. In a few minutes, Tom would lose his property.

'Oh, you fucking bitch!' he wailed.

The spout in the fire pit turned, crackled, weaved, and flickered. Out of the red and orange tumult emerged a suggestion of Joy Grace's profile. The profile turned to face him. *This isn't over yet.* A flaming hand wavered, as if reaching for the hair on the back of his scalp.

Tom wasn't surprised. In a way, he'd expected all along that he could never win.

THE GREAT INVOCATION
David Schembri

A tired gramophone labored as chorusing trumpets and piano scratched from its needle. It blared into the small auditorium thick with the scent of tobacco and aged wood. Harry Mogadino pranced onto the small stage, the tails of this dark coat dancing about his legs. In the glare of the lights, he gracefully presented a hand toward the back of the stage. On cue, his faithful fox terrier, Benny, ran out into the spotlight, his frilly white collar bouncing with every padded step. Harry tapped the breast of his coat, and Benny leapt into his arms. Synchronized to the scratchy music, The Great Mogadino threw up a white-gloved hand, Benny let out a high-pitched bark, and the two awaited their applause.

One could hear a pin drop.

Harry glanced around the auditorium. His heart sank. Only a dozen or so pale faces were scattered about the seats.

The music sprang back into life, jolting him from his gloom, and he let Benny down so they could perform their first trick.

Benny ran to a box, and clamped an alarm clock between his teeth. Harry tapped on a small table and Benny trotted over and set the clock upon it. Covering it with a small black cloth, Harry looked towards the pitiful audience. Sighing, he turned on his heel and flung the cloth away. In time with the recording, the trumpets blared *ta da!* to reveal that the clock had disappeared. Harry tapped on his breast, Benny leapt into his arms, and they appealed for their applause.

Cough... Cough...

The rest of the show was torture.

Harry's spirits were deflated, but there was always hope in Benny. His wagging tail, and his little panting mouth suggesting a smile.

He'd never changed. There had been good times once; performing inside packed houses. Yet even though times had darkened, Benny didn't. He was the bright light in Harry's life, always devoted, always loyal.

The final chorus resounded over the auditorium. The audience gave a scattering of claps and coughs.

Harry groaned as heavy crimson curtains dropped, leaving them in a cloud of dust.

Benny licked at his cheek. The frill of the little dog's collar pinched at Harry's neck, and he couldn't help but chuckle as he eased him down.

'You've lost your touch, Mogadino,' said Cordel, the theater's owner.

'It was a tough crowd.'

'Crowd? I've seen more folks line up for the latrine!'

'So, I won't see any commission for tonight?'

Cordel laughed then puffed from a cigar and said, 'You don't fill theaters no more, Mogadino. Face it, you're finished. Let the younger showman take over.'

'I'm only thirty-five!'

'There are folks ten years younger doing a better job. But they won't be seen dead in my rat's nest. You should think about pushing a broom!'

Harry lowered his head to Benny. 'Up boy, time to go.' He tapped on his chest and Benny leapt into his arms once more.

'Don't come back, Mogadino. Another goon showed up this morning asking for you. I don't want no trouble around here!'

Harry said nothing as he removed Benny's frilly collar, and stepping out into the street, he let the cold breeze carry it away.

#

Harry and Benny's single-bedroom apartment was nestled in lower Manhattan. On the fourth floor on Fifty-Second Street, Harry fumbled with the locks before pushing the door open. Benny raced onto a pile of tangled blankets—his makeshift bed. He nestled himself into it, facing out to view Harry's whereabouts.

'Sorry there is no dinner,' Harry said. 'I'll check the fridge, but it looks like we'll have to settle for some old apples,'

'I understand,' said Benny, in his little, gruff voice. 'Could I trouble you for some water?'

Harry stepped over and gave him a pat behind the ears; Benny always loved that. 'You don't have to be so polite. Face it, I'm a horrible provider.'

'It's not your fault, Harry. You're trying. We'll get through this the way we always do.'

Harry huffed out a small laugh and went to the sink to fetch a dish of water. He crouched and watched Benny lick it dry. Benny looked up at him, his tongue flapping around his muzzle, catching the water that had collected around his whiskers. He panted, showing his undying smile. Harry gazed at him lovingly. Benny's head was mostly black, but for the small wisps of tan that brushed above his eyes, giving him a constant look of concern.

'Does it discomfort you to talk?' Harry asked. 'I would hate to have given you a curse.'

'Of course not, Harry. It was strange at first, but it has become easy. My thoughts, as you know, haven't changed. I'm just able to speak them in your tongue. I think it's a gift.'

'Indeed. But I don't know how long it will last. I acquired the spell in Europe and it didn't come with instructions.'

Benny stared. 'That's not what troubles you though. I see it in your eyes.'

Harry scratched Benny behind the ear and said, 'The guilt will always be there.'

'You're only human. Stop punishing yourself.'

Harry crossed his arms as he always did when the foreboding shadow of self-hate crept up his shoulders. 'It wasn't for the want to hear you speak that urged me to seek council with those cultists. It was greed. *The World's First Talking Dog!* I'd already had the posters drafted. I can't believe that it had to take our sinking ship, loosing money and years of sets and equipment, for me to see that. When we docked in New York on the rescue boat, we were left with nothing but the clothes on my back.'

'And my voice.'

'Which will never be sold. I was a fool. The show was doing well and we were set to retour Sweden. Yet, I was so easily seduced to sell your voice to packed theaters across the eastern seaboard.'

Harry retreated into the kitchenette. 'You've been given a bad deal, Benny. A money-hungry illusionist, and now a struggling showman that can't even feed you. Not to mention the debt. I owe my family a great deal of money,'

'Are you finished?' Benny trotted from his bed and sat at Harry's feet, looking up at him and cocking his head. 'Do you think me *that* shallow?'

'Shallow?' Harry crouched to him. 'I've taken you for a fool. I would deserve your abandonment.'

'Do you know that canines never fall in love instantly? Love is earned.'

'All I've ever done is work you to the ground and plot to use you. When have I ever earned your love?'

'I was a puppy. We lived in that nice place overlooking Central Park. You came home one day to find I'd torn your leather loafers into ribbons. You were cross, and you sent me to bed. But you never hit me, nor did you yell at me. You just cleaned the mess. You didn't stay mad at me for too long. You called me over, patted and fed me. Life went on as normal. That was so important for me.'

'Why?'

'You've had many friends in your life—all I've ever had is you.'

'That's a pity.'

'I have no regrets,' Benny said, and put a paw up on Harry's knee. 'You are my friend.'

Harry jolted as a rapping at the door echoed through the apartment. Benny's ears stood to attention. They shared a glance.

'A bit late for visitors,' grouched Benny.

'Go to the bedroom. I'll close you in. You'll be safe,'

'Safe from what?'

Harry got up. The door was rattling violently.

'In the bedroom! Now!' he whispered harshly, stabbing a finger at the door by Benny's bed.

Benny lowered his head and trotted off. Harry stepped over to the door, but when he looked back, he saw that Benny had settled into his blankets and was staring at the door, growling lowly.

Stubborn boy!

Harry unlocked the door. 'Hold on! I'm opening up!'

The door inched open and Benny let out a high-pitched bark when a heavy fist met Harry's jaw, knocking him to the ground. Three men in dark suits filled the room and slammed the door shut behind them. All wore fedora hats with rims draping shadows over their eyes.

'On your feet, magic man!' ordered one of the goons. He then turned to one of the others. 'Shut that mutt up, Paul!'

Harry's heart skipped as the largest of three men stomped over to Benny. He jabbed the side of his shoe into Benny's muzzle and yelled, 'Shut up, you little rat!'

Benny hurled backwards with a yelp, then charged at Paul's leg, sinking his teeth around the foot of his trousers.

'Hey!'

Harry cringed when Benny yelped again. Paul had belted him with the side of his firearm, and aimed it at his head.

'No! Don't!' Harry cried, getting to his feet.

'Hold it, Paul!' the goon nearest him said; he looked to be calling the shots.

Paul lifted his gun as Benny continued to bark.

'You kidding me, Stefano? That little mutt just tore my trousers! I just bought them!'

Stefano turned to Harry. 'Shut the mutt up. Now.'

Harry leaned toward Benny.

'Benny! Stop barking!'

Their eyes met.

'Listen to me,' he pleaded. Benny did so and sank into his blankets, growling up at Paul.

'I could have shut that thing up with one bullet,' said Paul. 'Now it's growling!'

'The boss wants them both,' Stefano said, stepping up to him. 'You kill the mutt, then the boss won't have anything to bargain with, *capiche?*'

He smacked Paul's hat off, revealing a head of shiny, black hair parted to one side. 'You gotta lot to learn, you schmuck. Get that mutt on a leash.'

'There's no need. He can come with me. He's well trained,' Harry said, eyeing Paul as he collected his hat from the floor.

Harry tapped on his chest. Benny ran and leapt up into his arms.

'Don't go trying anything funny. I was told to deliver you both alive, but that doesn't mean in one piece, got it?'

Harry nodded and they all proceeded out. Benny tucked his little head into Harry's neck.

'I'm sorry. You should have gone into hiding,' Harry whispered to him.

'I'm no cat.'

#

Aless paced impatiently below the marble staircase. Classical music drifted in from the main lounge of his uncle's mansion. The chatter of countless attendees rumbled like a distant railway. Everyone in the family was invited to seek a final audience with the great Philip Bonano. Aless had his hands berried deep into the pockets of this dark blue, pinstripe pants. He lifted the rim of his white fedora when he noticed someone coming down the stairs.

'Alessandro, your uncle will see you now,' said Joseph, his uncle's private butler. He stood over Aless holding a silver tray.

'It's about god-damn time!' Aless spat, stomping up the stairs.

'Not so quickly, Alessandro. There is a condition to the visit.'

'What?'

'Your dear uncle, on his death bed, demands that all visitors have a taste of his true passion before entering.'

'What the hell does that mean?'

'You must indulge in one of your uncle's delicacies before proceeding upstairs.'

Joseph offered up the tray.

Aless looked down at the single item and tried not to retch. 'I gotta eat that slop?'

'To reject this is to reject your uncle's heritage. It was caught fresh this morning from the fishing business founded by his great-grandfather. He grew up with these delicacies, the foundation of the empire. All must honor this if they wish to see him.'

Aless sighed. He hated oysters. Raw, cooked, or otherwise—but what choice did he have?

He collected the single shell from the tray—Joseph looking on in anticipation. Aless pinched his nose with thumb and forefinger, grimaced, and took in the oyster with one gulp. Then he coughed loudly as the slimy thing slid down his throat.

'Very good, Alessandro. Was it delicious?'

He spat into the shell with disgust, slammed it onto the tray, and stormed up the stairs, his shoes clapping on the marble.

He stepped into the dimness of Phillip Bonano's grand bedroom. A nurse busied herself with a small basin and cloth at his bedside, and his Auntie Gianna walked up to greet him.

'So good of you to come, Alessandro.'

'Auntie,' he whispered, and they greeted each other with a peck on each cheek. 'Can I speak with him?' he said, removing his hat.

'For a little. He's very weak.'

Aless nodded and stepped slowly to the bedside. His auntie ushered the nurse away with her. Uncle Bonano was breathing noisily. His silver hair was not in its usual neatness. His wrinkled cheeks, usually shaved smooth, were covered in white and grey bristles. Cataract eyes looked up at him.

'Alessandro?' he croaked. 'Did you have an oyster?'

Aless gulped. 'Yes, Uncle,'

'How was it?'

An itch crept up his neck—his uncle knew he hated them. 'Like all oysters. Cold and slimy.'

Uncle Bonano croaked a small laugh. 'Alessandro, you have never changed. You were always the nephew that wanted the prize but never thought to appreciate the game. You hate fishing, yet you eat fish?'

Aless sighed again. 'I don't understand what you're saying, Uncle, but we still haven't settled some business. I was hoping—'

'That's right, Alessandro. You've never understood!'

'Phillip?' Auntie Gianna said from across the room, hearing her husband's raised voice.

'Uncle, please,' Aless said, leaning closer. 'That heist uptown. I gave the tip. Everyone had gotten their share of the diamonds, so where's mine?'

'You little schmuck! Open your eyes for once.'

'What's going on here?' Auntie Gianna marched over to the bed.

Phillip let out another croaky laugh.

'Nothing, Auntie. Uncle here was just about to finish some

144

business by telling me where—'

'Business?' Auntie Gianna snapped. 'Have you no heart at all, Alessandro? You have to leave!'

She gripped his arm.

'Uncle? Tell me!'

Philip's croaky laugh grew louder.

'Leave!' she demanded.

Aless eased back. 'As you wish.' And with that, he stormed out.

Waiting for him at the foot of the stairs was Stefano, his hands deep in the pockets of his long, black coat.

'Hey, boss. How was your meeting with Mr. Bonano?'

Aless stepped to his right-hand man and snapped, 'I hope that old fuck dies the most painful death ever! I hope he vomits up his own shit!' he said, stabbing a finger up at the marble stairs.

Stefano just nodded, then leaned close. 'Boss? We got him. Just like you asked.'

Aless stood back and raked fingers through his hair to settle his temper. 'And the mutt?'

'Yes, boss. The boys have them in the basement of the old man's garage. No one will hear a thing.'

Aless straightened his jacket. 'Let's do this.'

#

It was quite a regal room for being beneath a garage, but one would expect no less from Mr. Bonano. Harry stood upon an elegantly weaved rug with Benny still trembling in his arms. The room was draped with crimson and had all the workings of a private club. There was a pool table, and in the corner was a bar with mirrored shelves filled from floor to ceiling with spirits and wine.

Harry eyed his captors. They were scattered about the room, either smoking or sipping whisky. He jolted as Stefano entered, followed by someone he hadn't seen since he was a teenager.

'So here he is,' Aless said, stepping in and lighting a cigarette. He took in a deep drag, then smoke streamed out of his nose and mouth.

Stefano shut the door. He stood with Aless, their black shadows stretched out over the rug. 'The magic man, huh?' Aless said, taking another drag. 'Remember me, cousin?'

145

Harry gulped. 'Of course.'

'How long has it been?'

Harry had to think. 'I'd say it was before we were eighteen?'

'That's a long time. I know we're far from close, but family knows family. Time for a reunion, don't you think?'

A shiver of fear raced up Harry's back.

'We've gotta talk, cousin. But first, you gotta lose the dog.'

'What?'

'You can make this easy, or we can make this messy.'

Harry looked over Stefano's shoulder to see one of the other goons bring over a birdcage fit to hold a parrot.

'That's Vinnie, by the way. He likes hurting things.'

'My dog will be fine with me, I assure—'

Benny let out a deafening yelp as Stefano gripped the scruff of his neck.

'All right, here!' Harry cried as he released Benny. The look in his little dog's eyes drove daggers into his heart. 'Easy! Don't hurt him!'

Stefano fed Benny into the cage and shut the door. Benny's little high-pitched bark echoed. Vinnie stood over him, nudged the cage with his foot and yelled, 'Shut up!'

'Hold on,' said Stefano, peering at Harry. 'You gotta make your mutt keep quiet. Do it again and Vinnie cuts out his tongue.'

Harry called out, his hands open with appeal, and sure enough, the barking stopped. But Benny stared up at Vinnie, baring his little teeth.

'Now we can talk, cousin,' Aless said, taking another drag of his cigarette. 'Do you need a drink?'

'No.'

'Suit yourself.' Aless snapped his fingers and called out over his shoulder. 'Paul! Whisky—no ice!'

Harry watched as the big brute delivered the drink. 'You look to have fallen on hard times, cousin,' he said, taking a sip.

'So it seems.'

'Well, *you're* the one that strayed from the family business. When me and the others were playing with G-Man guns, you were reading weird books.'

'I wanted to be a showman, not a crook.'

'Look where that got you. Right, boys?'

Their mocking laughter filled the room.

Harry froze, his gaze fixed on Benny in his cage. He was looking out at him, his small eyes screaming: *Get us out of here!*

'You got some nerve. We're businessmen, not crooks. We lost track of you when you went off to be a circus act, then what do you know? You and your dog are up on posters all over town. Doing big shows and making loads of bread.'

'That bothered you?'

'Of course. Out of respect, you owed Philip Bonano a share,' Aless shrugged. 'You don't understand how our world works. Before I got the chance to teach you a lesson, you go and disappear again. Off abroad, right?'

'I wasn't aware I was in debt then.'

'It's worse than debt—it's disrespect! Then what happens? You come back and grovel like a weasel for cash? You got some balls, cousin. I was shocked you didn't get whacked on the spot. I couldn't believe my uncle loaned you a dime! What did you do, hypnotize him?'

'Your mother and mine were cousins. They were close. He pitied me, I guess.'

'That's right—the shipwreck. Lost everything apart from that mutt over there.'

Harry nodded.

'The cash you owe the family is over three grand. It's paynight, cousin.'

'I just need more time, Aless.'

Harry's heart skipped as Stefano stepped up and punched him across the chin. He fell to the rug, landing hard on his side, his head spinning. Benny was just a blur in his cage, barking constantly.

'Get him up!'

Rough hands lifted him from under the arms. Paul closed in and fired a punch into his belly. Harry gasped for breath.

'That's enough,' said Aless.

Stefano let him go.

Harry staggered, clutching his gut, and Benny only let up barking when his master shot him a look.

'Just a little taste, cousin,' Aless began. He stepped up to him. 'You gotta big problem here.'

147

'You just need to give me some more time. I just need a few good shows and I'll have the money,' he said, rubbing at his bruised stomach.

'You got no money hiding in a bank somewhere? Did it all go down with the ship?'

'I have funds in a bank in Europe. I initiated a transaction before I set for home. I received a cable from the bank telling me it had failed. It's all still there. I just need to make enough funds here so I can open an account and recover the money into it!'

'How much are we talking about?'

'At least fifteen hundred.'

'Only half, cousin? That won't make your problem go away. But what if I told you that I, too, have a problem. Maybe we can help each other out?'

'How?'

'I need your magic.'

'You mean my illusions?'

'No.'

The smile vanished from Alessandro's face. He stepped close, too close for Harry's liking. 'You do more than that, and I know it. Do you think the family is stupid? They kept their eyes on you in Europe. You moved a large sum of cash to a private buyer.'

'It was fraud!'

'Bullshit! Sources said that you met up with some strange folk and bought something from them about a month before you set sail for New York. When I finally got the job of dealing with you, I dug a bit deeper, see? They were Latin, those folks. Religious. I heard all sorts of stories, and I don't know what to believe, but what I do know is that you bought something, and it has to do with spirits. You learned how to call them—how to make them do things.'

Harry paused, his eyes darted back and forth from Benny to Aless. 'You're wasting your time. It was a hoax. It didn't work.'

'*What* didn't work?'

'What I paid for. It was a stupid move and it cost me.'

'Lies, cousin. If whatever it was didn't work, why were you in such a rush to come back here? Your shows were doing well abroad. Why tour here? Why?'

Harry couldn't find any words, his mouth opened and closed, but nothing came out. His jaw ached.

'I thought so. You *did* learn something from those priests. You know how to rouse the spirits.'

'Even if I do, what then?'

'I've lost something, and I want you to call a spirit to find it. Did you hear about the big jewelry heist uptown?'

'No.'

'Well,' Aless scoffed. 'That operation was based on *my* tip. Those diamonds are worth millions. Everyone got their share but Uncle Bonano is yet to give me mine. He just feeds me riddles.'

'You're talking about me using invocation to summon a spirit to find your loot?'

'That's what I'm talking about. Or there's another option.' He snapped his fingers. 'Vinnie?'

Benny yelped as Vinnie booted the cage.

'Stop it!'

'You see,' Aless began, stepping up to Harry and forcing him backwards. 'We could always gut your mutt, then put you both in a box and make *you* fucking disappear! That's *my* kind of magic.'

'The only spirit capable of finding missing things is a demon. That's what you want me to try and bring into this room?'

'Vinnie!'

The flick of pocketknife cut the air and Vinnie began to kneel.

'All right! All right! Stop! I'll do what you say! I'll try.'

'There you go!' Aless laughed and patted Harry hard on the shoulder. 'It's all you got, cousin. It's all you got.'

#

Sweat beaded on Harry's brow. His requests were met—a table, the leather-bound notebook he had tucked in his coat, and an assistant were made ready. All the while, Benny barked from his cage.

'Could I ask for one more thing?'

'What is it?' Aless asked, not hiding his impatience.

'Could you please give me a moment alone with my dog? I can make him stop barking.'

Aless stared down at Benny. 'Two minutes. If it doesn't work, the

149

mutt gets it.'

Harry ran to the cage and took Benny to the bar, where they were left alone. Benny's barks turned into whines as he set the cage on the counter top.

'You need to be quiet,' Harry whispered.

'I'm scared,' Benny ruffed. 'They want to kill you.'

'Our only chance is for me to perform the ritual.'

'How do you know it will work twice?'

'I don't.'

'Please be careful. Did a demon really do this to me? Give me a voice?'

He gulped before answering. 'Yes. But don't worry about that. Worry about being quiet. You must promise me. Whatever you see from now on, be silent. I don't want them to hurt you. Promise me, Benny?'

He nodded his little head.

'Say it?'

'I promise I will be silent.'

'No matter what they do to me. Understand?'

Benny nodded again.

Harry returned Benny to the rug. Resuming his place at the other end, he rested his hands on the table and looked up at his assistant, whose shadow inked over the table.

'Why did you choose me?' Vinnie asked, his bottom lip flapping over his upper like a bulldog's.

'Because you're the most gorgeous, meat bag!' yelled Paul.

Laughter erupted.

'You want a knuckle sandwich, fuck face?' Vinnie bellowed back.

'Easy!' yelled Aless. 'Let's get this show on the road.'

As the laughter died down, Vinnie addressed him again. 'Seriously, why me? I don't want to be a part of your circus act.'

'Because you're the one with the knife, and I need you to cut off one of my little fingers.'

Benny let out his high-pitched bark and Harry stabbed a finger at him and pursed his lips. Benny whined and cowered in his cage.

'What the fuck?' said Aless.

'It's necessary,' said Harry as he slipped off his coat.

'I'd gladly cut anything off you,' began Vinnie. 'But you telling

150

me to? Kind of takes the fun out of it.'

'This is not about fun.'

Harry unbuttoned his cuffs and rolled up his sleeves. 'The ritual demands an offering of the flesh,'

'Wait a minute,' said Aless. 'If you've done this before, what else have you cut off yourself?'

'A toe from each foot.'

Harry opened up his small book and flipped through some pages.

'Mother of God, this guy's a fucking freak,' Vinnie said, taking a step back.

'What's with all the mutilation?' Aless asked.

'I didn't pick you for squeamish.'

'Screw you, cousin. I just want to make sure you're not trying to pull any funny business. Spill it! Why the finger cutting?'

'I'm not a true worshiper of Satan. I'm an intruder, inviting a demonic spirit into our world. I must offer a piece of me as a gift. I'm making my finger sacred. If this pleases the spirit, it may, in return, provide its services.'

Aless let out a sigh, rubbed his brow, and looked at Vinnie. 'Do what he says.'

Harry placed his right hand on the table and spread his fingers. Vinnie flicked out his pocketknife, the blade glinting in the amber glow. He gripped Harry's wrist with his free hand and brought the blade to the center knuckle of the little finger.

'Not there,' Harry began. 'As close to my hand as you can. The whole finger. All of it.'

'That's gonna be tougher to cut through. It's gonna hurt like hell.'

'That should please you then.'

Without further hesitation, Vinnie pressed the blade into the flesh.

Harry grunted as the crunch of bone pierced his ears. He squinted as Vinnie rocked the blade until the little digit came free, blood squirting. He snatched a handkerchief from his pocket and covered the burning wound, trembling and channeling the pain by grinding his teeth.

'You best back away now,' Harry groaned. 'I'll take it from here.'

Vinnie looked at him as though staring at something unfamiliar, then took a few steps back. Harry looked at the handwritten verses in his notebook. Sighing, he dipped a finger into the pooled blood and smeared an upside-down, five-pointed star enclosed within a circle upon the table's surface. He then looked at Benny, cowering in his cage with paws over his eyes. After clearing his dry throat, he allowed the Latin verses to roll off his tongue:

I conjure thee, spirit, to come and show thyself in fair and comely shape without guile or deformity by the name of Casmiel! By the name of beloved Lucifer! Find and bring forth the treasure we so longingly seek! By the dread day of final judgment! By the omen! By the changing sea of glass! By those beasts having eyes before and behind, and having one hundred hands! Seek, ye holy one! Seek!

Harry made a fist of his good hand and looked to the ceiling.

'Is that it? Is it here?' Aless asked, looking around as though trying to track a fretting fly.

'Don't interrupt. I'm not finished,' Harry hissed and continued in the loudest voice he could muster.

I beg you, ye holy one! Regal and majestic! Glorious splendor! Mighty arch-daimon! Denizen of chaos and Erebus, and of the unfathomable abyss! Haunter of sky-depths! Murk enwrapped, scanning mystery, and guardian of cults! Flame-fanning terror darter! Heart-crushing despot! Satanachia of daimons! Invincible Lucifer!

The silence deepened.

All the men looked at each other. Aless dropped his cigarette butt and snuffed it with his heel. Harry's heart raced, and the burning in his wound shot spikes up his arm.

'I have to hand it to you, cousin,' Aless said, reaching into his coat. 'You had me for a second, thinking you could actually do that, but it looks—'

'Wait!' Harry yelled. All of his flesh goosed and he felt a familiar chill. His knees began to wobble and his heart thudded harder. 'It *has* worked! We are in the presence of the divine. It will appear. It will seek your prize,'

'Really? How will it appear?' Aless said, his voice almost bored. He pulled out his revolver and pulled back the hammer with a click.

'Do any of you feel different?' Harry asked, looking at them in turn. 'The spirit has come through, but not in its true form. It should be in one of you!'

'I think we all got a bit of the demon in us—right, boss?' huffed Vinnie.

Laughter. The rest of them revealed their firearms.

'Vinnie?' Aless said, pointing his pistol down at Benny's cage. 'Shoot the mutt first.'

'You got it, boss.'

Harry trembled where he stood, his eyes wild as he watched Vinnie step over to the cage.

What's happening? The sensations were the same as last time. Where's the spirit?

Vinnie aimed his hand canon down at Benny, only to hesitate.

A growl—deep and throaty, as though from a tiger.

'Boss?' Vinnie said, staring down. The growls continued through bared teeth. Vinnie shook his head as though to shake away cobwebs.

Harry could swear Benny's teeth were getting longer.

'What the fuck has gotten into that mutt?' Aless asked, looking at Benny's eyes, which Harry could see had transformed into black orbs.

Vinnie started circling the cage, and Harry watched as bulges rose and sank around Benny's muzzle—was he growing?

'Put your guns away,' Harry said. *Of course,* his mind raced, *the spirit has come through a vessel that has received dark magik before. Like a familiar plane!*

Benny let out a deafening roar. His fur had begun to sprout like a rash of spikes about his back. His canine teeth grew down to dreadful points.

'Vinnie? Shoot the mutt!' Aless said, taking a step back.

Before Vinnie could pull the trigger, Benny's size had reached the limits of the cage and he broke through as though it were built of cardboard. He launched himself at Vinnie's broad throat and sank his newly-formed teeth in. The big man gurgled as razor jaws worked into his flesh like a meat shredder. He fell hard on his back and trembled as the blood fountained from his jugular.

Benny whipped his head back to Aless and growled.

'Holy shit!' Aless tried to shout, but it only came out as a terrified whisper.

Benny stepped over the trembling legs of the dying Vinnie and stalked Aless. Blood and saliva dripped from his fangs and gore hung from his paws.

Harry stumbled back and Stefano fired a round, but Benny lurched out of the way as though seeing the bullet in slow motion. Stefano kept firing but the blood-soaked canine swerved past every bullet and—running with unnatural speed—launched itself. The powerful jaws clamped the hand that held the gun. Benny ripped Stefano's arm from its socket, leaving a geyser of blood in its place. Stefano screamed and fell to his side.

Paul fired next, only to miss his mark and catch Stefano through his left eye. He fired again and again, and Benny ran for the nearest wall. Defying gravity, he raced up and over the ceiling like a spider, then dropped onto Paul's shoulders. His curved claws gripped bone and his maw expanded abnormally. The razor teeth bit into the top of Paul's head.

Paul wailed and his gun fired shot upon shot in all directions, forcing Harry and Aless to drop for cover. Harry cringed when the cracking of Paul's skull cut the air. The shooting ceased and Paul froze, his eyes wide and his mouth wider still. Blood poured from beneath his hat and covered his face—the final curtain.

Benny kept growling, baring his teeth and Paul's legs finally gave out. He collapsed with a thud.

Benny raised his head, thick blood stringing from his jaws, and his black eyes fell upon Aless again. The beast sprang, canine limbs twisting at impossible angles, and Aless fired helplessly before being knocked to the ground.

'Cousin! Call this fucking thing off me!'

Benny's muzzle dug into Aless's stomach.

'I don't understand!' Harry yelled. 'It should be searching for…'

Harry crawled away from the table and looked on in horror as both his dog and his cousin thrashed around on the rug. Alessandro's suit was growing bloodstains upon its jacket and trousers. Benny's growl had become gurgled and Aless let out a squeal. He was on his back, the canine perched on his pelvis, his jaws ripping at clothing and flesh. Aless punched Benny but to no avail. His attack slackened and his arms soon flopped like dead snakes.

Harry retched as he watched his possessed terrier feast upon the gut of his second cousin. His brow raised as the beast dug profusely at intestine and liver. Chunks of flesh and gore travelled out from between his hind legs, the way dirt would if he were digging for a bone in the earth.

Harry cocked his head, seeing that Benny had clasped onto something. He watched as Benny withdrew his muzzle and backed away, then dropped a morsel of flesh. He sniffed, pawed, and licked away at it. When it was clean, he picked it up with his teeth and trotted over to his master.

Harry fell to his knees to meet Benny, but the dog stopped short, dropped the morsel on the floor, and froze. Harry's heart lurched as Benny let out a woeful whine and shrank back to his former size, bones snapping and flesh shrinking before he collapsed to one side.

'No!' He took Benny in his arms and cradled him. 'Benny! Benny, no!'

A bloodied cough escaped the little dog's mouth and he whined. Harry hugged him tight, crying into his blood-soaked fur. He hadn't lost him after all.

'I'm so sorry, my friend. Are you still with me?'

'Let's...go home?' Benny croaked.

'Yes, Benny. It's home time. I'll get you cleaned up.'

'Harry? Don't forget what is at your knees.'

He eased back. Grimacing, he picked up the clump of flesh with his good hand. It was still warm.

He allowed it to settle in his palm, and his eyes widened.

He paused, tilted his head, and sniffed.

A large diamond.

And it smelt like fish.

DOMINION
Jeff Wood

'Honey? Do you hear something?'

'No.'

'Seriously. Listen.'

My wife sighed and muted the TV set.

'Now. Listen. Can't you hear it?'

'Hear what?'

'Crickets.'

She cocked her head to her side and listened for a few seconds.

'Nope. Nothing.' She unmuted the TV and resumed watching her program, my question already forgotten.

I've lived in the Midwest for two years now. I grew up in the Midwest—Albia, Iowa—but left when I was in my late teens. I lived in a succession of cities for the next several decades, first on my own as a single young man. Minneapolis, Chicago, St. Louis, Detroit. After I met my wife and formed my own family, we moved back to the Midwest, where I'd grown up, and settled in a little Iowa town called Keokuk.

I wanted to raise my kids in a wholesome setting. Small town, good people with old-fashioned family values, a community that believes in God and country.

Our first night in that house, as I watched my daughter chase lightning bugs in the front yard, giggling with pure joy and freedom, just as I had when I was her age, I knew I'd made the right decision.

#

I began hearing the crickets a few weeks ago, right after we

156

returned from my mother's funeral in Albia.

I sat down in my comfy chair in the living room at the end of the day, exhausted and grieving. My wife shooed the children away so I could have some alone time. She brought me a stiff drink, turned on the TV, gave me a chaste peck on the cheek, and went upstairs.

I woke up four hours later, at 2 am, to a darkened house. It took me a moment to regain my bearings and remember where I was—and who I was.

To remember where I'd been that day.

I'd buried my mother.

I looked at the static on the television. The station must have gone off the air. I didn't think stations did that anymore, not with the heathen 24/7 media landscape of the modern world. But there it was—a rectangular wall of white noise.

The static was overwhelmingly loud, so I took the remote control in hand and turned off the TV. The bright white visuals of the screen blinked off, but the noise remained, unchanged.

That's when I realized I wasn't hearing static.

I was hearing crickets.

#

I feared bugs as a kid.

My fright stemmed, if memory serves, from when I was a small child and looked down to see a cricket perched motionless on my arm. I studied it, unsure of what kind of insect it even was. I reached out a finger and touched it. The cricket responded by chirping loudly. Cute, I thought. I touched it again. It chirped again. So cute! I touched it a third time. The thing responded by leaping straight into my mouth. I coughed and choked and wheezed in panic. I could feel the insect probing the soft flesh of my mouth, looking for an escape. It poked. It scraped. It jumped.

Worse than the feeling of movement inside my mouth was the sound. The bones of my skull amplified the actions of the cricket, so that the muffled sound of its motions filled my head, drowning out every other noise in my tiny childhood world. His frenzied chirping sounded like a fire alarm.

Fire alarms reminded me of fire.

157

Fire reminded me of Satan and the blazes of hell.

And suddenly this wasn't just a struggle between a clueless child and a harmless insect but a battle between good and evil for my very soul. I clasped my palms against my temples, trying to contain this otherworldly brawl and take back control of my own head.

My mother finally saw what was happening, ran to me, and patted me on the back, trying to get the cricket out of my mouth. I was so deep inside my panic I reacted in the worst possible way—I swallowed the cricket. All that demonic poking and scraping and jumping moved from my mouth to my throat.

Satan had won.

My fear and panic intensified.

I couldn't breathe. My throat constricted around the still struggling insect. I felt my strength ebb, and the world grow dark. I prepared to die. I wondered if I'd see heaven, and what it might look like.

I awoke on the couch a few minutes later.

Was this heaven?

It was not. My brother told me I passed out, and once I passed out the cricket simply hopped from between my lips and into the yard. They'd brought me onto the couch to rest until I regained consciousness.

Before that day, I'd considered insects my friends—no different from birds or cats or my friends down the block. After the cricket incident, any creature with more than four legs was suspect. Ants, grasshoppers, mosquitoes, and yes, especially crickets. They now scared me more than any other insect. The jet-black color, the hard sleek carapace, the barbed back legs. Their ability to jump hundreds of times their height, to fly out of the foliage and hit you in the face, jump into your mouth, fall down your shirt, get tangled up in your hair. They were terrifying. So terrifying, in fact, that I shifted all my fearful attitudes about crickets and applied them to all insects.

Later in life, my therapist called this "transference".

Even my beloved lightning bugs didn't escape this sense of loathing. Where I used to love running across the back lawns of the neighborhood in early evening, chasing the recurring flash of the fireflies with my friends, I now hid in my room, fearful of not only the lightning bugs but of any other critter that might be hiding in the flowerbeds and the well-manicured lawns.

I lay on my bed and prayed instead.

I prayed for all insects to die.

#

After my wife told me she didn't hear crickets, I went to ask my daughter. She loved insects. All insects. She never stepped on them, never killed them. She was never afraid of them, not even those that stung. She gave them names. She built little houses for them. She'd even leave little pieces of candy for the bees.

I found her on the back porch of the house, playing with Lego.

I sat down next to her.

'Honey, do you hear anything?'

'Like what?'

'I'll tell you in a minute. First I want you to try and figure it out for yourself. I'll quit talking. Just listen and tell me what you hear.'

She paused, eyebrows theatrically furrowed, listening intently. Eventually, she turned to me and said, 'I heard birds. Singing birds.'

'What else?'

'Conner.'

'Conner?'

'The dog. The neighbor's dog, Conner. He was barking. He does that every time someone walks past the house.'

'Good job, sweetie. What else?'

'I heard the neighbors telling their dog to shut up.'

I laughed. 'What else?'

'Nothing. That's all I hear.'

'Think hard. Listen. Is there anything else you hear?'

'The ice cream truck!'

'No. Anything else?'

'No. Can we get ice cream, Daddy? Come on, please?'

I knew I'd never get her attention back onto the crickets now that the possibility of ice cream was raised. I dropped the subject and walked with her to the sidewalk.

By the time the truck arrived, the crickets in my head fully drowned out the sing-song melody coming from the truck's loudspeakers.

I pretended nonchalance and bought my daughter a Dreamsicle.

#

My mother may have passed her fear of insects to me.

I remember her squealing and jumping on a chair in the kitchen when I saw a cockroach and pointed it out to her.

I remember her refusing to go into the garage until my father had assured her he'd cleaned it of moths. After he assured her he had, and after she entered the garage, I remember her scream of terror as she came running back into the house after discovering an errant moth. She didn't talk to my father for several days.

I remember her getting stung by a wasp after the Sunday sermon and collapsing in tears on the immaculate lawn of the church. I remember kneeling next to her on the grass, trying to console her. I remember how, even in the midst of her sobbing, her eyes were large and round, examining the grass, terrified that a grasshopper or an ant or a centipede would crawl on her before she returned to the safety of the concrete.

I honestly don't remember if this was before or after the cricket incident. I do remember my mind conjuring an image of a hidden army of insects, crouching behind clovers and blades of grass, amassing around her to attack. I remember my great relief as the pastor reached down to help my mother back up, as my chagrined father watched from the sidewalk.

She began keeping a can of insecticide on top of the refrigerator. She kept it up there to keep it out of reach of the kids in the house, but her outsized fear of insects meant she used the can almost daily. I remember the cloying, oddly metallic scent. Or rather, two scents fighting each other—the sweet artificiality of the wintergreen the spray was meant to smell like, and the disturbing sulfurous scent hiding underneath the intended scent. The scent often showed up in our lunchboxes and at the dinner table. Once or twice, the taste of the insecticide found its way into the food. My little brother cried the first time he encountered it. The stuff made his mouth uncomfortably warm and tingly.

My mother started being more careful with using insecticide around the kitchen when she was making food, but my sense is, we simply got more used to the smell and taste of the stuff.

Insecticide was a big part of my childhood, literally intermixed with the food I ate and the air I breathed.

#

Now, as a father, I felt it important to keep my own fears away from the impressionable young mind of my daughter. Even as I cringed passing an anthill or a wasp's nest, I lectured her about not stepping on bugs, even if she was scared. They didn't deserve to die. They were just doing their job according to God's plan, being bugs. We had long, far-reaching conversations about what a bug's job actually involved. I taught her that bees carried pollen from one plant to another, and that's how we got flowers, and plants, and vegetables for the dinner table. We discussed how spiders and praying mantises ate other insects, especially mosquitoes. I asked her, we don't like it when we get mosquito bites, right?

She didn't.

I dropped my questioning about the cricket sounds because I didn't want to alarm her. After all, my wife hadn't heard it either. I found that I couldn't not hear it, unless I was asleep. But every morning, I woke up and the sound greeted me, even before my wife wished me a sleepy good morning.

She asked me to describe it once. That's not an easy thing to do. Even now I struggle with it. Here's what it reminds me of—a Las Vegas casino. If you've ever been inside one, you'll know what I'm talking about. A high-pitched, bell-like ambient sound hovers over everything. I assume it's the sound of the coins clinking against each other as well as the bells and sirens that go off whenever someone has won.

The crickets aren't as loud as all that, of course, but the noise they make has the same high-pitched metallic timber to it. The two noises share a certain variability as well. It's never one constant, unchanging tone, but rather one that seems to wax and wane. Pockets of sound flare up, first to the left of me, or the right, then behind me, in front of me, above me. I can place the sound in time and space. But that pockets dies away and another gains ascendancy before fading back into white insectoid noise. The overall result is that of a cloud of sound surrounding me on all sides, pitched right at the edge of my hearing, following me wherever I go.

And no one hears it but me.

And it's getting louder.

After I described the noise to my wife, she suggested—not unkindly—that perhaps I should see a therapist.

#

They suggested I get therapy when I was a child too.

This was right after I burned all those ants alive.

It was a different time back then, something I think it's important to stress. There was no PETA. Our neighbors left their dogs and cats outside, even in the snow and rain. The Bible told us, *Let them have dominion over the fish of the sea and over the birds of the heavens and over the livestock and over all the earth and over every creeping thing that creeps on the earth.*

Dominion over every creeping thing.

Insects were not our friends and fellow occupants of Spaceship Earth. They were pests.

So it seemed to me at the time no big deal when my friend Kyle squirted a glob of honey onto the middle of a piece of cardboard and put it down next to an anthill. We'd been in the grass, playing with plastic army men. Predictably, within minutes, scouting ants found the honey and delivered the news to the rest of the colony. Within half an hour, ants were swarming on the top of the cardboard, lines of them coming to and from the honey to the anthill.

Meanwhile, while we were playing with the army men, Kyle was preparing something in an empty metal drum. We didn't pay much attention until we heard the whoosh of the flames and turned to see fire leaping out of the barrel and up into our bright sunny suburban skies. While we were huddled around our army men, he'd thrown a bunch of scrap wood into the barrel, then doused it with charcoal lighter fluid for the grill. He threw in a lit matchbook and *whoosh!*

Giggling maniacally, Kyle yanked away the cardboard from the center of where we'd been huddled and put it on top of the flames. One of the other kids—whose name is lost to memory—cried out, 'It's a burning building! All those people on top of the building are dying!' He punctuated the statement with overexaggerated sounds of people being burned to death. We all laughed. Various boys added their own interpretation of what was happening, replete with agonized screams—napalm, aliens, nuclear war.

What we saw were ants. They didn't act like people. They didn't scream or dial 911 or try to save their loved ones or hatch an escape plan. They all responded to the exact same dumb animal instincts: they ran from the extreme heat at the center of the cardboard to the edges, not realizing the fire would spread to the edges in minutes. When the flames arrived, they died—simply and easily—going up in a tiny puff of yellow, as undramatic as a kitchen match.

I want to say I was horrified, but I wasn't.

They didn't evoke, nor did they deserve, our empathy.

Dominion over every creeping thing.

After all the ants had burned and the flames died down, we doused the fire with the garden hose. It wasn't until then that we looked up and saw Kyle's mother watching us from the kitchen window.

She sent us all home right away and called our parents. Kyle got in big trouble, and we weren't allowed to play with fire at his house anymore.

I had to go talk to the pastor of our church.

Then I had to see a therapist.

#

I got along better with the therapist I went to as an adult than the one I visited as a kid. My therapist-as-an-adult listened to me tell him all about the crickets.

Then he asked, 'Do you know what tinnitus is?'

I did not and told him so.

'It's commonly called ringing of the ears.'

'I don't think that's it. It doesn't sound like ringing.'

The therapist leaned forward. 'It can present as all sorts of different things. Ringing, yes. But it can sound like hissing. Or like rushing water. Ocean waves. Buzzing, clicking, even like music sometimes. So, of course, it can sound like crickets. It could sound like any number of bugs.' I shuddered. He took off his glasses. 'Look. The human body is complex and infinitely varied. I bet there

163

are as many types of tinnitus as there are people who have tinnitus. Every case is different. But the general shape of what you're describing sure sounds like tinnitus. Why don't you let me run some tests?'

I didn't want him to run some tests. He didn't understand. He wasn't in my head like I was. He couldn't hear it.

I pressed my case with him. 'How do you know it's not like, actual crickets?'

'Okay.' He leaned back into his chair and returned his glasses to the bridge of his nose. 'Let's say it's crickets. Does your wife hear them?'

I'd already told him she didn't. I shook my head.

'And your daughter? What about her? Does she hear them?'

Again, he knew she didn't. I shook my head.

'And I don't hear them either. So, if you're hearing actual crickets, you're the only person hearing them. It's possible, of course. Maybe you have extraordinary hearing. Maybe you can hear things at too high or too low a frequency for others. Again, I could run some tests and we could figure it out right now.'

I didn't want to figure it out right now. I already knew what was happening. I just wanted someone to believe me.

Ten minutes later, my session was up and I left his office. I never went back.

Things weren't too bad in the car on the ride home, but when I shut off the engine and opened the car door, a wall of noise hit me. It sounded as if the entire front and back lawn of my house was filled with crickets, chirping at top volume. The woods behind my house sounded like an entire army of insects hid behind the leaves. I ventured out back before going inside.

The level of sound physically hurt my ears. I'd never heard it this bad before.

#

We did other cruel things to bugs when I was a kid. Remember, this was rural Iowa, and we lived out in the country. It was a different time. Don't judge me.

We put Black Cat firecrackers in the holes of anthills. They didn't

164

do much—a puff of dirt, a small divot in the ground, and a few flying ant carcasses. We returned to using the firecrackers to add realism to our diorama of plastic army men set by the creek.

We squirted lighter fluid meant for my father's Zippo onto a hornet's nest once. The result was much more dramatic than with the Black Cats and the anthill. The nest hung from the limb of a tree in the woods behind our houses, about four feet off the ground. After we doused the nest, hornets swarmed outside the structure, immediately aware something was wrong.

Before they could abandon their home, Kyle lit a match and flipped it up onto the nest. Fire swooshed up over the sides and reached up to the leaves and limbs hanging over it. At the same time, angry hornets poured out of the nest and into the surrounding air.

Our first instinct was to flee the area to avoid being stung or burned, but the tree was on the verge of catching fire, as well as the rest of the surrounding woods. Violence against insects was one thing, but setting the woods on fire would definitely get us into trouble.

Remember—we have dominion over plants and animals—over every creeping thing. They are our responsibility.

Kyle ran and pulled the hose from the side of the house, stretching it as far as it would go. We got the hose close enough for the water to reach the tree and doused the whole area until no more flames leaped from the trees.

Remembering what had happened with the burning ants, we did our best to hide our adventure from the adults. We hid the charred trees limbs, branches, and leaves and spread dry dirt on the sodden and blackened scene of our crime.

No one found out.

The only living things that knew it had happened were me, my friends, and the hornets.

And God, of course.

God knew what we had done.

#

I don't tell my own daughter these stories. I don't want her to be cruel to insects or any living creature. Nor do I want her to be scared of them. So when I scheduled a visit from the pest control guy, I made sure she didn't hear me make the appointment.

A young, long-haired kid with a wrinkled Buganex uniform showed up at my door. His Buganex truck stood in my driveway, a giant cartoon bug still bouncing from the drive over.

'Are you sure it's not tinnitus?' was one of the first questions he asked me.

'No, I've been to a doctor about it, and he declared me free of tinnitus,' I lied.

'I don't hear anything.'

'It's not your job to hear anything. It's your job to kill bugs.'

He shrugged his shoulders and put on his mask and shoe protectors. He went downstairs and sprayed the basement, then upstairs to spray the attic. After that he went from room to room, spraying the baseboards.

He took off his mask and shoe protectors and walked outside. He pulled a different, larger canister from his truck and used it to spray the periphery of the house. He ventured to the edge of the yard and walked the edge of the property, trailing small puffs of insecticide in his wake.

When he was done, he showed me his work. I inspected the job, wrote him out a check, and showed him the door.

As he opened the door to leave, I asked him, 'How long will it take to work? The poison?'

'It should already be working. Look!' He pointed to several newly dead ants lined along the sidewalk. He added, 'It'll be effective for the next month or so. There's a thirty-day guarantee.'

And upon giving me a copy of the guarantee and the invoice, he left.

I didn't need to wait for dusk to know whether I'd hear the crickets. It was the middle of the day and I heard them already.

It would only get worse as the day progressed.

#

My mother convinced my father to seal the house. By that, she meant tight seals around all the doors and all the windows, and repairs to cracks and gaps in the walls and joints. This wasn't just due to her fear of insects. She'd shifted her focus in her later years to include dirt and dust and microbes as well. As kids we were never entirely sure what she meant when she said 'microbes', but the way she pronounced the word assured us we wanted none of them in our home.

My father dutifully added the chores to his to-do list. After he'd sealed the walls and windows and doors, he moved on to light fixtures and electrical plates, to the basement, to the attic.

When he declared himself finished, a helpful neighbor informed us that our house was too tightly sealed and we wouldn't be able to breathe. The neighbor told us our sealed home would quickly cause mold and mildew, a build-up of toxins, even carbon monoxide poisoning.

My mother immediately decided we needed a solution for our new problem.

We swapped our old furnace and air conditioner for a new model that came with multiple HEPA filters and a UV light air purifier, guaranteed to eliminate 99.98% of particulates. No more pollen. No more smoke. No more bacteria. No more bugs.

It cost my parents a lot of money and I heard them fighting over the kitchen table about it after I went to bed. I listened but could make out no specifics. All I discerned, and all I remember these many decades later, is the righteous anger and distrust in their voices, both of them convinced they were in the right. Neither of them willing to give an inch.

My father left the next morning before I woke. I haven't seen him since.

I learned something, listening to them that night.

In order to get your way, you must be unwilling to give an inch.

Stand firm.

Keep the devil at bay.

#

I inspected my property after the Buganex man left—front sidewalk to back fence, then all along the property line. Dead insects littered the driveway, sidewalks, and lawn. All kinds, from spiders and centipedes to ants and ladybugs. I didn't see a single living

167

insect. Only hundreds upon hundreds of dead ones. The air around the house had that familiar tell-tale odor. That cloying, oddly metallic scent I associated with the insecticide-tainted rooms of my youth. I found the smell evocative, and wonderfully comforting.

I still heard the crickets.

Even though I saw plenty of dead crickets, I still heard them.

They were so loud they were nearly all I heard.

I realized they were inside the house.

All of them.

They clung to the curtains. They hid under bedsheets. They jumped out of the closets when doors were opened, leapt to the light of the television when it was turned on. They even chirped from the toilet when the lid was raised.

I didn't know how they'd gotten inside.

That night, or rather early that morning, long after my family had gone to bed, I dressed, scooped my car keys off the dresser as quietly as I could, and drove to the 24-hour gas station. I bought three bright red, five-gallon gas cans and a Zippo lighter. I filled the three cans at the pump under the bored eye of the teenaged kid running the register. I drove home.

At home, I checked on my family. Everyone slept soundly in their beds. Most of the windows in the house had been opened. I assumed to rid the house of the smell of the bug poison. I kissed my daughter, told her I loved her. I did the same to my wife.

Then I closed and locked their windows. I locked the door to the house.

I retrieved the gas cans and the Zippo from my car and walked out to the edge of my property. Stars dotted the clear skies overhead. No moon shone that night, and the lights of the nearest city were tens of miles away, so the light from the stars reached my eyes unimpeded. I saw a shooting star. The contrails of a passing jet cut the sky in two.

I inhaled the early morning air—a heady combination of lavender and sage from the neighbor's garden mixed with the diesel fumes from the highway and the trace of petrichor from the rainclouds hovering far off on the horizon. The scent was lovely, almost wholly occluding the smell of deadly chemicals left by the Buganex man.

I still heard the crickets, of course. Whether I was outside or in, the sound level remained constant.

I unscrewed the cap of the first gas can and began to pour, walking backwards, carefully making my way around the edge of my yard.

#

My mother died in the house I grew up in.

My brother and I had left years ago, him to college, me to a job at the meat processing plant a couple towns over.

She died of asphyxiation. I had to ask the authority who called me what the word meant. It means to die by being deprived of oxygen.

I asked them if they suspected foul play. They said they did not.

They said the air inside the house was full of poisonous substances. Fumes from bleach and ammonia-based cleaners. Air fresheners—which apparently can be toxic in high concentrations. Insecticides, of course. Oven cleaner. Carbon monoxide from the space heater in the spare room. The house had been pumped so full of chemicals and sealed so tightly the fumes slowly built up and had not been allowed to dissipate.

She died quietly in her sleep.

Neither my brother nor my father came to the funeral.

The authorities said they didn't suspect foul play, but that was their job. I knew who was responsible.

#

It took a little over two cans of gas to douse the periphery of my property. I splashed the remainder of the gas in the last can up onto the porch of the house.

I came across the carcass of our dog as I poured the gas. He must have gotten too close to the poison. I'd have to bury him before my daughter found him.

I found several dead squirrels as I made my path around the house as well. I'm sure they were killed by the same poison that killed the dog—their bodies in the same state of muscular tension and extreme rigor. I knew that was brought on by bifenthrin, the active ingredient in the insecticide.

I'd need to bury them too.

Wouldn't want to disturb the neighborhood kids.

Below my property, on my neighbors' lawns, I saw more dead animals. Dogs, cats, squirrels, birds. Must have been the runoff. Perhaps the Buganex kid had put down a little too much insecticide.

No matter. Not anymore.

In order to silence the crickets, this needed to be done. We have been given dominion over the fish and the birds and the beasts and the bugs. This is our responsibility and our right.

By the time I'd finished, the smell of gasoline had overcome the delicate, nuanced mix of scents I'd admired earlier in the night. Gas was all I could smell.

The thunderclouds at the edge of the horizon had crept closer, blocking the ancient light of the stars, covering them with a pewter gray blanket of stratus.

It was just me and the clouds, the gasoline, and the Zippo.

The crickets wouldn't stop.

The crickets wouldn't stop.

I flipped up the lid of the lighter and spun the flint. A cool orange flame leaped from the wick of the lighter. I tossed the lighter into the yard and the blaze rose up from where I had drenched the grass with gas, like a thing turned suddenly alive. The sound of the conflagration was followed by silence, blessed silence, a final silence. No more crickets. No more chirping. I collapsed at the front of my home, my enemy eradicated, my property purified, my wife and child asleep and eager to meet my dead mother in the bright, barren, insect-free fields of heaven.

DIVINE LIQUOR
C.C. Adams

'The horrid mystery hanging over us in this house gets into my head like liquor, and makes me wild.' – Wilkie Collins

Tooting, South West London
19:41, 26/02/2014

With the last candle lit, Volante squared the matchbox up to the far corner of the mantelpiece and seated herself at one end of the table. Taking a half-day from the office to vacuum, clean, and air the house had proven to be a masterstroke. Now she sat as quietly as the room itself, in silent and almost predatory anticipation. Three candles stood solemn beneath solo flames, one at the centre of the mantelpiece and the other two near the centre of the table—walnut wood burnished to perfection. The remaining chairs, save the one opposite her, were neatly racked in the far corner. A serving of pork-fried rice sat neatly on her plate and was matched by an equally neat if slightly larger serving on the plate at the other end of the table for Trayvon; each meal partnered by an empty wine glass. She cocked a quizzical eye at his meal. *Probably more than enough.*

She gave herself a critical once-over. The black silk robe covered her generous curves—along with the bra and panties—but barely covered her ass. The new black leather heels were already starting to pinch, but she bit back the discomfort. Odds were good that when Trayvon got back, she wouldn't have to wear them much longer, and even if she did, she wouldn't have to stand up in them.

Volante folded her arms and let her head fall back, her hair falling off her shoulders to hang down her back. A tight-lipped glance at the wall clock revealed a time of thirteen minutes past eight. Traffic, like a number of things in London, Volante thought, was abysmal, but that didn't mean that you would just wait. No. Right now, Chilean Merlot would take the edge off.

She reached for the open bottle and poured herself a glass, savouring the first sip. Italian heritage meant, at least in Volante's case, that she and wine were old friends; from working in her uncle's restaurant to time spent bonding with girlfriends in university, and certainly from previous dates. Raven-haired and dark-eyed with a wry quirk to her smile, her *Match.com* profile garnered attention from plenty of men, and successful suitors, in a bid to impress, had opened her up to many a wine bar. Trayvon was different. He opened her up to true romance, the last episode of which had seen him mark the five-month milestone in their relationship with a visit to the orchid display at Kew Gardens. Each kiss on her cheek for each time she smiled at him had left her dangerously aroused. How much, she would never tell him. But tonight would at least help redress the balance of arousal. Volante ran through Trayvon's commute in her head: finishing his shift at the bar, Northern line southbound from Leicester Square to Tooting Bec, then a short walk…and then, the irony hit her. She couldn't wait for Trayvon to get home, and when he did, flirtation would be a taut and drawn-out affair until the two—

Knocking sounded at the front door.

Volante took another sip of wine before setting her glass down. She pushed to her feet, noting with some surprise how much time had passed since she last looked at the clock. Hands smoothing down her robe, she felt a modicum of relief as the fabric, hiked up while seated, had now slid back down over her ass.

'Hello?' A woman's plaintive voice, calling from outside the front door. 'Please?'

Her arousal waned. Who the hell was this? And where was Trayvon? Volante kicked off her shoes, sighing in relief as she went to investigate, her feet relaxed from the confinement of tight leather. Inky darkness filtered through the frosted glass window set high in the top of the door, which she opened to receive the chill February air. Then she faltered and clasped a hand to her chest, staring.

The woman was a few inches taller than Volante—easy enough when facing her five-foot-two frame. Frizzy ginger-blonde hair hung low, hiding her face and the floral-printed fabric of her dress hung in an ugly rip over her crotch, exposing a bloody smear across white panties. Viscous red stained the fabric.

'He…' She lifted her face to reveal tear-stained elfin features. A silver eyebrow piercing glinted above her left eye. 'He was…' Her voice broke. 'He tried to force himself on me.' She stretched out a quivering hand to rest against the doorframe. Volante's gaze swept down the woman, noting the trembling legs in particular. A murmured 'oh' would have been the verbal response had the word not been smothered by the need for action. Volante darted forward as the woman collapsed, catching her under the upper arm. She helped her to her feet—the unsteady stance reminding her of a newborn foal.

'Is he coming?' she murmured. 'Do you hear him?' She looked at Volante, her gaze vague and unfocused. 'I can't even keep my eyes open.'

'Come on,' Volante said, keeping her voice soft but firm. 'Come on.' One hand under the woman's arm, Volante led her inside and shut the door softly behind them. Through to the dining room, the woman continued to sob and mutter, seemingly oblivious when Volante pulled out the chair adjacent to her own and guided the newcomer into it.

Volante chewed at the corner of her bottom lip, thinking. 'Have you called the police?'

'No!' The woman flinched, seemingly spooked by the volume of her own voice. Fearful features relaxed somewhat and she dropped her gaze. She surreptitiously licked her lip. 'I'm sorry,' she said. 'I just can't. Not right now. Give me a while to…you know. Please?'

Volante narrowed her gaze a little. Despite the newcomer's skittish frailty, a feeling of wary scepticism gnawed at her. Her street stretched for over two blocks, and many of the other houses would have provided better refuge—so why settle for this one? While some of the houses stood dark and silent—as Volante had remarked when she opened the door, lamplight or flickering TV screens could be seen through the curtained windows of others. Brewster alone would have been a better choice, she decided. Shift work at God-knew-where meant erratic hours, but you could always rely on his speakers to let you know when he was at home. *Fucking reggae.*

Her attention reverted to her guest. Sure, the woman had suffered an ordeal, but she needed a little strength to face it, to open up about it. Even if it came from the bottle—Dutch courage. Volante reached for the Merlot and half-filled a glass, holding it out to the woman. 'Try a little. It will help calm your nerves. If you don't like it...' A wry grimace: the facial equivalent of a shoulder shrug. 'At least you'll have tasted some good wine.' As soon as the words left her mouth, Volante gave herself a mental forehead slap—was this not a crass thing to say at a time like this? Marco had warned his little sister about her careless tongue before.

The woman sniffled, thin lips curving into a gentle smile. Volante felt the urge to pat the woman but held it back. The last thing she wanted to do was render the woman skittish again. Palm face down, she clenched her fingers loosely into a fist. When the woman had sipped her way through half the measure of wine, she decided to press further. 'Better?'

'A little. Sort of thirsty, but I don't really have a head for wine. Too strong.' She cast a glance at Volante. 'Thank you.'

Volante shook her hand in a splayed-finger wave of dismissal. 'It's okay.' She paused, appraising the woman. The tear tracks on her cheeks had dried and the hitching sobs of her chest had subsided. 'What's your name?

She shot a look over her shoulder, hair fanning out in motion behind her, before turning back to Volante with a fearful gaze.

'Hey,' Volante said, a little sharply. 'It's okay. Really, it's okay.' She allowed time for her words to sink in. 'What's your name?'

She leaned back in her chair, eyebrows high in anxiety. 'You didn't hear anything?'

'No.' Volante gave what she hoped would pass for a benevolent smile and gently laid her hand on the table as if it were the arm of her anxious guest. She inclined her head, repeating her earlier question without voicing it.

'Heidi.' She sat silently for a beat, and then tapped an unmanicured fingernail on the base of her wine glass. 'Volante's got good taste, I see. You'll have to tell me where I can get a bottle of this.' Her gaze flicked up, revealing awareness of an etiquette faux pas. 'Unless you can't reveal your sources or something...?'

174

Another handwave to keep the conversation on course, Volante shifted in her chair. 'You want to tell me what happened tonight?'

The fragility of her smile gave way to subdued solemnity. 'Sorry,' she said. 'I wasn't even thinking. You've obviously...'—she glanced around the room, then bit her lip, shaking her head as though it would shake loose the phrase she was looking for—'...got plans?' Brows lifted in question and her piercing glinted in the candlelight.

Volante allowed herself a smile. 'He's great. He's *late*,' she said, her voice lifting as she glanced at the clock (*Jesus, the TIME*, she thought), 'but he's great.'

Heidi nodded. 'I get it. You wanted to do something special for him. He's gotta be some kind of special, right? For you to go to all this trouble?' She fussed with her hands in her lap. 'I wanted something like that. But you know how those arguments go. You want him to give more of himself, and he says he's already giving you enough and something that sounds like "what more do you want from me?"' She breathed an open-mouthed sigh, her gaze slightly vacant. 'We keep going around in circles with it, but it's always kind of alright—for a while, you know?'

Volante nodded. She and Trayvon had their share of arguments, and if she was being truthful with herself, they were usually due to her short temper. What she *was* trying to do now though was remember if she had actually told Heidi her name.

'So, we were walking down this little side street when he cuddled me. Said he was in the mood. I said we needed to talk. You know, when you get a guy's motor running, it's hard to keep him on track.' Volante shot her an eye roll and a thin smile of unspoken agreement borne of considerable experience. 'He didn't want to listen. He didn't want to listen.' Heidi's voice cracked, and she drew her cheek up to her shoulder while she averted her gaze. 'I asked him to stop— but he didn't. He kept pulling at my clothes, forcing himself on me.'

Volante leaned forward, slowly, assessing the damage. The rip through the hem of the dress was frayed and diagonal, leading back over one of Heidi's thighs. One side of the rip had torn sideways; possibly where the man had grabbed the fabric to pull it apart.

'I hit him. Ran away. You know, in those cheesy horror films, the woman screams. I couldn't.' Heidi shook her head, her crimped locks swaying. 'I couldn't do anything except run. I must have stopped when I lost him.' Candlelight lent a yellowing sheen to her eyes, and her gaze clouded. She reached for her wine glass, stroking the base of the stem where it stood. 'It's like the hero of the piece trying to get into Croglin Grange without a key, so they unpick the lead'—she mimed with her forefinger—'from one of the window panes and get in that way.' She eased her hand back, palm down, spreading her fingers. 'Nails like these, I couldn't even pick my nose.' She propped her elbow on her knee and rested her forehead in her hand. Her head swivelled across her palm and she sighed, releasing a faint rasp that along with the ticking of the clock was the only sound to break the heavy silence.

Volante stole another glance at the clock, alarmed to see that at least another half hour had passed without any sign of Trayvon. Not that he'd object to Heidi's presence, but she could hardly stay there all night. *So...*'Should I call you a cab—or call the police now? It would still give you a chance to freshen up.' Would the police need to take DNA or something before Heidi cleaned herself up? Volante wasn't sure.

A brief inhalation, as if considering a response. 'No, that's okay,' she sighed. She swept her hand across her forehead and tucked her hair back over her shoulder, a curtain of it falling back to frame the side of her face. 'It's not even my blood anyway.'

'Good for you!' Volante prided herself on assertiveness, and appreciated it in others. 'If he's stupid or crazy enough to try and force himself on you, then you go and scratch him or bite—'

'No, no, no. I mean it's Trayvon's.'

'Eh?'

'You heard me. It's Trayvon's.'

Volante's eyelids fluttered as she weighed the revelation. She craned her neck at the other woman, ensuring she wouldn't mishear anything. 'What? It's his?'

Heidi sat up in her chair, tossing her hair back in a practised manoeuvre. 'Okay, I'm going to show you something, but only if you keep a straight face. Okay?'

Volante gave a wary nod. Flickering candlelight, which started the evening as a seductive prelude, had now morphed into something eerie and ungainly.

Heidi slid one hand down the front of her dress, knuckles tenting the fabric as she fumbled between her breasts. She drew a vaguely cylindrical object out and placed it next to Volante's glass with reverence.

The first thought that entered Volante's mind on seeing the object was; *dog shit?* Closer scrutiny revealed loose and ragged crimson tissue at one end. A fingernail at the other. A silver ring just below the knuckle.

Nausea rose in her like a shorebound wave. 'Trayvon?'

Memories visited Volante in a fleeting yet vivid kaleidoscope: the first time she and Trayvon had kissed in a dark corner of Funki Necta, the diamante-look fascia he bought for her smartphone because she was always dropping it, the last time they made love, only for him to threaten her with a Dutch oven once they had both climaxed and relaxed, his deadpan expression when she told him about the latest reality TV show.

The severed finger on the table.

'Your scent was all over him. Faint, but it was enough. I just followed both trails here.'

Volante searched Heidi's face for the punchline, for something, anything that would explain the vulgarity on the table. Two yellowed eyes with pinprick pupils stared back at her above a snub nose of gaping nostrils; the nose looked more like the nasal cavity of a fleshless skull. Volante pursed her lips, struggling to keep from screaming, talking—even *swallowing*. Something told her any loud or sudden movement would end badly. Breathing began to feel like a conscious act.

Heidi folded her arms, tucking her hands into her armpits. The movement added to the swell of her breasts. 'Volante...you're getting me so thirsty right now.'

The sound of her name in the other woman's voice was jarring. Her lips parted but could form no words.

Thin lips, free of lipstick or gloss, curved in a smile. 'See, this is the predicament. Drinking is the easy thing. Not some glorified spirit,' Heidi said, tipping her head at the bottle, 'but blood. Warm...*divine* liquor.' She traced a finger down the length of her neck; a perverse metronome keeping time with the ticking of the clock. Her smile faded. 'You might get sweat or moisturiser first— like the bite of lime before a tequila shot. That's easy. What you savour, though, is how much fear you cultivate and actually taste when they take their last breath. That takes skill. And practice.'

She blinked. Her eyebrows gathered in a frown, and between parted lips, her tongue tip caressed the point of a fang. The finger held its position at the base of her neck. 'Do you know what I am?'

Lips pursed, Volante gave a slow, wide-eyed shake of the head. Not to respond in the negative, but simply because the enormity of her predicament proved too much to absorb at once. Unable to speak, her mouth drew into a wretched grimace.

Heidi planted her hands on the table and drew herself forward, with the slow deliberation of a cat stalking a mouse. The creases lining her cheeks from the sides of her nose deepened in a sneer. '*Liar.*'

Volante whimpered.

The enunciation of the word had been slow and deliberate, revealing fangs nearly an inch long instead of normal human canines. Volante already knew what Heidi was but simply couldn't bring herself to say it out loud. The rational mind balked at the idea of such things but had no problem rendering Volante as tense and taut as piano wire. Her heart hammered in her chest. Compounding the alarm was the fact that she had let Heidi into her home.

Invited? A wave of goosebumps crawled across her skin. Her bladder began to feel heavy. *Oh, God.*

Where Heidi's fingers had been splayed on the table's surface, she now eased her thumbs back and underneath its edge. 'Next question. Do you know what I'm capable of?'

Slowly, Volante let her head fall as if defeated. Without looking sideways, she weighed the room from the corner of her eye. Heidi sat adjacent to her and farther from the door, the door itself half-open—

'I can't say I admire your optimism. To be honest, I find it a little irritating that you're even thinking about it. I'd stay seated, if I were you.'

She bit her lip, frustrated. Frightened.

Terrified.

'Let's try again. Do you know what I'm capable of?'

Again, Volante shook her head, feeling tears well up in her eyes. Wood creaked, splintered and broke as Heidi tore off the edge of the table and cast it aside, its impact on the carpet prompting a yelp from Volante.

Nostrils flaring, Heidi's eyes half-closed. 'Mmmmm. You smell good.'

Heidi's arm whipped forward in a blur of speed, the hand locking around Volante's neck. Volante gagged and choked as she fought to pry the other woman's fingers off her throat, but the grip held firm with an inhuman strength. In her struggle to free herself, she knocked over the glasses, one shattering on the table, spilling its contents, the other falling to the floor with a trifling snap as the stem broke. Fruited scents of fermented grape seeped into the air. 'Don't think this would end any differently,' Heidi whispered. 'You're going to die here.'

The hand drew her forward until a few inches separated Volante from the yellow-eyed monstrosity before her. The thumb on her neck drew itself up to the base of her jaw and dug in. Shirking from the discomfort, Volante turned her head away...thereby exposing her neck. Realisation made her gasp as her bladder let go.

'See?' murmured Heidi. 'It needs to be cultivated just right.' She affected the tone of a lecturer satisfied that the lesson had been fully understood.

And then she sank her fangs into Volante's neck.

LANDSLIDE
Harris Coverley

Melissa woke at five-thirty that morning. Dan felt her rouse and sit up without the aid of the alarm, but he kept his eyes and mouth shut, sensing her just sat there, staring into nothing for minute after minute. The alarm went off at 6:15. Even though he had been awake the entire time, it still felt a terrible slog to reach out and switch it off before rising and slipping his naked legs over the edge of the bed, his toes landing on his slippers.

'Oh,' he said to her. 'You're up.'

'Mmmm,' Melissa replied blankly, not looking at him.

He wondered if she knew he'd been awake and waiting for the alarm. That would be just like her.

The appointment was for eight-thirty, but the drive was long and traffic unpredictable on the Snake Pass route to Sheffield. They ate a slice of brown toast each and drank a strong coffee at the kitchen table, before dressing in their most professional clothes—Dan a dark grey suit with a bright red-striped shirt, Melissa a navy pantsuit. His thick mop, greying a touch at the temples, was slicked back. Her dyed blonde hair was tied into a tight bun.

'Have you got the forms?' she asked him.

'They're in your handbag,' he replied.

'Are they?'

'Just check.'

She checked.

'They're not…'

It turned out that they were in the handbag, buried under some brochure, but he was too muggy to start an argument over it, as was she.

Everything else was double-checked, the back door relocked, and the front door banged shut at seven exactly, the noise echoing across their suburban close.

'Is there petrol in the tank?' Melissa asked on the driveway.

Dan replied, 'No, I thought we'd coast there.'

She looked at him with thin contempt before he admitted that he had filled up yesterday and that they should get going.

The drive through and out of town was quick and grey, the roads mostly empty but for a few lorries and the early morning buses. It had rained the night before, the dampness remaining.

They went up the big hill into high country, crossing the border into the Peake District, through Glossop onto the Snake Pass road across the moorlands.

On the high point by the Pennine Way trail, they passed several parked cars belonging to the most committed of hikers, and Dan shook his head.

'Crazy bastards,' he muttered.

Melissa was looking out her passenger side window. 'What was that?'

'Those hikers.'

'What about them?'

'They're mad, at this time, to be out there in this chill.'

'Mmmm...'

They had listened to the tail end of the news on BBC Radio Four, which had led into a documentary piece on black Canadian women's literature.

He had long vagued out from it, the volume low and non-intrusive. His mind turned back to some piebald horses in a keep they had passed a moment earlier. He recalled a hackneyed joke that someone had told him years ago: a husband and wife in bad spirits were travelling through the countryside and drove by a pastoral farm. The husband in an already acrimonious frame decided to have a go at his wife's family. 'You see those animals back there?' he asked. 'The pigs and the cows?' The wife answered. He then asked her, 'Do they remind you of any relatives?' To which she replied, 'Yeah—my in-laws!'

He chuckled and stopped. He knew now what would happen.

'What are you laughing at?' she asked him, snapping from her window.

'Nothing, just erm...' he struggled. He dare not tell her the joke—it cut too close to the bone.

'Just something that happened at work,' he recovered. 'It doesn't really—you'd have to have been there.'

'Why, what?' she insisted.

'Well, like I said—'

'What?'

He could see her eyes from the corner of his, piercing spikes forged from hazel glass.

'Well, erm, it was like the, erm, machine, the coffee machine, and it had run out of flat whites again, and we all thought it had been Kevin, 'cause he likes his flat whites, and erm, yeah, we just thought it was funny, me and James, and erm, yeah, it was that, just that.'

She stared at him some more and then turned the spikes away and back out of the passenger window.

'Yeah, well,' she said. 'I guess you're right—you had to be there.'

He breathed a soft sigh of relief.

As they descended from the moorland and entered the reclaimed forests, he planned their visit in his head. They would arrive just after eight. Park as close to the main building at Sheffield Hallam as possible, taking an acceptable hit on the ticket machine. Walk through to main reception and find out where the fertility clinic was—it had been a year since they had last visited and neither of them could remember where the place was within the labyrinthine complex of glass, redbrick, steel, wards, lifts, franchised shops, and giant dustbins. Get to the clinic in good time. Have appointment as close to the allotted time as appropriate. Either get a yes or a no on further treatment. Leave and be back home in time for lunch, or maybe have lunch there, depending on how Melissa was feeling.

The possibility of lunch at The Fox and Badger in Broomhill made him think—would there be time to pop into Clark's Groove Records? He had found himself listening to a lot of Brazilian hard rock and heavy metal online recently, and he was wondering if they might have anything on CD or even vinyl. Would they have the time? Would she allow it? It all depended on what the doctor would say—would things carry on or not, on or not, on or not...?

Dan had grown increasingly numb over time. Ten years earlier, he would have been ecstatic at the chance of fatherhood, devastated at a denial. Now, well, it was just another thing to do. An opportunity maybe to get a baby, that being *her* baby…

They were too old, sliding into middle age, married for fifteen years, but with the money to burn. Mortality creeping like a prowler in the bushes outside their comfortable new-build home. Broody—that was the term his father would have used for his wife, and he knew that he would have once vigorously denied being like his father, using his lingo, reflecting his values and his deeper meanings, but these days it was a different story. All things come in a damn circle—and yet still, where was the son to his fatherhood?

'Planned it all out,' Dan announced.

'Good,' Melissa said, implicitly knowing what he meant.

He considered leaning his hand over and putting it on her knee, but he thought better of it. She would most probably not appreciate it, even brush it away.

Watch the road, she would say, or something similar.

As they continued to descend, a hovering soup of mist abruptly enveloped them. He had his headlights on, but now he had to flick them onto full beam.

The mist kept getting thicker and steelier as they went down.

'Where the hell has this come from?'

'Mmmmm…watch it,' muttered Melissa, looking about.

He slowed down to a steady thirty miles per hour, well below the speed limit, taking the curves as easy as he could.

The road narrowed as they went through the invading pine forest, planted by local collaborators, the English oaks raped from the land centuries ago, and visibility beyond more than a dozen feet vanished utterly.

'Slow down, Dan.'.

'I'm going as slow as I can…'

'Go slower!' she snapped.

A series of sharper bends came up—always taking him by surprise even though he had driven the road many times—and they found themselves hurtling into a void, shaking from side to side.

'Stop!' Melissa shouted. 'Stop!'

'All right! All right!'

But it was too late. He came on a right curve through high patches of bushes on the sides of the road. He failed to see the temporary traffic light through the fog until a second before he was bound to hit it.

Melissa screamed.

He swerved right and stamped on the brake.

There was a colossal jolt and a great clanging wallop.

The engine stalled.

Dan opened his eyes and saw nothing but the fog through the windscreen.

He turned to Melissa. She was wrapped up in herself, shuddering.

'Are you okay?' He leaned over and felt her—she was shaken.

'Yeah,' she said, unclenching herself. 'Yeah, I'm just—just shocked. What about you?'

Dan felt his neck—he had escaped another nasty whiplash. He would never forget that car accident in his early thirties.

They had crashed against something relatively soft, and they were wedged on top of it, at an angle.

Melissa's fear gave way to a wave of rage.

'You stupid, stupid twat!' she yelled. 'What do you think you were playing at?'

'Look, it's okay, we're okay,' he puffed. 'Let me get out and take a look and—'

'You could have killed me—*us*, us!'

'Well, thank Christ, I haven't. Let me get out and—'

He opened the door with difficulty against the tilt, having to lean against it to slide out.

'I told you to slow down!'

'Just stay a moment!'

'What have you done?'

'Shit, I'm trying to find that out!'

Dan's polished dress shoes hit the tarmac.

He grinned to himself nervously as he noted the individual red road barrier they had hit. Set as part of a line, the left side of it was crumpled and lifted their left front wheel. The barrier's concrete base was certainly solid—the impact had only moved it an inch at most.

But what were the barriers protecting against?

He peered over the line of barriers and felt giddy. The grin faded.

No tarmac could be seen through the mist a couple of feet beyond the barrier line. There had clearly been a gigantic landslide, tearing away a third of the road for a stretch of thirty-odd metres. This had left a murky cliff face going straight down into a dank muddy pit. Straining to see through the mist, Dan could make out a lumpy pile of detritus streaked with an ochre clay at the bottom.

'It's a big hole out of the road!' he called to Melissa.

'Oh my god!' were the words he read on her lips through the windscreen.

'It must have fallen away in bad weather.'

It was odd—he had heard no reports of a landslide, and there had been no warning signs posted on the road. There were no workmen or any signs of attempted repair, only the barrier line itself.

Dan looked over to the other side of the road. The light had been a temporary traffic light on a frame to control the flow of vehicles through the narrowed road. It had switched from red to green and had now returned to red. He walked around the car to take a closer look at the damage. The crimson Ford Focus was a decade old, but it was Dan's pride and preference. He was relieved to find the damage was minor—his loyal mode of transport had suffered some scrapes, and likely the bumper would need replacing, but it would not fall off if driven away, and there appeared to be no axle or wheel damage. Even the headlight was sound, beaming onwards against the blanket of vapour.

He tapped on Melissa's window and she opened the door.

'Seems okay,' he said to her with confidence.

'What are we going to do?'

'We're going to reverse off the barrier.'

'Dan, I think we need to call somebody…'

'No, no, I can fix this.' He checked his phone. 'Besides, there's no bloody signal down here.'

'Can't you find somebody?'

He looked up and down the road, or at least what remained of it, but he could see no lights. He could not hear the sound of an engine or tyres on tarmac either.

'The whole place is dead,' he concluded

She began, '*We* will be dead if—'

Dan closed her door to escape her comment and rushed back around the car. He got into the driver's seat, put the car into neutral, and turned the key in the ignition.

'What are you doing?' she asked.

'Like I said, I'm going to drive it straight back off.'

'You can't do that!'

'It's easy!'

The engine turned over and started up under protest.

'Look, just calm down,' he said.

'You're telling me to calm down!' Melissa shouted, grabbing his arm.

He ignored her, put the car in reverse and gunned it.

The front wheels spun, the left whirling into the heavy plastic, the right burning rubber against the road.

'Stop, Dan!' she cried. 'Stop it!'

'Nearly there!' he replied, hoping the car was on the cusp of wrenching off and away.

He pressed the accelerator further as the ground at the front of the car suddenly quivered.

She howled and grabbed him. 'It's going! It's going!'

He pulled his foot off the pedal and the engine stalled.

They threw themselves out of the car and rushed back behind it, worried the car would go over the edge with them in it

They waited in silence for a few seconds, before walking to the front. Nothing had changed—the car had not moved, nor the barrier, nor the ground in front of it.

'I said you couldn't do it!' she snapped.

Dan shook his head. 'The bloody thing is just jammed in too tight. There's no traction.'

'We have to get somebody!'

'I told you my phone has no signal—what about yours?'

She got her handbag from the car and searched it.

'It's…it's not there.'

'What?'

'I must've left it at home.'

'Again?'

She scowled at him.

He looked around again. Vehicles could easily pass between their car and the light. They were not blocking the road. He recognised the walls and the fencing on the roadside and had an idea.

'I think the Snake Pass Inn is around the corner,' he said and walked over to the barrier. He squinted. The fog was now beginning to clear and he could make out the top of an adjoining hill. He went around the barrier, still squinting, and approached the edge.

'Are you insane?' Melissa shouted. 'The earth just tremored! The whole place is unsafe!'

'No way!' he dismissed, not turning to face her. 'That was probably just the car juddering…we freaked out just then.'

'Dan!'

'I think…I can see…we can walk there and—' Then the edge crumbled away and he lost his footing. He fell, his backside hitting the edge, his legs floating, and Melissa gasped as he slid down the steep incline on his back.

He landed in a muddy depression and for a moment had no idea what had happened, as if he had lost and regained consciousness on the way down. His head hurt like hell, so there was no doubt in his mind he had hit it against something hard.

He tried to gain his bearings and realised he was up against the pile of soil he'd noticed from above.

'Dan!' Melissa yelled. 'Dan! Can you hear me?'

She could not see him for she dared not to go further than the barrier.

'Yes!' he yelled back, wiping mud from his face. He felt the back of his head and groaned.

'Are you okay?'

'Yeah, yeah, I think so…I landed in earth. Soft and damp.'

'Oh…well in that case, you're—you're an idiot! What d'yer think yer playing at? You could've had us both over!'

'Thank you, love. I hadn't considered that.'

'What are we gonna do now?'

He pushed himself to his feet, uneasy and addled with a fresh headache, but not worse than one of his usual stress migraines.

Much of the earth had slid further down the hill into a stream. To his right there was an opening onto grass, and just down the slope a broken pathway leading into the trees.

He remembered there was a stile for hikers going through the woods.

'There's a pathway down here!' he yelled up into the mist.

'What?'

'A pathway! It goes up to the side of the road!'

'So?'

'So I can walk up it and come back to you!'

'How long will you take?'

'How should I know?! Maybe a few minutes…'

'What should I do?'

'Don't do a thing! Just wait in the car!'

'But what if it starts to move again?'

'It won't! Just stay in the car!'

'Are you sure you're okay?'

He moved forward and pain shot up through his right ankle—he had sprained it no doubt, but it was manageable.

'I said I'm fine!' he lied. 'Just stay there!'

'But what about the—!'

'Show me your hand!'

'What!'

'Just show me your hand! I want to know that you're safe!'

'But what if—'

'Just lean over the bloody barrier! Stretch it out! I'll see it!'

He could still make out the edge of the crack some twelve feet up. He sensed her hesitation, but a moment later, an arm poked above the dark line.

'Okay, go wait in the car.'

The arm vanished and he heard a car door clap shut a moment later.

Getting his wife to do anything in an emergency was hard, but now he had to negotiate this mountain of morass.

His ankle throbbed as he inched his way through the squelching loam, clacking against loose stones, mindful of the dirt trickling down the incline behind him. He looked into the pile, hateful of it. It did not look natural at all. Up close, it seemed a little too rectangular, synthetic. In fact, he quickly came to realise that it did not belong to the natural world at all—it was mostly metal.

'What the hell is this?' he asked.

Dan gradually tracked around the flatter side to a more pointed end, and he recognised a wheel just above his head—it was a car.

How did a car get in here? Had it been involved in the initial landslide? Why would it be left here like this?

A chill went up his spine. What if it had crashed into the disaster zone like they had? Had it driven into the mud off the crack from the other end of the road? Could there be…? But no, the barriers were all in place, except for the one he had hit—it made no sense.

Dan brushed away a patch of soil and rapped on the bonnet. 'Hello! Anyone in there?'

He got no response, even from Melissa up above, isolated in their own car.

He chuckled—he was being silly. The whole situation had shaken him up something rotten. He probably needed a trip to a hospital—and he chuckled again: he was already on his way to a hospital!

Goodbye clinic appointment, he thought.

His knocking on the bonnet had caused some of the dirt to fall away—the car was a reddish colour, crimson perhaps. He saw also that it was a Ford, apparently of the newer generation of Focus hatchbacks, just like his.

He shook his head. 'It could have been worse, way worse, I can see it clearly…'

Out of pure curiosity, he wiped away the layer of soil on the number plate, just to see how old it was, fresh mud caking his fingernails.

He read it: BD12 RDE.

For the first time in his life, he instantly remembered his car's registration number—no, not remembered, but *recognised*—because it was the very same as the one on the plate before him.

His sweat turned cold as the car rattled from within.

'What the—?'

He stumbled back into the ditch beneath the encrusted underside of the half-buried car.

'Hello?' he cried. 'Is anyone in there?'

Soil slid from near the top of the mound.

'It's okay! I'll help you out!'

Something inside Dan told him to run. The whole thing was just too weird, too uncanny—why the hell did this car have his registration plate? He could not though. He could not just limp away as fast as his sprained ankle would allow. Someone in a terrible mess needed help.

189

There was movement again, then dirt and clay and pebbles rained down as the driver's door opened, sweeping upwards on an angle.

Dan, slathered in muck and perspiration and looking up like a tiny child to a towering parent, saw against the eternal haze of the Snake Pass fog a figure in a clean grey suit rise…

#

Melissa waited, tapping her knees, no phone to amuse her, yet also too anxious to turn on the radio. She looked at the clock on the driver's side. It had been about ten minutes since Dan talked to her from down there.

'What's taking him so long?' she asked aloud.

What if things had taken a turn for the worse down there? Or what if something had happened on his way up the path?

She was selfish, she thought. A good wife would have searched for her husband through thick and thin, mud and bullets, fog and fire. She was sat there like a lump, a *barren* lump—the thought nearly had her cry.

She flipped it around. On the other hand, would a good husband drive like such a maniac? Be so reckless?

Her train of thought was interrupted by movement in the rear-view mirror. A passing car to flag down? A hiker or a cyclist?

She looked over her shoulder. Dan!

At this, everything was forgiven. A flood of love and gratitude engulfed her, and she really did cry. She rushed out of the car and walked as fast as she could on her high heels towards her husband.

'Oh, Dan!' she wept. 'Dan! I was so worried! Are you all right? Let me see!'

But she stopped five feet away from him—something was wrong. She sized him up—he was grinning, his hands in his jacket pockets. His clothes were spotless. Not a splash of mud on him.

He looked at her with bright eyes—yet they were empty and soulless, making her think of a freshly painted room void of furniture or decoration.

'Dan?' she asked, tears dripping down scarlet cheeks. 'Dan? What the—what is it?'

The man tutted, rocked on his heels, and stood aside, his back to the hill's slope.

Out of the mist came another figure, smaller, hips swinging.

The pantsuit, navy, clean, strands and specks brushed away. The hair, blonde; the bun tight. The mouth grinning like the husband's was.

Melissa stared at the woman and was vaguely aware of the man's words. 'Get a good look, because that's all for now!'

He took Melissa by her shoulders and rushed her backwards.

She was too stunned by what she saw to resist.

Her shoes clattered along the road and she screamed only when the back of her stocking-clad legs hit the barrier.

She toppled over the edge and disappeared into the mist.

#

The man was able to wedge a bit of rubber under the wheel, which was just enough to angle it off the crushed barrier when he reversed the car.

Before getting in, the woman gave him a round of applause.

Deciding it was roadworthy, he backed up to the temporary traffic light and waited for it to turn green before setting off, passing a saloon car waiting on the other side.

'The fog's clearing now,' he said, taking it gently around the corners.

'Good,' she said. 'I hate the fog.'

'We're probably gonna be late at this rate.'

'Mmmm, most likely. But it's okay. We'll wait, they'll see us. And if not, we can always reschedule.'

'Sure. There's no rush.'

His palm resting on the gear stick, she stroked her dainty hand over it.

'I love you,' she smiled.

'And I love you,' he replied, flashing his eyes to meet hers, but not leaving the road for any longer than necessary.

HOLIDAY HOME
Cameron Trost

Pierre brought his silver Porsche Boxster to a halt and stared through the windscreen at the padlocked wooden gates to the Garnier family holiday home. His car's bright LED headlights ruthlessly exposed every scratch and crack in the wooden gates and made the lichen and moss on the granite gateposts glow eerily. It was a dark January evening and the first time he'd left his chic Parisian flat for the wild coast of southern Brittany outside of the high season when "the August people" came in hordes. He wondered whether he hadn't made a mistake—the sky was more menacing than he'd expected and the darkness suffocating for someone used to passing the winter in The City of Lights—but after driving for six hours with only two short toilet breaks, it was too late. He fished for the key to the padlock in the right pocket of his St Marius jacket but his smartphone started vibrating in the left pocket. He pulled it out, saw that it was his fiancée calling, and marvelled at how she'd somehow sensed he'd arrived at that very moment.

'Darling, I've only just arrived. I haven't even opened the gate yet. How do you do it?'

'What can I say? We're soulmates.'

He rolled his eyes. He'd gone to mass every Sunday with his grandparents, even at the local church in Mesquer when the family was on holiday together, but he'd never believed in souls or spirits, and he was quite certain his grandpapa hadn't either, even if perhaps grandmama had.

'Soulmates indeed,' he answered. 'You're something else, Appoline. You really are.'

'Such a cynic. Call me when you're settled in.'

'I will.' A gust of wind whistled around the car. 'I hope there's some firewood.'

'Why would there be if no one ever goes there in winter?'

He frowned. 'Good point.'

'I packed a goose down duvet for you,' she reminded him. 'It will keep you warm.'

'You'd keep me warm, darling.'

'I'll be there in a week,' she said softly. 'It's not so long. You need to prepare the nest for your little hen—and don't forget to buy plenty of Lady's favourite dog biscuits and treats. She loves you so much.'

Pierre rolled his eyes—an act he never dared perform in front of his fiancée. 'More than you love me?'

'It's possible.' She laughed. 'No—don't be silly, honey. No one loves you more than I do.'

'She'll think she's in heaven here.' He shook his head—at least long walks along the beach would keep the two females busy. 'I'll stock up on Carnilove for her. Call you back in a few minutes, darling.'

'*Bisous*.'

Pierre ended the call and slipped the phone back into his pocket before fishing the key out and opening the driver's door. He got out and pulled his collar up to stop the chill air from biting his face and neck as he hurried over to the padlock. He inserted the key and twisted it, slipped the chain away, and pushed the gate open.

The headlights lit up the granite walls of the three-storey holiday home, making the white shutters shine like beacons in the night. The garden all around, with it's unkempt laurel hedges and towering maritime pines, was lost in obscurity, and the dormant camellias and hydrangeas he knew were there remained unseen. Beyond the house, only a faint line of retreating orange sunlight glowed on the cold horizon, and Pierre realised that once it had sunk out of sight, it would be as if nothing else existed out there at all.

It seemed like another world from the one he'd always known— sailing trips from the hidden port at Toul'Ru, swimming and sunbathing, and those summer nights with champagne and cocktails on the terrace followed by a barbecue or a seafood platter for dinner. He knew it wouldn't be quite the same, and night was closing in after all, but he hadn't been expecting it to feel so very *foreign*. The coast was a ghost town now. Not one of the extravagant abodes perched along the ten-metre-high sea cliff was occupied. It was a long and winding row of magnificent homes with every door securely bolted and every window shuttered.

He glanced around but shook off the feeling of discomfort before it could worm its way too deep into his consciousness. He'd go inside, give Appoline a quick call, and get settled in for the night. Daylight would remind him he'd made the right choice and that he'd be more productive working online for however long it took his lawyers to deal with the brouhaha in Paris.

He got back into his Porsche and parked it by the three timeworn stone steps leading up to the front door, then walked back to close the gate and slip the bolt into place. He took a small torch from the boot and switched it on, then grabbed his overnight bag and the pillow and duvet Appoline had prepared for him.

He opened the door to the house and the mustiness hit him before he'd even set foot inside—he'd have to air the place out first thing in the morning. The priority for now, however, was calling Appoline back and getting settled in for the night. A light meal and a glass of whatever looked good from the cellar would get him through to morning. He used his torch to find the electrical panel in the hall and switched the mains on. No lights came on, so he navigated his way through to the sitting room and located the light switch. He'd forgotten where it was—it was seldom necessary in summer—but he found it just above waist-height near the doorway.

Soft light from a single low-wattage bulb flooded the room and he was relieved to find that everything was as it had been five months ago. He'd heard of holiday homes being vandalised by locals who resented the prime real estate along the coast being left empty most of the year while working families struggled to find adequate housing. Perhaps worse than that was the risk of squatters breaking in and setting up camp. Eviction was a long and complicated procedure, especially during the winter truce. But it was clear that nothing at all had been touched since the summer. It was as though time held no sway in this borderland—a world trapped between land and sea, almost literally teetering at the cliff's edge. The only difference was the unfathomable darkness never experienced by the

August people.

Pierre glanced around the sitting room. The shutters were all closed. He would open them in the morning to let fresh air in and to appreciate the sea view, whatever the weather. There was a dusty bookshelf on the inside wall, opposite the windows, and the hi-fi they put on to dance the summer evenings away to—Charles Aznavour's obligatory holiday classic echoed through his head: '*Emmenez-moi au bout de la terre. Emmenez-moi au pays des merveilles...*' There was no television but the radio would be his source of local news, and the modem was the key to having the internet connection needed to work from home. There was no electric heating in the holiday house, but a smile crept onto his lips as he saw three small logs, a pile of dry twigs, and a box of matches by the fireplace at the far end of the room. That would be enough to keep him warm for that first night. He'd pull a mattress close—but not too close—to the fireplace and wrap himself up in the duvet.

Once the fire was blazing, he nestled onto the sofa and called Appoline.

#

Pierre's phone alarm woke him at eight. He'd slept well curled up in the duvet by the fire, but he'd put the third log on around midnight and it was now cold. He got up and switched the light on, then opened the windows and shutters. Dawn had not yet broken, but it wouldn't be long now. Of course, sunset was the glorious sight to behold from the house, but judging by the chill, damp breeze that confirmed the weather forecast displayed on his phone, he knew there probably wouldn't be much of a show that evening.

He left the sea breeze to fill the sitting room and retreated to the kitchen to fix himself a pot of coffee. The first order of business was to get his hands on a supply of firewood, and he regretted not phoning a local supplier in advance. He'd also need to buy some groceries.

He took his laptop into the kitchen and began sifting through the dozen emails he'd received during the night. Two cups of strong coffee later, he could see that the first glimmer of weak daylight now reached over the house and was chasing the darkness from the western horizon, so that the grey of the sky could be distinguished from that of the sea.

He closed the sitting-room windows, got dressed, and ventured outside to see if there was more firewood stacked in the garden shed.

The shed door groaned but gave way and Pierre spotted five logs and a wicker basket full of kindling wedged between the Bosch lawnmower and three kayaks. That would only be enough to get him through another evening, and with the weather the way it was, he'd want to light a fire long before dark. He looked around the shed and couldn't help but reminisce. The kayaks in particular held so many fond memories of exploring the coast with Georges and Constance. The three Garnier children used to visit sea caves and clamber up rocky escarpments, but they hadn't touched the kayaks in years. They'd lost that adventurous spirit over time.

At some point, the Porsche Boxster had replaced the kayak as Pierre's vehicle of choice, even in the summer—especially then, in fact. He made a promise to himself right then that he'd take his bright yellow kayak down to the beach and go for a paddle as soon as the weather improved. First of all, it was the Boxster that begged his attention.

He locked the house, drove the car out, and asked himself where he could find someone to deliver firewood. There wasn't another car in the street. No one walking dogs or going for a jog either. There was no sign of life whatsoever. He shivered, turned up the heating, and started along the road towards the oyster port of Kercabellec. He'd find locals there, perhaps at the Café du Port—if there was one thing he knew about provincials, it was that they never did an ounce of work without a dose of alcohol in the bloodstream. He could grab a dozen fresh oysters for lunch while he was there.

Five minutes later, Pierre parked next to a muddy tractor and trailer used for oyster farming. The contrast couldn't have been starker, and it didn't go unnoticed by the two men in green waders smoking and sipping white wine outside the café. One was in his late fifties or early sixties and puffing a pipe. The other—possibly his son, but there was no telling in these villages where everyone was somehow related—was in his thirties and had a rollie sagging from his lips. They were both staring at the sports car as though it were an oyster gone bad.

196

Pierre pretended not to notice as he got out and approached. He nodded and said hello, to which they grunted a reply, and entered the café to find the proprietor staring at the television fixed to the far wall, pretending he hadn't noticed the Parisian in his Porsche. He was making it clear he was listening intently to the weather report warning of dangerous conditions due to gale-force winds and a spring tide. He eventually acknowledged Pierre's presence and unenthusiastically greeted him with a *bonjour*.

Pierre returned the greeting and glanced around the bar, noting the tables set with upturned wine glasses and paper serviettes. Apart from the two smoking outside, there were no other clients, but perhaps the café was a hive of activity come noon.

'What can I get you?' He looked Pierre up and down, wondering what these rich types drank at nine o'clock in the morning—coffee with hand-picked beans from some sacred valley in Peru?

Pierre decided to surprise him. 'A muscadet.'

The proprietor suppressed a wry grin, took a small glass, and poured from the bottle he'd no doubt opened for the two regulars outside. He filled the glass to the brim, but not a drop overflowed, and he didn't ask Pierre to pay, assuming there'd be at least one more glass consumed.

The oyster farmers came inside and Pierre made sure he didn't make a fool of himself by spilling a drop as he raised the glass to his lips. Served a bit too cold but the wine was otherwise rather nice in fact. The two locals placed their glasses on the counter for a refill. The younger one rubbed his beard and looked sideways at the Parisian while the older one nodded vaguely at him, a hint of curiosity in the stoic grey eyes set on a weatherworn face.

The proprietor broke the uneasy silence once he'd filled the two glasses to the brim.

'Passing through?' he asked.

Pierre sipped as he considered his reply, but there was no way he could ask about firewood without letting them know who he was.

'I needed a break from Paris,' he admitted.

All three nodded appreciatively. Air pollution, constant noise, and immigrant gangs running amok. How could anyone live like that?

'I'm working from home for a while,' Pierre went on.

The older of the oyster farmers frowned. 'How's that?'

197

'Over the internet, you know.'

But he clearly didn't.

'You have a holiday home here?' the proprietor asked.

It wasn't hostility Pierre heard in his voice, but something else, and the three men exchanged an enigmatic look.

'Yes.' There was no holding back now. 'My family have a house along the coast, not far from Toul'Ru.'

Again the look between them, and Pierre had the dreadful feeling for a moment that they were waiting for him to invite them over.

'First time here in winter?' the proprietor asked. He ran a hand across the few remaining strands of hair on his head and turned his attention to the television. A reporter was interviewing a man wearing the unmistakable orange jacket of the national search and rescue organisation. Snow-white stubble covered his face, and there was an incongruously dark look in his eyes as blue as an August day.

'It is,' Pierre replied, draining his glass and placing it on the counter.

'It's a different world here during the off-season,' the younger oyster farmer mused.

'Almost unrecognisable. The weather isn't pleasant.'

Silence as they sipped their muscadet.

'There's no heating in the holiday home, for example, and I don't have any firewood. I was wondering if there was a way of getting a load delivered.'

'Ah...' the proprietor said, looking at the others meaningfully, finally understanding why this rich Parisian had come to the café—he needed help, of course.

'It must get terribly cold in those huge coastal houses once winter sets in,' the older oyster farmer said, the mock sympathy almost too subtle to be noticed. 'No need for electric or gas heating since they're abandoned before the first day of September.'

Pierre smiled awkwardly.

The proprietor picked up his land-line phone and made a call.

Once there was an answer at the other end, he made some small talk, asking about storm damage, and then explained the situation.

Pierre couldn't hear the voice at the other end but the supplier must have made a joke at his expense. The proprietor burst out laughing. The oyster farmers sipped their muscadet and watched

Pierre, gauging his reaction.

'I can get a cord of wood delivered Wednesday.'

'Wednesday?' Pierre asked wide-eyed. 'Today's Friday. I can't wait until Wednesday.'

The proprietor shrugged.

'Tell him I need it today. Tomorrow at the latest.'

He frowned. 'He says—oh, you heard?' He listened. 'I'll tell him.'

'Yes?' Pierre asked sharply.

'He'll have to rearrange his schedule if you want the wood today, and he won't be able to help you stack it. It won't be cheap.'

Three pairs of eyes fixed on Pierre. He knew this game—everyone loved to play "Milk the Rich Man".

'How much?' he asked, rolling his eyes.

'Eight hundred euros.'

'*Eight hundred* for a cord?'

'A cord delivered express,' the proprietor said flatly. 'Your call.'

It meant peanuts to Pierre but he didn't like being taken for a ride. Nevertheless, he wasn't going to give them the pleasure of getting worked up. 'It's a deal.'

'Address?' the proprietor asked.

Pierre hesitated before giving the street name and number.

The proprietor stared at the phone for a moment, his brow furrowed, and Pierre couldn't help but wince. The fleeting expression didn't go unnoticed by the oyster farmers.

'That's *Penn-Avel*, isn't it?' the proprietor asked.

The Garniers never bothered to refer to the house by its Breton name. Pierre couldn't even remember the meaning.

'It will live up to its name tonight!' He laughed, and the two others joined him.

Pierre recalled the meaning. *Windy Headland.*

The laughs soon faded into uncomfortable silence, broken by the proprietor making sure the address had been received and then hanging up.

'Early afternoon. Payment in cash.'

'Understood,' Pierre replied, knowing what was coming next.

'You're Garnier's grandson?'

'That's correct,' Pierre said quietly. He'd been hoping the proprietor wouldn't realise, but memories live long in a place like this. It had happened twenty-three years ago. Pierre had been a mere child, but he'd never forget—the worse oil slick to hit this stretch of the coast—an unprecedented environmental disaster. The beach had been cleaned of oil, debris, and countless dead fish, gulls, and cormorants by the time he'd arrived for the following summer holiday, but the stain would never be removed from the hearts of the locals.

'Your father is the chairman now?'

Pierre drew a deep breath—he was losing his patience now—but he let it out slowly and simply nodded. 'He is, but I'm not on the board. I have no interest in shipping. I work in media.'

'Oh.' The proprietor turned to the others. They replied with a shrug but didn't say what they were thinking. *Well, that's that then—no oil on his soft Parisian hands.*

'One more for the road?'

'Thank you, but I'd best be off,' Pierre said, fishing out his wallet.

'Suit yourself. Four euros, please.'

'We'd better get back to work,' the older of the oyster farmers said, slapping the younger on the shoulder. 'Our table set for lunch, Patrick?'

'You bet. Ready for the storm?'

'Always ready.'

Patrick turned to Pierre. 'Be careful if you go down to the beach this afternoon. This one's likely to be worse than the last. The Mor Braz has a vengeful streak. We wouldn't want anything to happen to you, would we? Best steer clear of the shore altogether. A young chap drowned during the storm.'

'I thought I heard that on the news.' Pierre nodded at the television. 'What was he doing out in stormy weather?'

The younger of the oyster farmers huffed and the older placed a hand on his shoulder again—not a slap this time but a gentle reminder.

'It's getting harder to make ends meet for a lot of folks,' Patrick explained as though talking to a dull child. 'Inflation and all that. It's particularly tough for fishermen. You have to work when you can, and sometimes a storm hits hard and fast.'

Pierre remained unconvinced. It sounded like the skipper had made a bad call, with fatal consequences.

The oyster farmers were still at the bar, waiting to hear the end of the conversation.

'The sea claims who she wishes,' Patrick said gravely, as though imparting some profound wisdom.

Pierre resisted pointing out the glaring flaw in logic. The sea could only claim those souls who venture out in wild weather, and Patrick had just warned him to be careful and stay off the beach until the storm had passed, thus admitting that his safety was in his own hands.

'It's worse every time,' the younger oyster farmer complained.

'We need to take action,' the older said firmly.

Patrick frowned but didn't reply. Likewise, Pierre decided to keep his mouth shut. He wasn't going to waste his breath explaining to them that it was already too late to stop climate change, and that if for argument's sake anyone did have the power to make a difference, it certainly wasn't them.

The oyster farmers bid farewell and left. Pierre offered Patrick a smug smile and thanked him for his sage advice, making sure the hint of sarcasm was noticeable, before saying goodbye.

As he left, he realised he'd forgotten to ask about buying a dozen oysters. It was too late now—the tractor was already trundling away. He kept walking, and when he reached his Porsche, he noticed a long smear of mud covering the lower part of the driver's side from under the rear-view mirror all the way to the rear wheel.

'Fucking peasants,' he muttered to himself. 'I'll buy my oysters at the supermarket, and I'll use the self-checkout.'

#

The storm warning hadn't been an exaggeration. The wind picked up shortly after midday with gusts buffeting the windows and making them rattle. He'd bought oysters at Carrefour, withdrawn eight-hundred euros in cash to pay for the firewood, and washed his car at the automatic car wash. Arriving home, he'd left the garden gate open and enjoyed the oysters, washing them down with a glass of chablis. After that, he'd lost himself in his work until he heard a lorry reversing up the drive just before two o'clock. He rushed outside to make sure the supplier didn't dump it too close to his

Porsche.

A head with a messy mop of hair as dark as seaweed and a face as pale as a cuttlebone peered back from through the window. He stopped, applied the handbrake, and jumped down from the lorry. He said hello as he joined Pierre at the rear and surveyed a flat spot of ground between the steps to the house and the trunk of a maritime pine. 'Here's good?'

'Yes,' Pierre said.

He climbed back into the lorry and the tray began to tip. 'Stand clear!' he shouted, shaking his head.

Pierre knew he was already a safe distance away but took a couple of steps back just to please him.

The wood began to slide slowly before picking up speed and coming down like a landslide.

The supplier jumped down again, walked over to Pierre without a word, and put his hand out for the cash.

'Any chance you can give me a little help?'

The smile was unadulterated mock sympathy. 'Very sorry, but the storm's only going to get worse and I have a lot to do.'

Pierre sighed loudly as he pulled the notes from his pocket.

The supplier brushed a twisted lock of hair from his eyes before taking the money and counting the notes aloud. 'One, two, three, four, five, six, seven, eight. Thank you, sir. Best put a couple of logs on now if you want this big old place warm before evening.'

Pierre grunted and took a log in each hand. By the time he came back for the next two, the lorry had disappeared.

He stacked forty logs by the fireplace, took a break and made himself a cup of coffee, then went back and stacked another forty inside the garden shed. The wind was growing and it carried cold rain with a spattering of hail now. The top branches of the maritime pines were thrashing wildly and he was worried one might come crashing down on top of him. What would Patrick and the oyster farmers have to say about that once news the Parisian had been killed in the garden of his holiday home reached Kercabellec? They would probably have a good laugh over a glass of muscadet—or something stronger.

He decided it was best to retreat to the sitting room, and once he'd got a fire going, he pulled a chair up to the window to watch the show. He'd never seen the sea so agitated. Beyond the gorse hedge, there was nothing but the endless expanse of green water rising and falling. No sooner had a foamy peak formed in one place than it dispersed, only to be replaced by another here, and there, and now there, over and over—impossible to count. Pierre couldn't help but think of the dead fisherman and how foolish it was to go out at all when a storm was forecast. Looking around now, he saw no boats. Apart from the sea, there was only a low rocky reef about half a mile offshore. It had always been there, of course, but he'd never seen it like this—white sprays of salty water rising high into the air as wave after wave crashed into it.

From the safety of the sitting room, with the trembling window pane protecting him from the unrelenting wind, the onslaught was exhilarating to behold.

For several hours, he alternated between watching the storm, tending to the fire, and getting some work done. The legal team was dealing with the situation in Paris. When you worked in media and came from a notable family, accusations of corruption were an occupational hazard—much like going overboard was for a fisherman. He called the head lawyer and was reassured they were making headway. All he had to do was stay put and take advantage of being at the beach. Pierre rolled his eyes but didn't bother to ask the lawyer whether he'd ever been to Brittany in winter.

The sun hadn't made much of an appearance that day—not even a cameo—but the faintly glowing patch of cloud that had been slowly sinking towards the horizon suddenly drowned some time after five o'clock. Darkness set in and it soon became difficult to distinguish the sky from the sea. The distant red and green pinpricks of bobbing buoys were the only sources of light to be found. His day's work would be far from finished in the city, but time felt different here, at times slower, but then quite abruptly fast-forwarded. Without streetlamps and illuminated shopfronts, it seemed night had fallen like the blade of a guillotine.

Pierre went to the kitchen and poured himself a glass of chablis. He stopped by the rattling window and considered closing the shutters but decided to keep that eye on the sea open. He switched the reading lamp by the bookshelf on, turned the main light off, and stoked the fire, then decided to put the radio on to get the latest news on the storm. It had died down a little in late afternoon but judging by the rattling of the shutters and window, the wind was growing again, coming in violent gusts.

After a string of advertisements for local businesses, there was an update on the storm. It was intensifying with the spring tide, the announcer explained, which would reach its peak in an hour's time. There were power outages to an estimated ten thousand households, and one unoccupied car had been crushed by a falling tree limb near Damgan. No loss of life had been reported. Inhabitants were warned to stay indoors.

'Don't go fishing for fuck's sake,' Pierre murmured to himself, shaking his head.

He checked his phone, wanting to call Appoline, but there was no network signal. No internet either. Thank heavens for old-fashioned radio. He walked along the bookshelf, sipping his wine and browsing the books, most of which had been bought over the years by his grandfather. They touched on nautical matters by and large—the old man's lifeblood.

Blood. Oil. Life... Death.

He missed the old man. Hardly warm and cuddly, but he'd shown his love for his family the only way he knew how—by being emotionally stable and by spoiling them. He'd been small of stature but always held himself with dignity—arrogance, the envious might say—even after The Slick. He'd always come to the holiday home in summer. As far as Pierre was aware, he'd never set foot in Brittany at this time of year, and he'd never referred to the house by name, like Patrick at the café had that morning. *Penn-Avel.*

There weren't many books about the area—its traditions, its history. He spotted two squeezed in at the end of the top shelf. He read the spine of the first one, a pastel blue paperback in mint condition. *Naufrageurs et contrebandiers des côtes bretonnes.* An untouched book on the wreckers and smugglers on the Breton coast. The second book was an old green hardcover with a gilded spine, but the lettering had faded. He pulled it out and opened it to the yellowed title page—*Légendes de la mer.* One book about peasants committing crimes and the other about peasant superstitions. He closed the book of sea legends and dropped it carelessly onto the bottom shelf.

He sipped his wine and wandered over to the window, but before he reached it, the reading lamp flicked off and the radio went dead.

'Oh, just great!'

He managed to reach the chair by the window and place his glass on it before spilling any of the chablis, then he turned around and studied the darkness that reigned in the sitting room. No light other than the flickering fire. At least he had that. Radio silence—not even static.

'Ten thousand and one,' he remarked.

He told himself it might be a fuse. Wishful thinking most likely, but he'd fetch his torch and have a look. He was trying to remember where he'd left the torch when a bright light caught his attention. It danced on the ceiling—coming from outside.

He turned back to the rattling window and looked beyond where he knew the terrace and the gorse hedge at the cliff's edge to be, but it was all utterly black now apart from the drunken red and green pinpricks. Then he saw it again—flashing torchlight. It seemed more distant this time. Where was it coming from? Not the garden. Not that close. Not the beach either, because it couldn't be seen at all from the ground floor of the house. He judged it to be out in the water, not far out, but in this weather? Was someone trapped on a rocky reef or in a boat run aground, getting pounded by the storm surge?

Flash. Flash. Flash. Flaaaash. Flaaaash. Flaaaash...

Pierre didn't know Morse code but realised he wasn't being invited to a cocktail party on a private yacht.

Flash. Flash. Flash. Flaaaash. Flaaaash. Flaaaash. Flash. Flash. Flash.

There it was again, aimed straight at the window—the only window along that stretch of coast that had the shutters open. Someone was in grave danger, and as much as Pierre wanted to sip his chablis and pretend he remained blissfully unaware, that simply wasn't an option. He had to call for help, but of course, he couldn't. No signal. He returned to the sofa and saw the firelight reflected on the screen of his smartphone. He snatched it up, unlocked it, and hurried back to the window. The light flashed against the trembling pane again as he held his phone up—no signal, and the battery was low.

Panic set in. He was going to have to go down there. If he could help without putting himself in danger, he would. If not—what? He'd have to drive for help. He imagined the thick, knotted limb of a maritime pine penetrating the windscreen of his Boxster like a battering ram through a portcullis, his head crushed and bleeding against the headrest.

He shook the image away, took his jacket and his torch, pulled on a pair of blue and white striped wellies, and opened the door leading onto the terrace. The door knocked him back and he had to fight his way outside, head down against the gale like a rugby player about to be tackled, but with his light build, there was more chance he'd be blown clear off his feet than pinned to the ground.

Across the terrace. Along the gorse hedge. Through the rickety wooden gate. Down the narrow, treacherous path, using the torch to make sure he didn't twist an ankle on a rock or root. It was a matter of seconds, but it felt like aeons. He reached the concrete steps, steep and slippery, leading down onto the beach, and there it was, the flashing light, out on the water—in a boat! He couldn't sea the boat, or who was in it, but the light was bobbing violently.

He shouted, not really aware of just what he was saying, but the gale snatched the words from his lips and sent them hurtling against the cliff. He stumbled forwards, pointing his torch at the light fixed on him, not flashing now but a constant beam. He was at the water's edge now, but it wasn't really an edge—pelting rain, rabid foam, bursting waves—water everywhere. He was already drenched and his wellies were fuller than a freshly poured glass of muscadet. He knew he wasn't *in* the sea—not far out in any case—because he could still feel the squelchy sand beneath his feet, but he knew he couldn't go much further.

The light was on his face—in his eyes. Blinding. Disconcerting.

'Hey!'

The next thing he knew, he was being held. It wasn't the wind, which buffeted and shoved and bit. This was substantial. He was being gripped tight. One, two—on his shoulders. Three, four—at his left elbow and wrist. Five, six—at his right elbow and wrist.

'Get off me! What are you doing?'

Not a word. Only the wailing wind.

He wanted to shine his torch at them but he no longer held it. He

206

struggled against the hands but they were pulling him now, forcing him into the thrashing water and towards the light. They were powerful hands. There was no breaking free. He could tell they were wearing life jackets, but he couldn't see their features, except in fleeting glimpses when the light brushed their faces—he recognised the thick mop of dark hair to the left.

What was this? The book about wreckers and smugglers came to mind. Was this a flipped take on the tradition? Instead of luring ships to the rocks during storms, had the locals now turned to luring the rich from their holiday homes? He was being kidnapped. An extravagant ransom would be communicated to his father. Dirty money—cash stained by more than sixty thousand tonnes of crude oil. This was extortion and revenge wrapped up in one horrendous package.

He yelled at them to stop. He begged. To no avail.

The panic that had set in before he left the house had grown to a state of terror now. Three sturdy men. Six hands that showed no sign of yielding. Pierre soon gave up trying to break loose, because when he did, strong fingers sank into his flesh. They were leading him into the water. There was no knowing how deep it was. A wave crashed over them and brine stung his eyes and mouth, the backwash then pulled at his legs and waist but the hands kept him steady. Even if he lost his footing, they would hold him up and keep him moving towards the boat.

They were almost there. It looked to be a small speedboat and Pierre could now hear the sound of its powerful outboard motor—or perhaps there were two—over the din of the storm and through the water in his ears.

The pilot was looking down on him, and as he raised the torch so the others could see what they were doing, Pierre caught a glimpse of his whiskered face and vaguely recalled those piercing blue eyes. Then the light swept right and blinded him again, and the six hands hauled him into the boat. They climbed in and held him down, flat on his back, and the boat was off, bouncing and rolling, sending jolts of pain through his body.

He had no idea where they were taking him, but as it turned out, it wasn't far. The boat slowed a little further out to sea and the pilot kept control of it, levelling his torch as best he could while two of the others clambered out into the water. A moment later, the third pulled Pierre up and he saw that the others were no longer in the water but standing on rocks dangerously close to the boat. Each gripped a heavy metal chain with one hand and reached out to take Pierre with the other.

He was shoved from behind and then dragged clear of the boat by the two on the reef. There was no doubt in his mind that it was the same reef he could see from the safety of the sitting room.

Why here? It made no sense. He wasn't being held for ransom—so what was this?

He was on his back now. The rocks were digging into his back and salt water rushed over him with each crashing wave. He was so cold now he could hardly feel his body at all. There was a series of dreadful metallic clicks and he realised that his wrists and ankles were held tight not by hands now but by shackles. He tried to see but his eyes were stinging. He tried to bring his hands to his face but the chains held his arms stretched out past his head.

'It's almost time,' a voice yelled over the roar of the wind. 'Take our off—, morga—' Pierre couldn't make out all the words, but it wasn't the words that had caught his attention—it was the voice.

'Let's go!' the other replied, a voice belonging to a younger man.

The oyster farmers!

A wave crashed against the rocks and he closed his eyes and mouth tight. Once it had passed, in the seconds before the next one came, he knew he was now alone on the reef, and he roared with all his might until the water came rushing over the rocks again.

Swooosh!

He drew a deep breath as the wind wailed and used it to call out for Appoline, but her name was cruelly whisked away. He pulled with all the strength he had left against his shackles, then drew another breath as the next wave pounded against the reef.

Swooosh!

He breathed out and heard a watery whisper in his ear. The words belonged to no tongue he had ever heard but the whisper was strangely soothing. When the next wave rushed over him, something slippery in it caressed his lips and the last sensation he had was of being taken from the reef—torn painlessly from the shackles and carried away.

Meanwhile, back on the beach, locals were hunkered down at the base of the sea cliffs, waiting to welcome the crew of four as heroes. When the boat came into view, scores of figures dressed in hooded fisherman's smocks and carrying storm lanterns strode down to the water. They were smiling, taking comfort in the knowledge that the sea had been appeased.

#

It wasn't like Pierre to ignore her calls, not for a whole weekend. Appoline arrived at the holiday home with her Australian shepherd, Lady, early Monday afternoon. She found his Porsche parked by the house, undamaged but covered in leaves and twigs, and a pile of soaked firewood by the stairs. She left Lady in the car while she went to try the front door, but it was locked. She walked around the house and found the terrace door wide open and the floor inside flooded.

She hesitated before entering but refused to let the gnawing sense of dread overcome her.

'Pierre!'

Dead silence.

She walked slowly into the sitting room. Nothing was broken. There were no indications of violence. Nothing looked out of place. Nothing except that one book lying at the edge of the bottom shelf, not put away in its rightful spot.

She picked it up. *Légendes de la mer.* She couldn't remember whether she'd read that one before. Had Pierre been reading it? Not his usual fare. She flicked through the first few pages. The book was about the legends of Brittany's sunken cities and sea creatures. There were illustrations of fabulous beings, and one in particular caught her eye—a beautiful mermaid. The text, however, explained that the *morganez* was a spiteful creature that fed on the souls of men and conjured storms if not given satisfaction.

Appoline realised Lady had started to bark, so she closed the book and ran back to the car to let her out. The sleek, mottled dog darted over to the pile of firewood and sniffed about before dashing around to the terrace. Appoline did her best to keep up and was expecting Lady to enter the house, but she followed a trail along the hedge instead and disappeared down the path leading to the beach.

'You've found him?' she asked as she reached where the water was lapping gently at the beach, but the glimmer of hope quickly drowned as Lady worked herself into a frenzy, barking at the deep green sea.

HER MOTHER'S LULLABY
Micah Castle

The Boar's Den door closed behind me, deafening rowdiness. The weighty quietness of the town fell over me like a stone quilt. The streets were empty, and all the shanty homes were shuttered. Sprouting from the rising walls of the valley the village was built within, the cluttered pines were silent. Not a hint of wind.

The chill wasn't bad—in the heart of summer—so I decided to walk off the drink. Might as well try to be as sober as I can before returning to Alice, already fast asleep at home.

I followed the main dirt road running through town. The mud hadn't dried, and I thanked the heavens for my boots. Not a cloud could be seen in the night sky, and the full moon hung low. Everything was ghostly, pale.

I looked at the calm, dark lake at the end of the way—and halted.

A petite girl stood before the water, wearing only a white sleeping gown. No shoes. Her long, light hair seemed to glow in the moonlight. She put a violin to her shoulder and put the bow to its strings.

I neared as she began to play soothingly eerie, melancholy notes. Her music felt tangible, the rising and falling chords like hung sheets in a gentle breeze, like a waxing and waning tide. Her music glided over the sleeping village, the still lake.

I was transfixed until her tune came to its end and she lowered the instrument to her side.

'Miss?'

She spun around, and sniffled. 'Yes?'

I wanted to ask about the song, or where she learned to play so beautifully, but something bothered me even more. 'Where are your shoes?'

She looked at her feet, as if she hadn't noticed they were bare hitherto, then faced me. 'I haven't any.'

'Where's your father?'

'At sea,' she said.

'And your mother?'

'Home, sleeping.'

I knelt before her, and could make out the mud staining the hem of her gown, the dirt smearing her face. Filth and uncleanliness hid beneath her blond hair. But the violin and bow were seemingly new. 'If you tell me which house is yours, would you mind if I carried you there? On my back, that is. Girls oughtn't be out at night, especially alone and without proper clothes or shoes.'

She glanced over her shoulder at the lake for a heartbeat, turned back to me and nodded. I gave her my back and she jumped on, her hands around my neck, legs around my waist. Whispering in my ear, she told me where her home was.

#

Her house had two windows, one without glass and boarded, the other webbed with cracks, and a warped front step leading to a door hanging on a hinge. It was a sorry sight, and sadness crept inside me just looking at it. The girl had fallen asleep during the trip, yet she still held her instrument tightly.

I awoke her gently, and set her on the step.

'Thank you,' she said.

I nodded. 'Aye, not needed. Now run inside and throw a log on the fire, if you have it. Warm your feet.'

She smiled, and when she opened the creaking door, the sour reek of an overflowing chamber pot wafted out. I grimaced but kept my composure out of respect for the child.

After she was safely inside, I rushed away from the smell, back to my own home.

#

Another night at the Boar. Another night of having an overly plentiful share of drink. I left so others could catch up. Like times before, it was the middle of the night. The homes across the road began to tilt, and the cloudless sky and near full moon started to rotate. I shook my head, rubbed my eyes. The world righted itself. Had to make it home to my Alice. My beautiful, sleeping Alice.

Stomping through the muck towards the lake, I found the girl again standing at the calm waters, already prepared to play. She wore the same soiled gown, and her bare feet were caked in mud.

I strode towards her, becoming frustrated—not with the poor girl, but her mother. Who would allow a child out at night like that? What sort of parent wouldn't wash her clothes or her hair, or give her a pair of damn shoes? Before I reached her, she began to play and the sweet music flowed over me like honeyed waves. I stopped. The melody made my skin clammy, my spine prickle, and it washed away the frustration that had rampaged through me only a second ago.

Once she'd finished, I stood by her. We stared out over the lake for a while, neither speaking. Eventually, I asked, 'Does your mother know you come here at night?'

She shook her head, her gaze not leaving the water.

'How long has your father been gone?'

'A long time,' she said.

'Was he a sailor?'

She nodded.

Ah, a tale as common as the Witches of Brislock in this damned place. Men leaving their families for the sea, in the hopes of a better life.

Poor child.

Her stomach grumbled. She put her hand holding the bow to her belly.

I grinned. 'Have any food at home?'

She shook her head.

'Would you like some? Alice baked some bread yesterday—still good, not hard yet—and we have some cheese left. Milk, too.'

'No,' she said, then added: 'Thank you.'

I shrugged. If she didn't want to eat, then let her go hungry. Alice wouldn't approve of force-feeding her.

We stood in the quiet again for some time. It must've been long for I became a lot less drunk. I stretched my lower back, inhaling the cold air sharply. 'Would you like me to carry you home now?'

'Yes, please.'

And so I did, like before. Carried her to the front step of her home. She didn't fall asleep this time. After setting her down, she thanked me and quickly went inside. The same rancid stench hit me like a carriage when the door opened, and I wondered, as I started for home, what could cause such a smell? It was far worse than an overflowing chamber pot.

#

I arrived early at the Boar and got my share of drink, enough to warm my belly and push the doldrums of life away. I left early, too, before the regulars staggered in, and went to the spot where the girl had been the last two nights. It was empty, but the imprints of her feet remained in the grassy mud.

The looming moon cast everything in a deathly glow.

'What are you doing?' a familiar voice caught my attention.

I turned to find the girl standing in the same filthy clothes. Though, now, her bangs were tucked behind her blackened ears. 'Came to see you play,' I said, 'and talk, if that's all right with you.'

She didn't answer and walked around me, and placed her feet onto the footprints like sliding on a pair of worn boots.

The child peered over the lake in silence. The palpable stillness became awkward.

'Aren't you gonna play?'

'It's not right.'

'What's not right?'

'Time,' she said.

'How do you know when the time's right?'

'My father taught me,' she said. 'I just know.'

I took a deep breath, and like Alice does when I come home too late, I pried. 'Where was the ship heading for, the one your father was on?'

'To sea.'

'Yes, but where to?'

'An island. With magic.'

214

'Magic?' I held back a laugh.

She nodded. 'Yes, magic.'

'And, what sort of magic does this island have?'

She shrugged. 'He will come back. He said it true.'

Most sailors don't return once they depart. There's far more out there than a sordid village in the middle of a no-name valley. The only attractions were a pub and the loud, dirty drunks who occupied it. Folks only came here when there was nowhere left to go; the poor fools who were born here never left, unless the sailor's life was a welcome one. Even in death, they remained, buried in the cemetery along the narrow road leading out of the valley—to better places.

'Will he come back on another ship or—'

'It's time.'

She began to play the soft, sweet song. Each note rolled over the lake like waves of its own. It might've been the ale or a trick of the moonlight, but I swear to the heavens that the water rippled with each crisp cord. Maybe there wasn't only magic on this island, but in her hands as well. The song rose and fell, rose and fell, my breathing matching its rhythm. It felt like coming out of a winter storm and settling before a blazing hearth, like sinking your cold, cold bones in a warm bath. Things not many can say they have or ever had here.

Her song ended and I waited to say, 'Where did you learn to play that song?'

'My mother played it when I was a child, to help me sleep. My father taught me to play it when she couldn't.'

'Can you play any others?'

She shook her head. 'No.'

The child faced me. Her eyelids drooped, and her body moved as though she were at sea. I didn't want to bother her any longer, so without asking, I turned and she got onto my back.

#

I arrived at the Boar earlier than I ever had before. Night hadn't fallen yet, so the usuals weren't churning in the bar's belly.

Tables and chairs were empty, the fire small, but the smell of sour ale, vomit, and piss still lingered and grease coated seemingly everything.

215

Billy Boar—the owner—came out from the door to the back, polishing a bare pint with a dirty rag. A bear of a man with wide-set dark eyes and no chin, wearing an oversized stained shirt and ragged pants. I hadn't had a drink yet so a part of me cared that the glass would never be clean, but I knew soon I wouldn't. But not yet, I came early for another purpose.

I hunched over the bar. 'Aye, Billy. I have a question.'

'Ya, what is it, Drunk Jack?' He stomped over, set the glass onto the counter and grabbed another from under the bar.

'You know about a girl—a young girl—who stands out by the lake at night? She plays music.'

He laughed. 'Everyone does, Jack. I'm surprised you don't. She's the Lady of the Lake, though not a man has made her a proper lady yet.'

A shiver of revulsion ran through me. Sober, Billy was horrible. Drunk, he was the hilarious heartbeat of the Boar.

'*Lady?* She's a child! Does she have a name?'

'Joanne's her name.'

'Her father, did you know him?'

'Ya, John Graystone. Before he left on the Liminal for his magic island, that is.' He spit into a glass, polished, and grabbed another. 'Always talkin' about that stupid, damn island.'

'A magic island?'

'He spoke about it all the damn time, drunk or clean. Said, he did, that there was an island far off the coast, somewhere in the Black, that he read about in some book. A book!' He gave a throaty chuckle. 'He never mentioned where it was, but swore the Liminal was headin' that way.' Billy leaned over the counter. A ripe, pork odor stung my nose. 'So, he said, he signed up to be a crewman—a sailor, if ya will. He said he'd make it to that bloody, magic island and return with its magic. But has the bastard returned? No, never once in all this time.' Billy straightened. 'Probably drowned or killed himself. Ale was his air, spirits his blood. A day clean would've been maddenin' for him, I'm sure. Too much to bear and all that.'

I ignored Billy's rant, for nearly all men in town were the same. 'What about the magic? Did John say anything about the magic?'

Someone came into the pub. I heard chortling outside, and knew more were coming.

216

'No, never did. Wait, ya—now I recall. He said it was somethin' with evolution. Or, no, wait—it was an odd word…tra…trans…'

'Transformation?'

'That be it!' Billy grinned, revealing yellowed teeth, and pointed at me. 'That be the one! *Transformation!* Bloody hell what that means, right?'

I laughed, nodding. More men entered the bar. Though there were no windows, I knew night must've come. Like the changing of time gave permission to change from one person to another, I ordered a pint, then a second.

#

Three, four at most, drinks was all I stomached until I departed and walked to Joanne's spot. The lake gave way to the ocean on the horizon. I wondered what book John read that spoke of a magical island. Was he reading fiction? And, where would've he gotten such a book in this village? Books like that only came from the cities. Day travel from here.

'You're here again?' She wore the same clothes and dirt.

'Aye, I am. Come to hear you play—if that's all right, that is.'

I stepped aside to let her take her spot.

'When it's time, you can.'

We waited in silence until she played.

#

'Why do you play in the same place, at the same time, child?' I asked Joanne after she had finished playing. I hadn't revealed that I knew her name, or her father's. Being nameless oddly felt like it suited our relationship more.

The wind sighed and the cold bit into open skin. Not enough ale that night to warm my blood. She shivered and her grip on the violin and bow tightened. If I owned an extra coat, I would've given it to her. Maybe we'd find spare kindling on the way to her home.

'My father told me to. He said that if I played at the lake every night at the same time, he would hear it and come back.'

I didn't dare ask how many nights it had been. 'Ready to get out

217

of the cold?'

She nodded and I gave her my back. It took longer for her to get a solid grasp around my neck, for her fingers trembled. It felt like icicles on my throat.

I hurried her home. The cold was unforgiving, autumn was on its way. I smelled it in the air. The mud was drier, sharper, worse than Hell to walk through without slipping and possibly breaking an ankle. I found no sticks or branches, or wood of any kind during the trip.

We made it, and I set her down on the stair. She went inside without saying goodbye. The same rancidity drifted from the open door before closing.

I glanced down the road, over the abandoned shanties. Not a soul awake; not even smoke from crooked chimneys.

I crept and gently opened the door a little, peeking in. This close, the odor burnt my nose and made me want to retch. I clenched my teeth to keep from vomiting.

A small, iron stove burned dimly in the corner. There were more holes in the walls than there were rotten boards. The waterlogged ceiling bowed towards the floor. A pile of mismatched lumber sat against the wall, and a heap of rotting apples, moldy bread, and cheese lay near. In the far corner was a layer of dark straw, upon which someone lay, covered by a thin, black and green sheet. At the foot of this pauper's bed, Joanne slept on the hardwood floor with her legs tucked to her chest and her head resting on her arm.

I took another step, pushing the door open more.

By Joanne was a hillock of human waste. Flies buzzed and created a frenzied cloud around it. I bit my lower lip—couldn't retch yet. I tiptoed to the sheet, checking every moment that Joanne's eyes remained shut. Standing before what must be Joanne's mother was like entering a smog of death, reeking of festering rot. It was unbelievable that she stank worse than their waste.

I pinched the top of the sheet, knowing what I would find already. Knew that Joanne's mother was not asleep, like the girl believed. Knew the child was more alone than I imagined. I pulled it down, only revealing the head. I fought the instinct to run away. Never liked the dead. Never liked how they looked, like their souls were sucked out of them and every ounce of humanity gone. A shell. Something meant to be buried or burned or sent overboard.

The flesh had decayed and a black tear circled her skull. Her gaping torn lips were bruised with dry black. A scarlet stain drenched the straw under her head. Only a few wisps of her light hair remained. Her eyes were closed, and I blessed the heavens for that.

This was enough for me. More than enough. I'd never wanted to be at the Boar so badly in a long, long while. I covered her and snuck from the hovel, closing the door behind me.

In the street, I fell to my knees and vomited. My legs trembled when I stood again and a clamminess coated my skin. I wiped away tears and snot and forced my feet to carry me to the Boar in the hopes of drowning and flushing out the horrid image of the woman from my mind.

#

Alice tried to convince me to stay home that night, but I left anyway, going to Joanne's spot. I had to talk to her, had to convince her to come live with me and Alice. Where she lived was not a place for a child, no less a girl. I'm not her father, and I may be Drunk Jack, but I'm still breathing, still in town, still can put a roof over her head and warm food in her belly.

The dark, cloudy sky spat rain. The wind howled. Not a soul was out. I hugged myself as I waited for her to arrive. The black lake was a sheet of nothing, and the horizon was lost in the deluge. Thunder boomed in the distance, lightning crackled over the valley.

When I glanced at where she stood, she was there. I hadn't even heard her come. Her gown was soaked through and plastered to her body. Water dripped from the tip of her bow. Her wind-whipped hair stuck to her scalp.

'Why don't you come to my home tonight?' I shouted.

She shook her head, keeping her wincing eyes forward.

'Your father's not going to come tonight! Not in this storm.'

The rain straightened, and thunder closed in, exploding over the village, shaking the ground. I caught flashes of ripples in the lake when lightning struck, over and over again.

'Please! Come to my home. There's food and a fire!'

Either she didn't or couldn't hear me, or the girl had ignored me. Nevertheless, she began to play.

Not a single note could be heard. Not one of the sweet chords. If I couldn't hear it, sure as hell her father couldn't. Frustration swelled inside me. Selfish, stupid little girl, like all children. Her father wasn't coming home, didn't she realize that? I was standing out in a storm, offering a warm place to sleep and eat and she just played her silly music.

But silly or not, I refused to let her die the way her mother had, refused to let her waste her days away at the lake for a drunk of a father who'd probably been thrown overboard, refused to allow her to be remembered only as the Lady of the Lake—not as Joanne.

I grabbed her arm, and she cried out. I spun her towards me, ripping the bow from strings. 'You're coming home with me! I'm getting you out of here!'

She tore her arm from my grasp and faced the lake. A flash of light revealed her smile. She walked towards the edge of the bank, her lips moving as though speaking.

'No—wait!' I made for her, but another sound—wet, craggy, like crumbling stone, crashing boulders—pierced the air, stopping me.

A giant shadow blocked the abrupt light. It towered over us, the town. I'd never believed something could be darker than the night— never believed something could be taller than the surrounding hills. My jaw dropped. My eyes widened, numb to the rain. Lightning flashed.

It was like a sea mountain had grown limbs. Gray-speckled coral ran up one rocky side, growing across what must've been half of its head. Red starfish clung to it. Wet silt, sand, and water drained from hundreds of pockets along its other side. Patches of seaweed hung like damp hair from oceanic protrusions. Its deep-seated face—if it was a face—if it was anything that could be believed to be a face— had craters burning with emerald, citrine, and aquamarine smoke. Below, a cavern filled its entire chest, revealing a cerulean light that silhouetted a frenzy of stalactites inside.

The world turned upside down. I stumbled back, slipped, and fell on my ass.

The glow from the titan brightened, basking Joanne crossing the lake, her open arms stretched towards the monster. I called for her to come back. Its light blared like an exploding star and a gurgling roar sounded from somewhere deeper than any ocean. For a moment, it was a green-tinged day without a sun, then an overwhelming gloom crashed over everything..

The taste of copper told me I was still screaming, the saltiness of my tears and snot let me know I was still crying, and the reek of feces told me I had shat myself.

Then, the world went away and I was nowhere—I was nothing.

#

It was dawn when I came to. Mud oozed between my fingers when I pushed myself to my feet. My knees popped, my back ached, and I smelled of shit. Mist floated over the calm lake, seeping through the hillside trees. Something like a stick or branch stuck out of the water near the bank.

I wrenched it from the earth. It was Joanne's bow, and partially hidden under long, wet grass, was her violin. I whipped the mud from the bow, brushed the water from the instrument.

Standing in silence, I looked to the horizon. Memories of the monster flashed through my mind, followed by more of Joanne, of her walking towards it with arms outstretched.

I had listened to her music so many times I could hum it by heart. I put her violin to the crook of my neck and shoulder, set the bow to the strings. I wanted to play, I wanted the melody to flow out like a fall breeze; I wanted to call her back from the sea, like she'd done with her father.

I dropped the instrument to my side. But would she return? Would she want to? The child finally got what she had been wanting for years, to be with her father at long last, and what would she be returning to? A dead mother, a dilapidated house, a drunk who'd befriended her, and a dead-end village full of even more drunks. I didn't know where her father had taken her, or what he could do in his form, but I believed whatever it was, it was far better than what she'd left behind.

When the sun rose, I turned away from the lake, and returned home, bow and violin in hand.

AUTHOR BIOGRAPHIES

David Turnbull is a member of the Clockhouse London group of genre writers. He writes mainly short fiction and has had numerous short stories published in magazines and anthologies. His stories have previously been featured at Liars League London events and read at other live events such as Solstice Shorts and Virtual Futures. His near future dystopian novella, *HUSks*, is currently on release.
indienovella.co.uk/product-page/husks-david-turnbull

Edward Lodi has written more than thirty books, both fiction and non-fiction, including six Cranberry Country Mysteries. His short fiction and poetry have appeared in numerous magazines and journals, such as Mystery Magazine, and in anthologies published by Cemetery Dance, Murderous Ink, Main Street Rag, Rock Village Publishing, Superior Shores Press, and others. His story, *Charnel House*, was featured on Night Terrors Podcast. He is a member of the Short Mystery Fiction Society and a frequent contributor to their blog.

Kev Harrison is a writer of dark fiction and English language teacher from the UK, living and working in Lisbon, Portugal, where he resides with his partner in crime, Ana, and their two cat overlords. He's previously lived in various cities in the United Kingdom, as well as Turkey and Poland. He is the author of two novellas, *Below* and *The Balance*, as well as a short fiction collection, *Paths Best Left Untrodden*. His début novel, *Shadow of the Hidden*, arrives in March 2024 through Brigids Gate Press. His fiction has been published in a variety of magazines, podcasts, and anthologies, and he is a staff writer for This is Horror.

Matthew R. Davis is an author and musician based in Adelaide, South Australia, with over seventy short stories published around the world to date. He has been shortlisted for a Shirley Jackson Award, the WSFA Small Press Award, and multiple Aurealis and Australian Shadows Awards, winning two Shadows in 2019. His books include *If Only Tonight We Could Sleep* (horror stories, Things in the Well, 2020), *Midnight in the Chapel of Love* (novel, JournalStone, 2021), *The Dark Matter of Natasha* (novella, Grey Matter Press, 2022), and *Bites Eyes: 13 Macabre Morsels* (flash chapbook, Brain Jar Press, 2023).
www.matthewrdavisfiction.wordpress.com

Sam Dawson's job is as a journalist, but he's been quietly writing (and illustrating) fiction for quite a while now. *Humus* was his first ever story, back in 1997. It has been reworked slightly here, in particular to be a little fairer to Morris dancers. His collection *Pariah & Other Stories* is published by Supernatural Tales.

A longtime resident of the American South, **Elizabeth Broadbent** lives in Virginia with her three sons, three dogs, and very patient husband. She has published essays in *The Washington Post*, *Time Magazine*, and *Insider*; her TV and radio guest spots include CNN, MSNBC, and 'All Things Considered' on National Public Radio. Since turning to fiction, her work has been published by, or is upcoming in, among others, Flash Fiction Magazine, Penumbric, Tree and Stone, Wyldblood Press, Wyld Flash, Ghostlight Press, and AntipodeanSF.
writerelizabethbroadbent.com

Meg Belviso holds a BA in English from Smith College and an MFA from Columbia University. She is a Staff Editor at *Angels on Earth* magazine and has written for various fiction and non-fiction properties, including several biographies in Penguin's best-selling *Who Was...?* series. She is a regular presenter at the Sirens fantasy conference, where she has written on a variety of topics such as ghosts, hauntings and monsters. She is determined

to one day speak Russian fluently.
amazon.com/stores/Meg-Belviso/author/B002BM8RNW

Two-time international Bram Stoker Award-nominee®*, **Greg Chapman** is a horror author and artist based in Queensland, Australia. Greg is the author of several novels, novellas, and short stories, including his award-nominated début novel, *Hollow House*, and collections, *Midnight Masquerade* (IFWG Publishing International) and *This Sublime Darkness and Other Dark Stories*. He is also a horror artist and his first graphic novel, *Witch Hunts: A Graphic History of the Burning Times* (McFarland & Company) written by authors Rocky Wood and Lisa Morton, won the Superior Achievement in a Graphic Novel category at the Bram Stoker Awards® in 2013. He was also the President of the Australasian Horror Writers Association from 2017-2020.
  * Superior Achievement in a First Novel for *Hollow House* (2016) and Superior Achievement in Short Fiction for *The Book of Last Words* (2019).

Angelique Fawns is a journalist and speculative fiction writer. She began her career writing articles about naked cave dwellers in Tenerife, Canary Islands, and hosting a radio show in Mooloolaba, Australia. Now she works full-time making television commercials for Global TV in Toronto. She writes fiction for fun and uses her journalism skills to promote editors, publishers, and authors. She lives on a farm north of the city with her husband, daughter, horses, goats, chickens, and a Potcake rescue dog. You can find her work in Ellery Queen Mystery Magazine, DreamForge, and a variety of horror anthologies.

Deborah Sheldon is a multi-award-winning author, anthology editor, script editor and medical writer from Melbourne, Australia. She writes across the darker spectrum of horror, crime and noir. Published fiction includes poems, drabbles, flash, short stories, novelettes, novellas and novels. Deb's short fiction has appeared in various magazines and "best of" anthologies, been translated, and received numerous award nominations. Her latest titles are *The Again-Walkers*, *Liminal Spaces: Horror Stories*, and *Man-*

Beast. As editor, her latest anthology, *Killer Creatures Down Under: Horror Stories with Bite*, is out now. Other credits include feature articles, TV scripts and stage plays.
deborahsheldon.wordpress.com

David Schembri is an author, artist, comic creator, and poet from Australia. He is the author of *Unearthly Fables* (The Writing Show, 2013), the Australian Shadows Awards-nominated collection *Beneath The Ferny Tree* (Close-Up Books, 2018), and the comics, *Splitting Sides: Tales of Humorous Horror*, and *Crowman*. His first novella will be released in 2023. David's short fiction has been published by Chaosium Inc, Horror World Press, Things in the Well, Black Beacon Books and Midnight Echo. His poetry has been published in Spectral Realms, Midnight Echo, Silver Blade Magazine, and anthologies by Rainfall Books. David also created the Black Beacon Books logo.
davidschembri.net

Jeff Wood lives in Colorado Springs, where he spends way too much time staring at the night sky, and a little too much time watching baseball. His stories have appeared in over thirty publications, such as Boston Phoenix, New York Press, Wild Musette, Fiction at Work, Bright Desire, The Greyrock Review, Bellowing Ark, and Java Journal. He has a children's play included in the anthology *Childsplay*, in the company of such authors as Sam Shepard and Maya Angelou.
jeffmwood.com

London native **C.C. Adams** is the horror/dark fiction author behind books such as *But Worse Will Come*, *Forfeit Tissue* and *Downwind, Alice*. A member of the Horror Writers Association, he still lives in the capital. This is where he lifts weights, cooks, and looks for the perfect quote to set off the next dark delicacy.
ccadams.com

Harris Coverley has had more than eighty short stories published across dozens of periodicals and anthologies. A former Rhysling nominee, he has also had over two hundred poems published in journals around the world. He lives in Manchester, England. Twitter: *@ha_coverley*

Cameron Trost is an author of mystery and suspense fiction best known for his puzzles featuring Oscar Tremont, Investigator of the Strange and Inexplicable. He has written two novels, *Letterbox* and *The Tunnel Runner*, and three collections, *Oscar Tremont, Investigator of the Strange and Inexplicable*, *The Animal Inside*, and *Hoffman's Creeper and Other Disturbing Tales*. Originally from Brisbane, Australia, Cameron lives with his wife and two sons near Guérande in southern Brittany, between the rugged coast and treacherous marshlands. He runs the independent publishing house, Black Beacon Books, and is a member of the Australian Crime Writers Association.
camerontrost.com

Micah Castle is a weird fiction and horror writer. His stories have appeared in various magazines, websites, and anthologies, and recently his novelette, *Reconstructing a Relationship*, was published by D&T Publishing. His forthcoming début novel, *The World He Once Knew*, will be published by Fedowar Press in 2023. While away from the keyboard, he enjoys spending time with his wife, playing with his animals, spending hours in the woods, and can typically be found reading a book somewhere in his Pennsylvania home.
micahcastle.com

Also Available from Black Beacon Books

A cataclysmic anthology of post-apocalyptic tales!

For news, reviews, competitions, author interviews,
and exclusive excerpts

Visit our website
blackbeaconbooks.com

Like us on Facebook
facebook.com/BlackBeaconBooks

Join us on Twitter
@BlackBeacons

Find us on Instagram
instagram.com/blackbeaconbooks

Subscribe on Patreon
patreon.com/blackbeaconbooks

Discover All our Social Media Links
https://linktr.ee/blackbeaconbooks

www.ingramcontent.com/pod-product-compliance
Lightning Source LLC
Chambersburg PA
CBHW020611180626
46810CB00007B/2724